EROTIC
STORIES

EDITED BY ROWAN PELLING

EVERYMAN'S POCKET CLASSICS
Alfred A. Knopf New York London Toronto

THIS IS A BORZOI BOOK
PUBLISHED BY ALFRED A. KNOPF

This selection by Rowan Pelling first published in
Everyman's Library, 2013

www.randomhouse.com/everymans
www.everymanslibrary.co.uk

ISBN: 978-0-375-71239-5 (US)
978-1-84159-614-3 (UK)

A CIP catalogue reference for this book is available from the
British Library

Typography by Peter B. Willberg
Typeset in the UK by AccComputing, Wincanton, Somerset
Printed and bound in Germany by GGP Media GmbH, Pössneck

EROTIC
STORIES

Contents

EXTRA-MARITAL EXCURSIONS

Preface

NO STRAND OF literature seems so thronged with pitfalls as that dealing with sexual intimacy. One writer's notion of an erotic frisson can easily be a thousand readers' anaphrodisiac; for every book lover who thrills at the baroque excesses of the *Story of O*, there are plenty who seek gentler refuges for sensual pleasure. So I was only too aware that compiling this volume would prove no easy task. The eight years I spent editing an erotic literary magazine served to tell me how few lubricious tales appeal to the great majority of readers, or stand the test of time. Disputes over taste in humour seem minor compared to quarrels about what could judiciously be called sexy, or, indeed, gratuitous. It is hard not to hear the pained voice of the prosecutor in the Lady Chatterley obscenity trial enquiring whether this were the kind of book 'you would wish your wife or servants to read'.

Nevertheless, I discerned firm threads of consensus on the genre: the finest erotic stories are honest to the point of discomfort, even if that truth is emotional, rather than factual; they make you marvel at the author's simultaneous audacity and vulnerability; they are paced with such finesse that narrative peaks prove as cathartic as the culmination of a true seduction and they offer a master class in the language of desire – whether that vernacular be subtle or explicit – invoking all five senses. There must be leeway for the more unsettling reaches of sensation, yet the passions described should be disconcertingly familiar.

I have tried my hardest in this volume to track down

literary works that best reflect the irrepressible drive of erotic desire in all its illogical, tender and torturous manifestations. From the pastoral playground of *Daphnis and Chloe* to the adulterers' basement in Hanif Kureishi's 'Nightlight', every stage of seduction is traced – even to the point of the first flickering intimation of ennui. It is extraordinary to feel the nervous joy and innocence of first love leaping fresh as paint from Longus's prose nineteen centuries after his death. Who knew that Edith Wharton, mistress of erotic undercurrent, could be so explicit in her private writing? 'My Little Girl' was found among Wharton's unpublished papers after her death and is as highly charged as any sex scene written in our supposedly liberated age. As for amorous obsession, who can match Junichirō Tanizaki's description of the man whose most cherished fantasy is to stare uninterrupted at the pure white skin of his wife?

It's sobering to reflect that some tales in this book were not generally available until the second half of the twentieth century, due to opprobrium and censorship. Or, as Philip Larkin noted, 'Sexual intercourse began/ In nineteen sixty-three ... Between the end of the Chatterley ban/ And the Beatles' first LP.' It is also impossible to ignore the stark contrast between E. M. Forster's constrained allegory of gay passion, 'Dr Woolacott' (written at a time when homosexual acts were illegal), and Allan Gurganus's visceral, expansive story about a married man lured into the woods by a cocksure youth. The debate will long continue as to whether cultural restrictions and the challenge of taboos have often compelled writers to greater imaginative heights; consider the fantastical seduction of the woman who takes a djinn, in the form of a snake, as a lover in Alifa Rifaat's 'My World of the Unknown'. Whatever the truth of the matter, readers of these tales can be left in little doubt creativity is born of the act of love.

EROTIC
AWAKENINGS

LONGUS

from:
DAPHNIS AND CHLOE

Translated by Ronald McCail

AND NOW IT was the beginning of spring: the snow thawed, the earth was laid bare, and the new grass peeped forth. The herdsmen drove their animals out to pasture, and before them all went Daphnis and Chloe, because *they* were servants of a Greater Shepherd. Straightaway they sped to the Nymphs and the cave, then to Pan and the pine-tree, and after that to the oak, under which they sat down and watched their flocks, and kissed and caressed each other fondly. Afterwards, wishing to make garlands for the gods, they went to look for wild flowers; these were just being coaxed from the ground by the fostering breath of the west wind and the warming rays of the sun, but they succeeded in finding violets and narcissi and pimpernels and other tributes that earliest spring is wont to bear. They also took new milk from some of the nanny-goats and ewes, and poured the Nymphs a drink of it when they garlanded their statues. They made another kind of offering by playing their pipes, as though trying to provoke the nightingales to begin their music – whereupon those singers sounded faintly from deep within the thickets, and little by little and ever more clearly framed the name of Itys, as if remembering their song after the long winter's silence.

On all sides the flock bleated and the lambs skipped joyously before kneeling down to suck their mothers' teats. Meanwhile the rams were galloping after those ewes which had not yet been mothers – they would straddle them and tup them, choosing a different partner every time. Among

17

the billy-goats, too, there was pursuing and amorous mounting of the she-goats – they even fought over them, and each one had his own harem and took care not to let it be invaded when his back was turned. Scenes like these would have made even old men feel frisky; and our two adolescents, who were in the heyday of their blood and had long been looking for a way to consummate their love, kindled at the sounds and melted at the sights and tried to think how they, too, could do something better than kissing and embracing. Daphnis, in particular, was beset by these thoughts; charged as he was with animal spirits after his confinement indoors and his enforced idleness during the winter, the kissing made him feel wanton and the embracing made him feel lascivious and he was meddlesome and impudent enough for any devilry.

And so he asked Chloe to grant him everything he wanted and lie naked with him for a longer time than they had done before – for, said Daphnis, of Philetas' instructions for administering the only cure for love, they had tried everything else but this. Chloe wanted to know what else there could be besides kissing and embracing and simply lying down, and what he intended to do after they were both naked and he had lain down with her.

'What the rams do to the ewes and the he-goats to the she-goats', said Daphnis. 'Don't you see how, after they've done what they do, the females don't run away from the males any more and the males don't weary themselves going after them, but from that time on they graze side-by-side as though they had enjoyed some kind of pleasure together? So what they do must be something sweet, that puts away the bitterness of love.'

'That's all very well, Daphnis,' quoth Chloe, 'but don't *you* see that the she-goats and the he-goats and the rams and the ewes do what they do with the males standing up, while the females stand up and let them do it – the males jumping up and the females making a back for them? Whereas you're expecting me to *lie down* with you and take my clothes off into the bargain, even though the ewes' coats are a lot thicker than my clothes are when I have them on!'

Daphnis gave in, and lay down with Chloe; for a long time he lay there without having the slightest idea how to do any of the things that he longed for so passionately. And so he made Chloe stand up again, and clung to her from behind in imitation of the billy-goats. But that only made him feel more baffled than ever; so he sat down and wept, to think that even the rams knew more about the deeds of love than he did.

Now Daphnis had a neighbour who farmed his own land, by name Chromis. This man's youth was far behind him, but he cohabited with a woman from the town – she was young and pretty and too delicate for her rustic surroundings, and her name was Lycaenion. She saw Daphnis daily, when he drove his goats past her house in the morning on their way to graze and when he returned with them in the evening, and she took a fancy to make him her lover, by enticing him with gifts. Following this plan, she waylaid him once when he was alone and gave him pan-pipes and a honeycomb and a knapsack made of doeskin; but she hesitated to speak, because she had guessed that he was in love with Chloe, from observing how enamoured he was of the girl's company. Their lively glances and their laughter told her to begin with. Then, early one morning, she told Chromis that she was going to visit a neighbour whose baby was due, but instead shadowed Daphnis and Chloe and hid in the bushes to avoid being seen – she heard all that they said, and saw all that they did, and was looking on when Daphnis burst into tears. Lycaenion was touched by their obvious unhappiness, and at the same time she knew that she had been presented with a double opportunity – she could be the means of salvation to them, while getting what she dearly wanted for herself. So she went to work in the following way.

Next morning she left the house under the pretence of paying another visit to the expectant mother, went quite openly to the oak-tree where Daphnis and Chloe were sitting, and gave an accomplished performance in the role of a woman distraught.

'Oh Daphnis,' she cried, 'whatever shall I do? Help me, please help me, Daphnis! You know my twenty geese – well, the pick of them has been carried off by an eagle! Its weight was too much for him, though, and he couldn't carry it aloft to his eyrie on that high crag, but fell with it into the forest down here. So I beg you by the Nymphs and by Pan yonder, come into the woods with me – because I daren't go alone – and save my goose! You mustn't let me be minus a bird! And maybe you'll kill the eagle too, and stop him stealing all those lambs and kids you keep on losing! Chloe will watch your herd meantime ... I'm sure the goats all know her, because she's always so thick with you in the pasture.'

Little suspecting what was in store for him, Daphnis jumped up without hesitation, took his crook, and followed Lycaenion's retreating figure. She led him as far from Chloe as she could; and when they came to the heart of the wood she made him sit down beside a spring and said:

'Listen, Daphnis: I know you're in love with Chloe – I heard all about it from the Nymphs, last night in a dream. They told me how you wept yesterday, and they've given me my orders – I'm to save you by teaching you the deeds of love. But the deeds I mean are not kissing and embracing and behaving like rams and billy-goats: they're another kind of leaping altogether, and it's a much nicer kind than what goes on in the herds, because you feel the pleasure for a longer time. So if you want to banish the blues and sample the delights you've set your heart on, all you have to do is make yourself my pupil, and I'll give you a lesson, as a favour to the Nymphs, our neighbours.'

Now Daphnis was only a country boy, just a humble goat-herd, and he was young and in love; and when he heard what Lycaenion was proposing, his joy knew no bounds – he flung himself down at her feet and begged her to teach him there and then the art of doing to Chloe the thing he wanted. And, as though he were on the point of receiving some great and truly god-sent teaching, he promised to give her a stall-fed kid and some soft cheeses made from the first squirts of milk from a she-goat, plus the goat herself. 'That's a bonus!' thought Lycaenion, who had never expected a goatherd to be so affluent. And then she began to teach Daphnis, like this:

She told him not to stand on ceremony, but to sit down beside her and kiss her as he usually kissed Chloe and just as often – and when he was in the middle of kissing he was to put his arms round her and lie down on the ground as he did so. After Daphnis had sat by her, kissed her, and lain down with her in his arms, Lycaenion could tell that he was able for love-making and all athrob with desire; so she made him raise himself a little from where he lay on his side, slid her body expertly under his, and guided him into the road which had eluded him till then. After that she didn't bother to do anything exotic – there was no need, because Nature herself taught him how to complete the act.

As soon as the lesson in love was over, Daphnis – who was still a shepherd-boy at heart – wanted to run hot-foot to Chloe and do what he had been taught without a moment's delay, as though he were afraid that he might forget it if he lingered. But Lycaenion kept him back, and spoke again:

'You still have something to learn, Daphnis. I felt no pain this time round, because I'm a woman, not a girl – another man taught me this lesson long ago, and took my maidenhead as his recompense. But when Chloe struggles with you in this wrestling-match, she'll wail and weep and lie in a pool of blood. You mustn't fear the blood, though; but when she has agreed to let you have your way with her, bring her here, so that if she cries out, no one will hear, and if she weeps, no one will see, and if she bleeds, she can wash in the spring. And always remember that I made you a man before Chloe did!'

(3.12–19)

MICHÈLE ROBERTS

COLETTE
LOOKS BACK

I WAS MY MOTHER'S youngest child, her darling. I was her Rapunzel and she my tower. Her arms encircled me, swooped me up to bed at night, held me safe.

Every evening she unravelled my hair. Loosened, it reached my hips. She brushed it out. It sprang alive, crackling and flaring, and she struggled with it, subduing it, tugging at knots. I was a meadow of dried cut grass and she raked me up and I snapped back. Then she twisted the crisp mass into two thick plaits which lay docilely on my shoulders, ready for the night.

My mother called my long, rippling hair her treasure. But my hair was my own treasure first, and then Jean-Luc's. In the barn that day I held the tips of my plaits in my hands, stretched them out and embraced him. I tied him to me with my ropes of hair.

I'd followed him in to find the cat and her new kittens. Stacked golden bales loomed over us. White sunlight knifed in through the half-open door from the yard outside. Grain dust, soft underfoot, silted up the corners. Fragrance of hay: sweet, almost fermenting. Heat pressed onto our shoulders, felled us. Down we dropped. High above us, the branching timbers of the roof. We lay on a bed of parched stalks covered with empty flour sacks. Coarse linen paler than his brown face, brown hands. I want to kiss you, I said. We were eleven years old. I'd never yet kissed a boy. He was the first.

The village school was just two streets away from my

parents' house, near the church, on the far side of the market-place. Childhood meant wildness, going barefoot all summer if I wanted, freedom to roam the woods and fields on my own; tearing madly home at dusk after staying out too late. In the school yard, in between lessons, boys and girls played together. Once we turned ten years old, however, new rules issued up from nowhere and constricted us, separated us. We ran and swaggered in separate gangs, stuck to different games. Boys no longer joined in girls' elaborate hopscotch and skipping rituals. Girls who, a year before, had linked arms with boys, screaming and whooping, to play wars – a line of children swooping towards the opposite enemy line, determined to crash into it, crush it – were banned now from kicking balls about or leapfrogging over rows of bent backs. Girls whispered in groups by the black stove in the centre of the classroom. Boys hunted in packs outside.

I'd always been a tomboy. I didn't have to care about pleasing grown-ups. My father, the tax collector, accepted me as his fellow dreamer, his companion on trips in the horse and cart to outlying villages and farms. My mother, the god-dess of the hearth, acknowledged my temporary freedoms, tolerated my scabbed knees and dirty face as long as she could grasp me between her knees at night and re-do my hair. My long plaits might fly out behind me when I ran pell-mell down the cobbled hill to our house, but to me they simply meant I was a runaway horse with reins trailing. I scowled rather than smiled when casually-met grown-ups chucked me under the chin and cooed at me. My black school overall was always ripped, inkstained, with buttons missing. My boots were always scuffed.

I wanted to remain a tomboy, not to have to grow up, turn into a mincing young lady with corsets and hair pieces and rouge pots; not to feel forced to compete with my friends.

I felt girls begin to betray me, lining up for the prettiness-and-pleasing stakes. They frightened me too. They seemed like sleepwalkers. In turn I frightened them: they considered me too rough, and backed off. When I seized them by the hand and whirled them across the playground they'd fall over and start crying. I leaned against the wall, sulking, watching the others play. Part of me wanted to be like them, and so not to be excluded; that made me run faster and shout louder than ever. I heard them talking about me once: oh, she's weird, but not a bad sort, if only she didn't use such long words.

How could I help it if I loved reading? I loved my father, and loved being near him. He let me into his study, let me read whatever I liked, and I worked my way through his complete library. Botany, geology, biology, I learned about them all; learned their vocabularies. Such precision, a kind of poetry, fascinated me. The tiniest part of something had its own distinct name. I learned this through living in the house, and also through living in my father's books. My mother named plants, animals, foodstuffs, implements, my father the stars and the layers of the earth. They named and separated things; that was how you knew things. You had to keep them apart. They weren't in charge of explaining girls, explaining boys. Those words didn't matter to me while I was still a girlboy, a boygirl.

I noticed Jean-Luc because sometimes he too hung about on his own. How do you know what first attracts you? I'd known him all my life as one of the boys who came in to school from the farms outside the village. We learned our hierarchies early on: the sons of shopkeepers fought the sons of peasants, just as the girls from the village looked down on the girls from the outlying hamlets. Jean-Luc managed to keep a certain distance from these feuds. I began to see him as himself, not just part of a group who chased and tormented any girl crossing their path. He had a thin, bony face, brown as a hazelnut. Fair hair cropped short, hazel eyes, a beak of a nose. He was wiry, but not tall. I began to notice other things. How he used his nimble tongue to get out of trouble with the bullies but fought when he had to, fierce as any driven terrier worrying a rat. He could be funny. He had a way of cracking jokes quietly, laughing without making a sound, lips pressed together, laughing with just his eyes, his whole body shaking with mirth. I tried not to laugh, not to acknowledge I was listening to repartee directed only at boys, but I could tell he knew he had my attention.

He lived with his father and mother, on a farm two kilometres outside the village, a little way into the forest. Wild boar ran to and fro in its depths, emerging to trample and eat the young tips of crops. The men hunted them down, shared out the meat. The forest gave us chestnuts, and mushrooms, and bilberries. The deer trotted out of it, seeking water, and could be shot in season. In late winter we cut young birch branches there, dragged them home, sorted them into bundles that we tied with wire to make brooms. We picked up kindling from the sides of the paths. The forest provided for us: larder and playground; boundary. Beyond it lived people we didn't know. Another country. Beyond that: Paris.

One July afternoon, Jean-Luc arrived at my parents' house in the village main street with a wooden-topped basket containing two dead cockerels sent by his mother as a gift. Gifts knotted our little community together in a tight mesh of obligation and gratitude. Perhaps the gift had something to do with the fact that my father was the local tax collector. I didn't know. Jean-Luc flipped up the two centrally hinged lids of the basket to show us the contents. With my mother I inspected the two red combs, the glossy feathers, the limp, gnarled legs, the bunched claws. Jean-Luc said, in response to my mother's questioning, that he had killed the cockerels himself. In our household it was my mother who slaughtered the poultry, hanging them up by their trussed feet from a hook on the back of the shed door and then slitting their throats with the knife she kept in the pocket of her apron.

Wait, my mother said: let me find some pots of preserves for you to take back with you.

She vanished up the outside steps to the grenier, the granary turned store-room, where all such things were kept, and Jean-Luc and I stood in the back garden at the top of the flight of stone steps that led down to the flowerbeds and vegetable plot.

I studied him. How clean he looked. Scrubbed up for this visit, as though he were off to Mass or catechism class. Ironed blue shirt and blue trousers. Well-blacked boots. Suddenly my arms wanted to open, take him in as knowledge: he was part of the gift. His mother had sent him to me.

I pestered him with questions. He told me that yes, he knew how to handle a gun, how to kill and skin a rabbit. He'd helped his father with the lambing, had watched cows give birth.

Our cat's just had kittens, he said.

My mother stepped rapidly down the wooden staircase from the grenier, heels clacking. She held out two earthenware jars of redcurrant jam. She didn't want to be too beholden for the gift of the cockerels and so she wished to send something back in exchange. Presents worked like that. They went back and forth instead of money.

My mother sent me off with Jean-Luc, the basket and the pots of jam. Her arms closed against us, her hands clapped and she shooed us away. I was my mother's treasure and she was giving me to Jean-Luc.

Remember, you're to be back well before it's dark, she instructed me. Remember your manners.

We went the long way round to his farm. In order not to waste time we should have gone direct. We should have taken the main road between the fields where everybody was out harvesting, but we chose the back route: more interesting and more private. In fact there was so much to see that ours turned into the very longest way possible, rambling and roundabout with plenty of stops. I encouraged these. I didn't want our walk to end. Mindful of how girls were supposed to behave, I pretended the opposite. Fiddling my fingers over the cool twist of the basket's handle, I tried to sound indifferent whenever I spoke to him.

We turned off the path by mute consent and plunged through a thicket of cow-parsley down towards the stream that ran between banks of wild mint.

Won't you get into trouble for dawdling? I asked: your mother must have been expecting you sooner than this.

We were stabbing sticks through the green scum of water weeds clogging the edges of the lazy stream. Crouching next to him I felt the sun strike, scorch, burnish the back of my neck. It burnished him too. The sun made us equal, as did the fact that we were the same height. Both of us skinny and sturdy. Both able to run fast, whistle, and use our fists.

He shrugged.

I don't care.

We had made our way through the leafy tunnels that formed the lanes linking meadows, the hedgerows growing so high that their tops met overhead. Every spring they were cut back to keep the path clear for moving herds of cows between pastures, and every midsummer they sprouted full and thick with greenery again. They would become overgrown in a single season if allowed to grow unchecked, like the briar hedge swallowing up Sleeping Beauty's palace. Swinging the basket, bumping it rhythmically against my thigh, I liked the feeling of dissolving into all that green. We picked bunches of coarse weeds and whipped each other's bare legs with them, then bandaged each other with dock leaves. We held buttercups under each other's chins, tickled each other's wrists with thorny twigs, tied our feet together with laces of vetch and tried to run three-legged. Horse flies wove buzzing clouds above our heads and we had to slap them away. I smelled cattle, and cowpats, and wild garlic in the ditches, and hot grass, and him, very close to me as we dawdled along the rutted track, our elbows brushing. He smelled of carbolic soap, and of his own sweat breaking through. Fresh sweat's a good smell. Like on horses. I snuffed it up.

Finally we reached a path that skirted the forest on one side and had fields full of grazing sheep on the other. We pushed through the rusted iron gate and into the yard. The dog barked and bounded up to greet us. His mother, summoned by the dog's joy, came out of the kitchen. Heat stained her face red. Escaped strands of scraped back hair caught under a plain white cap looked lank and wet. She wore a faded blue-checked dress with a grey pinafore over it.

Where have you been!

I could tell she felt she had to be more polite to me than she wanted; as a result she spared Jean-Luc a scolding. She took back her basket, studied the jars of redcurrant jam in it, thanked me unsmilingly.

I'll bring the jars back to your mother once they're empty, she said.

So it would go on. Back and forth. Back and forth.

Jean-Luc's mother was a tall, thin woman, with deepset blue eyes. A faded blue, like the colour of her dress, like the pattern on old plates after many washings. She wore her sleeves rolled to the elbow, hooked back with pins. Her arms were wiry and muscled as a man's. How strong she seemed. My mother was strong too, but she hid it under bustles and trailing skirts. This woman, standing legs apart, feet planted in clogs, looked tough enough for anything. I glanced at her big hands, her floury knuckles, her short fingernails crusted with dough. If you tried to get near those kneading hands you'd be clouted away. Mind my pastry! Whereas my mother's hands captured me, caressed me, knew me, clenched me close, didn't let me go.

Say thank you to your mother.

She nodded dismissal, stalked off towards her kitchen. I looked at her back, the determined set of her shoulders.

Jean-Luc was due to bring the cows in for milking a little later on, but first of all he took me all around the farm. Deserted: his father and brothers were out working on the harvest. He'd been let off to come over to my house, but tomorrow he'd have to work extra hard to make up for it. Patiently he showed me everything I wanted to see: the donkey, the pony, the hens and ducks, the sheep. Patiently he explained what everything was for: the harnesses, the tools, the tubs and buckets.

We circled back to the yard and went into the hot, dark barn. No cat and kittens visible. Cats moved their kittens from time to time, to keep them safe, I knew that. Picked them up, one by one, by the scruff of their necks, shifted them to new hiding-places.

Let's play horses, I proposed.

Jean-Luc seized the ends of my plaits as reins. I galloped, neighing, around the central space inside the toppling bales of hay, pulling him after me. Then I turned round, and snared him. I stretched out my hands, holding the tips of my long plaits, and caught him. I tied him to me with my ropes of hair.

We sank down together, winded. Under our different clothes, under our skins, we were alike, that was what I felt, we were kin, we belonged together, and so it was natural first to hesitate and then to lean closer, to say: I want to kiss you. I touched my mouth to his. Immediately he gripped me and kissed me back.

Later on his mother screamed for him and he went off to fetch in the cows and I walked home. I helped my mother pluck and draw the cockerels, pull out the gooey red mess of their insides.

Jean-Luc and I played together all through that summer, whenever he could skive off his various jobs around the farm. On those occasions his mother spotted me, she tolerated me frowningly. Watched me with a suspicious eye. He and I kept out of her way as much as possible. We climbed trees, made dens in the hedges, set traps for mice and rats, fished in the stream, explored the tumbledown sheds behind the farmyard. He showed me the disused cottage at the edge of the property, where his grandparents had first lived, before they built the farmhouse. The forest towered over it. It seemed to me like a fallen tree-house, surrounded by a beech hedge, dandled among greenery, nettles and brambles twining it into themselves. Soon it would fall into complete disrepair. I wanted to make it go the other way: I wanted to mend it. I wanted to change it into a house people could live in again. I didn't like seeing it turn to rack and ruin.

Every so often we ended up in the barn. I learned him, like a geography lesson at school. I recited him, like tables. I spelled him out, tracing him with my finger. We learned each other: speechless, mouth on mouth, arms round each other, legs wound together. Then at length I'd sit up, drowsy with heat and kisses, smoothe myself down, race across the yard, run home along the forest path.

Late one afternoon, when I'd spent too long at the farm, when Jean-Luc should have been helping his brother muck out the cowshed, his mother came searching for the truant, caught us hugging each other on our bed of straw. A clip round the head for him, a cold shoulder turned on me. Scolding furiously, she drove him towards the house.

My mother frowned at my flushed face.

Where have you been? What have you been up to?

Nothing, I said.

I glowered.

What a mess you're in, she said: your hair's all undone and full of bits of hay.

She pulled me onto her lap and began unbraiding my plaits. She smacked the brush through my tangles. Little wretch, little tearaway, little rebel, oh my bad girl, my precious one, my treasure.

After that, Jean-Luc and I made the tumbledown cottage our hiding-place. The forest held us, all summer long, until autumn arrived.

Years passed. Once we both left school I hardly ever saw Jean-Luc. I went on knowing him: my hands knew him and so did my mouth. My skin still knew him. My plaits remembered how they had twirled round him and captured him. Did he remember me? I didn't know. I knew he was going to get married to a local girl and bring his bride home to his parents' house. I glimpsed his fiancée at market one day, when I accompanied my mother there to help her with the shopping. My mother casually pointed her out, standing next to a big basket of eggs. She wasn't anyone I remembered from school. The spitting image of his mother she seemed to me: tall, slender, fair hair pulled back in a bun, neat feet in polished clogs. I saw her glance at my young lady's get-up: smart serge skirt, sailor blouse, beret with a rosette. She's called Agathe, my mother said, noticing me looking. A saint's name sounding like agate; hard and burnished as a jewel. Jean-Luc chose her as his jewel. I thought that perhaps I remained the secret pebble he carried in his pocket; a souvenir. Jewel in one pocket; pebble in another.

Before I was twenty years old I became engaged to Willy. Stout, moustachioed, licentious, Parisian Willy, the journalist, the entrepreneur who kept a factory of impoverished literary hacks churning out the novelettes that made his fortune. Willy, who was my escape route from my adored, all-possessing, country-goddess mother.

Willy of course believed, given my youth, that I remained an innocent little savage, that my family delivered me up to him as a virgin sacrifice, that I'd never seen a naked man before and certainly not one with an erection. On our wedding night he'd be the teacher and I his docile pupil. I'd prance for him on the stage of our bed, watch my shadow tremble on the wall, watch my dark shape waver as the shadow of his huge cock loomed up beside me. Oh oh oh! Oh la la! Blah blah blah and so on and so forth.

I was due to get married in late autumn. First of all I had to get ready. All through September I hemmed my new petticoats and chemises, my new sheets. October: season of picking, bottling, preserving. In my mother's garden the cherry tree leaves turned golden, pink, orange. Red fruits studded the apple trees. We shook them down onto canvas sheets. In the mornings spiderswebs, beaded with brilliant dewdrops, laced the hedges, the scarlet points of rosehips and haws.

Then the weather changed. Often now it rained, long sweeping showers of grey, and the mists wrapped themselves around the house and crept along the village street. The sun appeared only at mid-day, glimmering pale gold, and then vanished again. October melted into November, the coming of winter.

Four days before my wedding to Willy I sent a message to Jean-Luc, entrusting it to one of the village children, bribing him with a bag of macaroons. Two days before my marriage, I told my mother one afternoon I needed a walk, then slipped out when she wasn't looking, so that she couldn't point out that it was raining, and didn't see what direction I took.

Wrapped in my father's big coat, a big cap hiding my face and hair, I went towards the forest. I made for the farm, for the disused cottage where Jean-Luc waited for me. I squelched over mud, over mashed leaves. Once I entered the forest, greyness muffled the world. Fog hung under the trees. I stepped carefully: I could hardly see a metre ahead. The world shrunk to impenetrable grey mist. On either side of the deep rutted track enormous toadstools sprouted, red ones with white spots, luminous blue-mauve ones, fluted like trumpets. The air, steeped in moisture, put clammy hands to my face. I smelled wet earth, wet leaf-mould. Such silence! Inside it I heard tiny sounds. I heard rain dropping. Pattering on leaves, on fallen logs. No birds. A veil of silence: no light. The thick mist banished the afternoon; made night come early. I stumbled and slid on the narrow path clogged with fallen leaves on top of soft mud; unstable and very slippery.

I turned into the lane that led to the cottage. Into a tunnel of darkness I plunged, tree branches meeting overhead, rain soaking my shoulders through my coat. The light of a lantern shone through the darkness. I trod through the opening in the beech hedge. The forest loomed above me like a circle of wolves with open mouths. I fumbled with the latch. The wet stone wall felt solid with cold. I pushed the door open and went in.

The cottage smelled of damp. At first we kept our coats on. He wore a big coat, a bit too big for him, green and felted as the covering of walnuts you gather early for pickling. Water streamed from our coats onto the mud floor. He lit a fire with kindling and branches he told me he'd brought across the day before. In front of the fire he made us a bed with ferns he'd cut and stacked to dry. A thick mattress of springy ferns smelling of greenness, and some clean linen sacks laid on top. The fire roared up and chased away the cold. Nobody will see the smoke through the mist, he said: we're safe.

Years later I'd write my girly porno for Willy, about my childhood in the village, the goings-on at school. I'd fake it, to please him, I'd work up salacious details, to titillate him, earn my pin-money. Whereas with Jean-Luc it wasn't like that at all.

At first I told myself I just wanted to say goodbye. Years, perhaps, before I'd see him again. He looked exactly the same. Brown and complete as a hazelnut. We blurted out a few bits of nonsense. Circled each other, keeping plenty of space between us. Then I screwed up my courage and went closer. His smell hadn't changed.

I want to kiss you, I said.

I leaned towards him. Meaning, I think, to give him just a swift kiss. Whatever I intended didn't matter. Immediately, he seized me. His wide, light tongue filled my mouth. My hands flew up. I pulled off my cap, shook and loosened my plaits. I tore them apart with my fingers. I unravelled my hair and wrapped it around us. Covered by my streams of hair we sank down onto our makeshift bed. We knew each other so well: no fumbling and no fuss. His cock felt dry and warm. It swung up between my hands. I pulled him into me as he pushed inside me. We played a new game of animals who could speak, we made a new animal between us. Warmth concentrated and rose inside me, slowly bloomed like a gold flower.

He walked me back to the edge of the forest and I squelched home. Wedding nerves, such nonsense, darling, scolded my mother: you could have caught your death of cold. She ripped off my sodden coat, my blouse and skirt, stripped off my soaked muddy stockings, towelled me dry. She tutted over the blood on my petticoat: that's what the matter is, you've got your period, that's all.

The road ahead divided: the road I took and the road I didn't. If I'd married Jean-Luc, become a farmer's wife, borne his children, stayed all my life in one place, would I ever have had other adventures? In any event, he didn't ask me. He said goodbye to me and I to him.

I went ahead and married Willy and with him I boarded the train for Paris and very soon afterwards I cut my hair.

SARAH WATERS

from:
TIPPING
THE VELVET

BY NOW IT was December – a cold December to match the sweltering August, so cold that the little skylight above our staircase at Ma Dendy's was thick with ice for days at a time; so cold that when we woke in the mornings our breath showed grey as smoke, and we had to pull our petticoats into bed with us and dress beneath the sheets.

At home in Whitstable we hated the cold, because it made the trawler-men's job so much the harder. I remember my brother Davy sitting at our parlour fire on January evenings, and weeping, simply weeping with pain, as the life returned to his split and frozen hands, his chilblained feet. I remember the ache in my own fingers as I handled pail after frigid pail of winter oysters, and transferred fish, endlessly, from icy sea-water to steaming soup.

At Mrs Dendy's, however, everybody loved the winter months; and the colder they were, they said, the better. Because frosts, and chill winds, fill theatres. For many Londoners a ticket to the music hall is cheaper than a scuttle of coal – or, if not cheaper, then more fun: why stay in your own miserable parlour stamping and clapping to keep the cold out when you can visit the Star or the Paragon, and stamp and clap along with your neighbours – and with Marie Lloyd as an accompaniment? On the very coldest nights the music halls are full of wailing infants: their mothers bring them to the shows rather than leave them to slumber – perhaps to death – in their damp and draughty cradles.

But we didn't worry much over the frozen babies at Mrs Dendy's house that winter; we were merely glad and careless, because ticket sales were high and we were all in work and a little richer than before. At the beginning of December Kitty got a spot on the bill at a hall in Marylebone, and played there twice a night, all month. It was pleasant to sit gossiping in the green room between shows, knowing that we had no frantic trips to make across London in the snow; and the other artistes – a juggling troupe, a conjuror, two or three comic singers and a dwarf husband-and-wife team, 'The Teeny Weenies' – were all as complacent as we, and very jolly company.

The show ended at Christmas. I should, perhaps, have passed the holiday in Whitstable, for I knew my parents would be disappointed not to have me there. But I knew, too, what Christmas dinner would be like at home. There would be twenty cousins gathered around the table, all talking at once, all stealing the turkey from one another's plates. There would be such a fuss and stir they could not possibly, I thought, miss me – but I knew that Kitty would if I left her for them; and I knew, besides, that I should miss her horribly and only make the occasion miserable for everybody else. So she and I spent it together – with Walter, as ever, in attendance – at Mrs Dendy's table, eating goose, and drinking toast after toast to the coming year with champagne and pale ale.

Of course, there were gifts: presents from home, which Mother forwarded with a stiff little note that I refused to let shame me; presents from Walter (a brooch for Kitty, a hat-pin for me). I sent parcels to Whitstable, and gave gifts at Ma Dendy's; and for Kitty I bought the loveliest thing that I could find: a pearl – a single flawless pearl that was mounted on silver and hung from a chain. It cost ten times as much as I had ever spent on any gift before, and I trembled when

I handled it. Mrs Dendy, when I showed it to her, gave a frown. 'Pearls for tears,' she said, and shook her head: she was very superstitious. Kitty, however, thought it beautiful, and had me fasten it about her neck at once, and seized a mirror to watch it swinging there, an inch beneath the hollow of her lovely throat. 'I'll never take it off,' she said; and she never did, but wore it ever after – even on the stage, beneath her neck-ties and cravats.

She, of course, bought me a gift. It came in a box with a bow, and wrapped in tissue, and turned out to be a dress: the most handsome dress I had ever possessed, a long, slim evening dress of deepest blue, with a cream satin sash about the waist and heavy lace at the bosom and hem; a dress, I knew, that was far too fine for me. When I drew it from its wrappings and held it up against me before the glass, I shook my head, quite stricken. 'It's beautiful,' I said to Kitty, 'but how can I keep it? It's far too smart. You must take it back, Kitty. It's too expensive.'

But Kitty, who had watched me handle it with dark and shining eyes, only laughed to see me so uneasy. 'Rubbish!' she said. 'It's about time you started wearing some decent frocks, instead of those awful old schoolgirlish things you brought with you from home. I have a decent wardrobe – and so should you. Goodness knows we can afford it. And anyway, it can't go back: it was made just for you, like Cinderella's slipper, and is too peculiar a size to fit anybody else.'

Made just for me? That was even worse! 'Kitty,' I said. 'I really cannot. I should never feel comfortable in it . . .'

'You must,' she said. 'And, besides' – she fingered the pearl that I had so recently placed about her neck, and looked away – 'I am doing so well, now. I can't have my dresser running round in her sister's hand-me-downs for ever. It ain't quite the thing, now, is it?' She said it lightly – but all at once I saw

43

the truth of her words. I had my own income now – I had spent two weeks' wages on her pearl and chain; but I had a Whitstable squeamishness, still, about spending money on myself. Now I blushed to think that she had ever thought me dowdy.

And so I kept the dress for Kitty's sake; and wore it, for the first time, a few nights later. The occasion was a party – an end-of-season party at the Marylebone theatre at which we had spent such a happy month. It was to be a very grand affair. Kitty had a new frock of her own made for it, a lovely, low-necked, short-sleeved gown of China satin, pink as the warm pink heart of a rose-bud. I held it for her to step into, and helped her fasten it; then watched her as she pulled her gloves on – aching all the time with the prettiness of her, for the blush of the silk made her red lips all the redder, her throat more creamy, her eyes and hair all the browner and more rich. She wore no jewellery but the pearl that I had given her, and the brooch that had been Walter's gift. They didn't really match – the brooch was of amber. But Kitty could have worn anything – a string of bottle-tops about her neck – and still, I thought, look like a queen.

Helping Kitty with her buttons made me slow with my own dressing; I said that she should go on down without me. When she had done so I pulled on the lovely gown that she had given me, then stepped to the glass to study myself – and to frown at what I saw. The dress was so transforming it was practically a disguise. In the half-light it was dark as midnight; my eyes appeared bluer above it than they really were, and my hair paler, and the long skirt, and the sash, made me seem taller and thinner than ever. I did not look at all like Kitty had, in her pink frock; I looked more like a boy who had donned his sister's ball-gown for a lark. I loosened my plait of hair, then brushed it – then, because I had no time

44

to tie and loop it, twisted it into a knot at the back of my head, and stuck a comb in it. The chignon, I thought, brought out the hard lines of my jaw and cheek-bones, made my wide shoulders wider still. I frowned again, and looked away. It would have to do – and would have the merit, I supposed, of making Kitty look all the daintier at my side.

I went downstairs to join her. When I pushed at the parlour door I found her chatting with the others; they were all still at supper. Tootsie saw me first – and must have nudged Percy, beside her, for he glanced up from his plate and, catching sight of me, gave a whistle. Sims turned my way, then, and looked at me as if he had never seen me before, a forkful of food suspended on its journey to his open mouth. Mrs Dendy followed his gaze, then gave a tremendous cough. 'Well, Nancy,' she said, 'and look at you! You have become quite the handsome young lady – and right beneath our noses!'

And at that, Kitty herself turned to me – and showed me a look of wonder and confusion that it was as if, just for a second, *she* had never seen me before; and I do not know whose cheeks at that moment were the pinker – mine, or hers.

Then she gave a tight little smile. 'Very nice,' she said, and looked away; so that I thought, miserably, that the dress must suit me even less than I had hoped, and readied myself for a wretched party.

But the party was not wretched; it was gay and genial and loud, and very crowded. The manager had had to build a platform from the end of the stage to the back of the pit, to carry us all, and he had hired the orchestra to play reels and waltzes, and set tables in the wings bearing pastries and jellies, and barrels of beer and bowls of punch, and row upon row of bottles of wine.

We were much complimented, Kitty and I, on our new dresses; and over me, in particular, people smiled and exclaimed – mouthing at me across the noisy hall, 'How fine you look!' One woman – the conjuror's assistant – took my hand and said, 'My dear, you're so grown-up tonight, I didn't recognize you!': just what Mrs Dendy had said an hour before. Her words impressed me. Kitty and I stood side by side all evening but when, some time after midnight, she moved away to join a group that had gathered about the champagne tables, I hung back, rather pensive. I wasn't used to thinking of myself as a grown-up woman, but now, clad in that handsome frock of blue and cream, satin and lace, I began at last to feel like one – and to realize, indeed, that I *was* one: that I was eighteen, and had left my father's house perhaps for ever, and earned my own living, and paid rent for my own rooms in London. I watched myself as if from a distance – watched as I supped at my wine as if it were ginger beer, and chatted and larked with the stage-hands, who had once so frightened me; watched as I took a cigarette from a fellow from the orchestra, and lit it, and drew upon it with a sigh of satisfaction. When had I started smoking? I couldn't remember. I had grown so used to holding Kitty's fag for her while she changed suits, that gradually I had taken up the habit myself. I smoked so often, now, that half my fingers – which, four months before, had been permanently pink and puckered, from so many dippings in the oyster-tub – were now stained yellow as mustard at the tips.

The musician – I believe he played the cornet – took a small, insinuating step my way. 'Are you a friend of the man-ager's, or what?' he said. 'I haven't seen you in the hall before.'

I laughed. 'Yes you have. I'm Nancy, Kitty Butler's dresser.'

He raised his eyebrows, and leaned away to look me up and down. 'Well! And so you are. I thought you was just a kid. But here, just now, I took you for an actress, or a dancer.'

I smiled, and shook my head. There was a pause while he

sipped at his glass and wiped at his moustache. 'I bet you dance a treat, though, don't you?' he said then. 'How about it?' He nodded to the crush of waltzing couples at the back of the stage.

'Oh, no,' I said. 'I couldn't. I've had too much cham.'

He laughed: 'All the better!' He put his drink aside, gripped his cigarette between his lips, then put his hands on my waist and lifted me up. I gave a shriek; he began to turn and dip, in a clownish approximation of a waltz-step. The louder I laughed and shrieked, the faster he turned me. A dozen people looked our way, and smiled and clapped.

At last he stumbled and almost fell, then put me down with a thump. 'Now,' he said breathlessly, 'tell me I ain't a marvellous dancer.'

'You ain't,' I said. 'You've made me giddy as a fish, and' – I felt at the front of my dress – 'you have spoiled my sash!'

'I'll fix that for you,' he said, reaching for my waist again. I gave a yelp, and stepped out of his grasp.

'No you won't! You can push off and leave me in peace.' Now he seized me, and tickled me so that I giggled. Being tickled always makes me laugh, however little I care for the tickler; but after several more minutes of this kind of thing he at last gave up on me, and went back to his pals in the band.

I ran my hands over my sash again. I feared he really had spoiled it, but couldn't see well enough to be sure. I finished my drink with a gulp – it was, I suppose, my sixth or seventh glass – and slipped from the stage. I made my way first to the lavatory, then headed downstairs to the change-room. This had been opened tonight only so that the ladies should have a place to hang their coats, and it was cold and empty and rather dim; but it had a looking-glass: and it was to this that I now stepped, squinting and tugging at my dress to pull it straight.

I had been there for no longer than a minute when there came the sound of footsteps in the passageway beyond, and then a silence. I turned my head to see who was there, and found that it was Kitty. She had her shoulder against the door-frame and her arms folded. She wasn't standing as one normally stands – as she usually stood – in an evening gown. She was standing as she did when she was on stage, with her trousers on – rather cockily. Her face was turned towards me and I couldn't see her rope of hair, or the swell of her breasts. Her cheeks were very pale; there was a stain upon her skirt where some champagne had dripped upon it from an over-spilling glass.

'Wot cheer, Kitty,' I said. But she did not return my smile, only watched me, levelly. I looked uncertainly back to the glass, and continued working at my sash. When she spoke at last, I knew at once that she was rather drunk.

'Seen something you fancy?' she said. I turned to her again in surprise, and she took a step into the room.

'What?'

'I said, "Seen something you fancy, Nancy?" Everybody else here tonight seems to have. Seems to have seen something that has rather caught their eye.'

I swallowed, unsure of what reply to make to her. She walked closer, then stopped a few paces from me, and continued to fix me with the same even, arrogant gaze.

'You were very fresh with that horn-player, weren't you?' she said then.

I blinked. 'We were just having a bit of a lark.'

'A bit of a lark? His hands were all over you.'

'Oh Kitty, they weren't!' My voice almost trembled. It was horrible to see her so savage; I don't believe that, in all the weeks that we had spent together, she had ever so much as raised her voice to me in impatience.

48

'Yes they were,' she said. 'I was watching – me and half the party. You know what they'll be calling you soon, don't you? "Miss Flirt".'

Miss Flirt! Now I didn't know whether to cry or to laugh.

'How can you say such a thing?' I asked her.

'Because it's true.' She sounded all at once rather sullen. 'I wouldn't have bought you such a fine dress, if I'd known you were only going to wear it to go flirting in.'

'Oh!' I stamped my foot, unsteadily – I was as drunk, I suppose, as she was. 'Oh!' I put my fingers to the neck of my gown, and began to fumble with its fastenings. 'I shall take the dam' dress off right here and you shall have it back,' I said, 'if that's how you feel about it!'

At that she took another step towards me and seized my arm. 'Don't be a fool,' she said in a slightly chastened tone. I shook her off and continued to work – quite fruitlessly, since the wine, together with my anger and surprise, had made me terribly clumsy – at the buttons of my frock. Kitty took hold of me again; soon we were almost tussling.

'I won't have you call me a flirt!' I said as she tugged at me. 'How could you call me one? How could you? Oh! If you just knew –' I put my hand to the back of my collar; her fingers followed my own, her face came close. Seeing it, I felt all at once quite dazed. I thought I had become her sister, as she wanted. I thought I had my queer desires cribbed and chilled and chastened. Now I knew only that her arm was about me, her hand on mine, her breath hot upon my cheek. I grasped her – not the better to push her away, but in order to hold her nearer. Gradually we ceased our wrestling and grew still, our breaths ragged, our hearts thudding. Her eyes were round and dark as jet; I felt her fingers leave my hand and move against my neck.

Then all at once there came a blast of noise from the

49

passageway beyond, and the sound of footsteps. Kitty started in my arms as if a pistol had been fired, and took a half-dozen steps, very rapidly, away. A woman – Esther, the conjuror's assistant – appeared on the other side of the open doorway. She was pale, and looked terribly grave. She said: 'Kitty, Nan, you won't believe it.' She reached for her handkerchief, and put it to her mouth. 'There's some boys just come, from the Charing Cross Hospital. They are saying Gully Sutherland is there' – this was the comic singer who had appeared with Kitty at the Canterbury Palace – 'they are saying Gully is there – that he has got drunk, and shot himself dead!'

It was true – we all heard, next day, how horribly true it was. I should never have suspected it, but had learned since coming to London that Gully was known in the business as something of a lush. He never finished a show without calling into a public-house on his way home; and on the night of our party he had been drinking at Fulham. Here, all hidden in a corner stall, he had overheard a fellow at the bar say that Gully Sutherland was past his best, and should make way for funnier artistes; that he had sat through Gully's latest routine, and all the gags were flat ones. The bar-man said that when Gully heard this he went to the man and shook him by the hand, and bought him a beer, then he bought beer for everyone. Then he went home and took a gun, and fired it at his own heart . . .

We didn't know all of this that night at Marylebone, we knew only that Gully had had a kind of fit, and taken his life; but the news put an end to our party and left us all, like Esther, nervous and grave. Kitty and I, on hearing the news, went up to the stage – she seizing my hand as we stumbled up the steps, but in grief now, I thought, rather than anything warmer. The manager had had all the house-lights lit, and the band had lain their instruments aside; some people were weeping, the cornet-player who had tickled me had his arm about a trembling girl. Esther cried, 'Oh isn't it awful, isn't it *horrible*?' I suppose the wine made everybody feel the shock of it the more.

I, however, did not know what to make of it. I couldn't think of Gully at all: my thoughts were still with Kitty, and with that moment in the change-room, when I had felt her hand on me and seemed to feel a kind of understanding leap between us. She hadn't looked at me since then, and now she had gone to talk to one of the boys who had brought the news of Gully's suicide. After a moment, however, I saw her shake her head and step away, and seem to search for me; and when she saw me – waiting for her, in the shadows of the wing – she came and sighed. 'Poor Gully. They say his heart was shot right through . . .'

'And to think,' I said, 'it was for Gully's sake that I first went to Canterbury and saw you . . .'

She looked at me, then, and trembled; and put a hand to her cheek, as if made weak with sorrow. But I dared not move to comfort her – only stood, miserable and unsure.

When I said that we should go – since other people were now leaving – she nodded. We returned to the change-room for our coats; its jets were all flaring now, and there were white-faced women in it with handkerchiefs before their eyes. Then we stepped to the stage door, and waited while the doorman found a cab for us. This seemed to take an age. It was two o'clock or later before we started on our journey home; and then we sat, on different seats, in silence – Kitty repeating only, now and then: 'Poor Gully! What a thing to do!', and I still drunk, still dazed, still desperately stirred, but still uncertain.

It was a bitterly cold and beautiful night – perfectly quiet, once we had left the clamour of the party behind us, and still. The roads were foggy, and thick with ice: every so often I felt the wheels of our carriage slide a little, and caught the sound of the horse's slithering, uncertain step, and the driver's gentle curses. Beside us the pavements glittered with frost, and each street-lamp glowed, in the fog, from the centre of its own yellow nimbus. For long stretches, ours was the only vehicle on the streets at all; the horse, the driver, Kitty and I might have been the only wakeful creatures in a city of stone and ice and slumber.

At length we reached Lambeth Bridge, where Kitty and I had stood only a few weeks before and gazed at the pleasure-boats below. Now, with our faces pressed to the carriage window, we saw it all transformed – saw the lights of the Embankment, a belt of amber beads dissolving into the night; and the great dark jagged bulk of the Houses of Parliament looming over the river; and the Thames itself, its boats all moored and silent, its water grey and sluggish and thick, and rather strange.

It was this last which made Kitty pull the window down, and call to the driver, in a high, excited voice, to stop. Then she pushed the carriage door open, pulled me to the iron parapet of the bridge, and seized my hand.

'Look,' she said. Her grief seemed all forgotten. Below us, in the water, there were great slivers of ice six feet across, drifting and gently turning in the winding currents, like basking seals.

The Thames was freezing over.

I looked from the river to Kitty, and from Kitty to the bridge on which we stood. There was no one near us save our driver – and he had the collar of his cape about his ears, and was busy with his pipe and his tobacco-pouch. I looked at the river again – at that extraordinary, ordinary transformation, that easy submission to the urgings of a natural law, that was yet so rare and so unsettling.

It seemed a little miracle, done just for Kitty and me.

'How cold it must be!' I said softly. 'Imagine if the whole river froze over, if it was frozen right down from here to Richmond. Would you walk across it?'

Kitty shivered, and shook her head. 'The ice would break,' she said. 'We would sink and drown; or else be stranded and die of the cold!'

I had expected her to smile, not make me a serious answer. I saw us floating down the Thames, out to sea – past Whitstable, perhaps – on a piece of ice no bigger than a pancake.

The horse took a step, and its bridle jangled; the driver gave a cough. Still we gazed at the river, silent and unmoving – and both of us, finally, rather grave.

At last Kitty gave a whisper. 'Ain't it queer?' she said.

I made no answer, only stared at where the curdled water swirled, thick and unwilling, about the columns of the bridge beneath our feet. But when she shivered again I moved a step closer to her, and felt her lean against me in response. It was icy cold upon the bridge; we should have moved back from the parapet into the shelter of the carriage. But we were loath to leave the sight of the frozen river – loath too, perhaps, to leave the warmth of one another's bodies, now that we had found it.

I took her hand. Her fingers, I could feel, were stiff and cold inside her glove. I placed the hand against my cheek; it did not warm it. With my eyes all the time on the water below I pulled at the button at her wrist, then drew the mitten from her, and held her fingers against my lips to warm them with my breath.

I sighed, gently, against her knuckles; then turned the hand, and breathed upon her palm. There was no sound at

53

all save the unfamiliar lapping and creaking of the frozen river. Then, 'Nan,' she said, very low.

I looked at her, her hand still held to my mouth and my breath still damp upon her fingers. Her face was raised to mine, and her gaze was dark and strange and thick, like the water below.

I let my hand drop; she kept her fingers upon my lips, then moved them, very slowly, to my cheek, my ear, my throat, my neck. Then her features gave a shiver and she said in a whisper: 'You won't tell a soul, Nan – will you?'

I think I sighed then: sighed to know – to know for sure, at last! – that there was *something to be told*. And then I dipped my face to hers, and shut my eyes.

Her mouth was chill, at first, then very warm – the only warm thing, it seemed to me, in the whole of the frozen city; and when she took her lips away – as she did, after a moment, to give a quick, anxious glance towards our hunched and nodding driver – my own felt wet and sore and naked in the bitter December breezes, as if her kiss had flayed them.

She drew me into the shadow of the carriage, where we were hidden from sight. Here we stepped together, and kissed again: I placed my arms about her shoulders, and felt her own hands shake upon my back. From lip to ankle, and through all the fussy layers of our coats and gowns, I felt her body stiff against my own – felt the pounding, very rapid, where we joined at the breast; and the pulse and the heat and the cleaving, where we pressed together at the hips.

We stood like this for a minute, maybe longer; then the carriage gave a creak as the driver shifted in his seat, and Kitty stepped quickly away. I could not take my hands from her, but she seized my wrists and kissed my fingers and gave a kind of nervous laugh, and a whisper: 'You will kiss the life out of me!'

She moved into the carriage, and I clambered in behind her, trembling and giddy and half-blind, I think, with agitation and desire. Then the door was closed; the driver called to his pony, and the cab gave a jerk and a slither. The frozen river was left behind us – dull, in comparison with this new miracle!

We sat side by side. She put her hands to my face again, and I shivered, so that my jaws jumped beneath her fingers. But she didn't kiss me again: rather, she leaned against me with her face upon my neck, so that her mouth was out of reach of mine, but hot against the skin below my ear. Her hand, that was still bare of its glove and white with cold, she slid into the gap at the front of my jacket; her knee she laid heavily against my own. When the brougham swayed I felt her lips, her fingers, her thigh come ever more heavy, ever more hot, ever more close upon me, until I longed to squirm beneath the pressing of her, and cry out. But she gave me no word, no kiss or caress; and in my awe and my innocence I only sat steady, as she seemed to wish. That cab-ride from the Thames to Brixton was, in consequence, the most wonderful and most terrible journey I have ever made.

At last, however, we felt the carriage turn, then slow, and finally stop, and heard the driver thump upon the roof with the butt of his whip to tell us we were home: we were so quiet, perhaps he thought we slumbered.

I remember a little of our entry into Mrs Dendy's – the fumbling at the door with the latch-key, the mounting of the darkened stairs, our passage through that still and sleeping house. I remember pausing on the landing beneath the skylight, where the stars showed very small and bright, and silently pressing my lips to Kitty's ear as she bent to unlock our chamber door; I remember how she leaned against it when she had it shut fast behind us, and gave a sigh, and reached for me again, and pulled me to her. I remember that she wouldn't let me raise a taper to the gas-jet – but made us stumble to the bedroom through the darkness.

And I remember, very clearly, all that happened there.

The room was bitter cold – so cold it seemed an outrage to take our dresses off and bare our flesh; but an outrage, too, to some more urgent instinct to keep them on. I had been clumsy in the change-room of the theatre, but I was not clumsy now. I stripped quickly to my drawers and chemise, then heard Kitty cursing over the buttons of her gown, and stepped to help her. For a moment – my fingers tugging at hooks and ribbons, her own tearing at the pins which kept her plait of hair in place – we might have been at the side of a stage, making a lightning change between numbers.

At last she was naked, all except for the pearl and chain about her neck; she turned in my hands, stiff and pimpled with cold, and I felt the brush of her nipples, and of the hair between her thighs. Then she moved away, and the bed-springs creaked; and at that, I didn't wait to pull the rest of my own clothes off but followed her to the bed and found her; so shivering there, beneath the sheets. Here we kissed more leisurely, but also more fiercely, than we had before; at last the chill – though not the trembling – subsided.

Once her naked limbs began to strain against my own, however, I felt suddenly shy, suddenly awed. I leaned away from her. 'May I really – touch you?' I whispered. She gave again a nervous laugh, and tilted her face against her pillow.

'Oh, Nan,' she said, 'I think I shall die if you don't!'

Tentatively, then, I raised my hand, and dipped my fingers into her hair. I touched her face – her brow, that curved; her cheek, that was freckled; her lip, her chin, her throat, her collar-bone, her shoulder . . . Here, shy again, I let my hand linger – until, with her face still tilted from my own and her eyes hard shut, she took my wrist and gently led my fingers to her breasts. When I touched her here she sighed, and turned; and after a minute or two she seized my wrist again, and moved it lower.

Here she was wet, and smooth as velvet. I had never, of course, touched anyone like this before – except, sometimes, myself; but it was as if I touched myself now, for the slippery hand which stroked her seemed to stroke me: I felt my drawers grow damp and warm, my own hips jerk as hers did. Soon I ceased my gentle strokings and began to rub her, rather hard. 'Oh!' she said very softly; then, as I rubbed faster, she said 'Oh!' again. Then, 'Oh, oh, oh!': a volley of 'Oh!'s, low and fast and breathy. She bucked, and the bed gave an answering creak; her own hands began to chafe distractedly at the flesh of my shoulders. There seemed no motion, no rhythm, in all the world, but that which I had set up, between her legs, with one wet fingertip.

At last she gasped, and stiffened, then plucked my hand away and fell back, heavy and slack. I pressed her to me, and for a moment we lay together quite still. I felt her heart beating wildly in her breast; and when it had calmed a little she stirred, and sighed, and put a hand to her cheek.

'You've made me weep,' she murmured.

I sat up. 'Not really, Kitty?'

'Yes, really.' She gave a twitch that was half laughter, half a sob, then rubbed at her eyes again, and when I took her fingers from her face I could feel the tears upon them. I pressed her hand, suddenly uncertain: 'Did I hurt you? What did I do that was bad? Did I hurt you, Kitty?'

She shook her head, and sniffed, and laughed more freely. 'Hurt me? Oh, no. It was only – so very sweet.' She smiled. 'And you are – so very good. And I—' She sniffed again, then

57

placed her face against my breast and hid her eyes from me. 'And I – oh, Nan, I do so love you, so very, very much!'

I lay beside her, and put my arms about her. My own desire I quite forgot, and she made no move to remind me of it. I forgot, too, Gully Sutherland – who three hours before had put a gun to his own heart, because a man had sat through his routine unsmiling. I only lay; and soon Kitty slept. And I studied her face, where it showed creamy pale in the darkness, and thought, *She loves me, She loves me* – like a fool with a daisy-stalk, endlessly exclaiming over the same last browning petal.

GAMES OF
SEDUCTION

CHODERLOS DE LACLOS

from:
LES LIAISONS DANGEREUSES

Translated by Richard Aldington

The Vicomte de Valmont to the Marquise de Merteuil

I WAGER THAT ever since your adventure you have every day been expecting my compliments and praise; I have no doubt but that my long silence has put you a little out of temper; but what do you expect? I have always thought that when one had nothing but praise to give a woman one can be at rest about her and occupy oneself with something else. However, I thank you on my account and congratulate you on yours. To make you perfectly happy, I am even willing to admit that this time you have surpassed my expectations. After that, let us see if on my side I have at least partly fulfilled yours.

I do not want to talk to you about Madame de Tourvel; her slow advance displeases you. You only like completed affairs. Drawn-out scenes weary you; but I have never tasted the pleasure I now enjoy in this supposed tardiness.

Yes, I like to see, to watch this prudent woman impelled, without her perceiving it, upon a path which allows no return, and whose steep and dangerous incline carries her on in spite of herself, and forces her to follow me. There, terrified by the peril she runs, she would like to halt and cannot check herself. Her exertions and her skill may render her steps shorter; but they must follow one upon the other. Sometimes, not daring to look the danger in the face, she shuts her eyes, lets herself go, and abandons herself to my charge. More often her efforts are revived by a new fear; in her mortal terror she would like to try to turn back once again; she exhausts her strength in painfully climbing back a short distance and very soon a magic power replaces her nearer the danger from which she had vainly tried to fly. Then having no one but me for guide and for support, without thinking of reproaching me for the inevitable fall, she implores me to retard it. Fervent prayers, humble supplications, all that mortals in their fear offer to the divinity, I receive from her; and you expect me to be deaf to her prayers, to destroy myself the worship she gives me, and to use in casting her down that power she invokes for her support! Ah! At least leave me the time to watch these touching struggles between love and virtue.

What! Do you think that very spectacle which makes you rush eagerly to the theatre, which you applaud there wildly, is less interesting in reality? You listen with enthusiasm to the sentiments of a pure and tender soul, which dreads the happiness it desires and does not cease to defend itself even when it ceases to resist; should they only be valueless for him who gives birth to them? But these, these are the delicious enjoyments this heavenly woman offers me every day; and you reproach me for lingering over their sweetness! Ah! The time will come only too soon when, degraded by her fall, she will be nothing but an ordinary woman to me.

But in speaking to you of her I forget that I did not wish to speak of her. I do not know what power attaches me to her, ceaselessly brings me back to her, even when I insult it. Let me put aside the dangerous thought of her; let me become myself again to deal with a more amusing subject. It concerns your pupil, now become mine, and I hope you will recognize me here.

For some days I had been better treated by my tender devotee and in consequence, being less preoccupied with her, I noticed that the Volanges girl is indeed very pretty; and that if it was silly to be in love with her like Danceny, perhaps it was none the less silly on my part not to seek with her a distraction rendered necessary by my solitude. I also thought it just to pay myself for the trouble I am giving myself for her; I remembered too that you had offered it to me before Danceny had any claims to it; and I thought myself authorized to claim some rights in a property he only possessed through my refusal and rejection. The little person's pretty look, her fresh mouth, her childish air, even her awkwardness fortified these sage reflections; I resolved to act upon them and the enterprise was crowned by success.

You are wondering already by what means I have so soon supplanted the cherished lover; what seduction is suitable to this age, this inexperience? Spare yourself the trouble, I used none. While you skilfully handled the arms of your sex and triumphed by subtlety, I returned to man his imprescriptible rights and overcame by authority. I was sure of seizing my prey if I could come at it; I needed no ruse except to approach her and that I made use of hardly deserves the name.

I profited by the first letter I received from Danceny for his fair one, and after having notified her of it by the signal agreed upon between us, instead of using my skill to give it her I used it to find means not to give it; I feigned to share the impatience I had created, and after having caused the difficulty I pointed out the remedy for it.

The young person's room has a door opening on the corridor; but naturally the mother had taken the key. It was only a question of getting possession of it. Nothing could have been easier to carry out; I only asked to have it at my disposition for a couple of hours and I guaranteed to have one like it. Then correspondence, interviews, nocturnal rendezvous, all became convenient and certain. However, would you believe it? the timid child was afraid and refused.

Another would have been nonplussed by this; but I only saw in it an opportunity for a more piquant pleasure. I wrote to Danceny to complain of this refusal and I acted so well that our scatter-brain had no rest until he had obtained, exacted even, from his timorous mistress her consent to grant my request and to yield wholly to my discretion.

I confess I was very pleased to have changed parts in this way and to have the young man do for me what he thought I should do for him. This idea doubled the value of the adventure in my eyes; therefore as soon as I had the precious key, I hastened to make use of it; this was last night.

After making sure that everything was quiet in the *Château*, I armed myself with a dark lantern, made the toilet which suited the hour and was demanded by the situation, and paid my first visit to your pupil. I had caused everything to be prepared (and by herself) to be able to enter noiselessly. She was in her first sleep and in the sleep of her age; so that I came up to her bedside without awakening her. At first I was tempted to go further and to try to pass as a dream; but fearing the effect of surprise and the noise it brings with it, I preferred to arouse the pretty sleeper cautiously, and in fact I succeeded in preventing the cry I feared.

After having calmed her first fears, I risked a few liberties since I had not come there to talk. Doubtless she had not been well informed at her convent as to how many different perils timid innocence is exposed, and all it has to guard to avoid a surprisal; for giving all her attention and all her strength to defending herself from a kiss, which was only a false attack, she left all the rest without defence. How could I not profit by it! I therefore changed my movement and immediately took post. Here we were both very nearly lost; the little girl was terrified and tried to scream in good faith, fortunately her voice was quenched in tears. She also threw

66

herself towards her bell-rope, but my skill restrained her arm in time.

'What are you doing?' I then said to her. 'You will ruin yourself for ever. Suppose someone comes; what does it matter to me? Whom will you convince that I am not here by your wish? Who but you could have given me the means of coming in? And will you be able to explain the use of this key I hold from you, which I could only have had through you?'

This short harangue calmed neither her grief nor her anger; but it brought about submission. I do not know if I achieved the tone of eloquence; it is at least true that I did not have its gestures. With one hand occupied by force and the other by love what orator could pretend to grace in such a situation? If you imagine it correctly, you will at least admit it was favourable to attack; but I do not understand anything and, as you say, the simplest woman, a mere school-girl, leads me like a child.

For all her distress she felt she had to adopt some course and come to terms. Since prayers found me inexorable she had to come to offers. You will suppose that I sold this important post very dearly; no, I promised everything for a kiss. It is true that, having taken the kiss, I did not keep my promise; but I had good reasons. Had we agreed that it should be taken or given? After much bargaining, we agreed on a second and it was said that this should be received. Then I guided the timid arms around my body, I held her more amorously in one of mine, and the soft kiss was indeed received, well received, perfectly received, in short, love himself could not have done better.

Such good faith deserved a reward; and so I immediately granted the request. The hand was withdrawn; but I do not know by what chance I found myself in its place. You suppose that there I was very eager, very active, do you not? Not at all. I have begun to like slow methods, I tell you. Once certain of arriving, why hurry on the journey so fast?

Seriously, I was very glad to observe for once the power of opportunity, and here I found it divested of all other aid. Yet she had to combat love, and love supported by modesty or shame, fortified above all by the annoyance I had given, which was considerable. Opportunity was alone; but it was there, all was offered, all was present, and love was absent.

To make certain of my observations I was cunning enough to use no more force than she could combat. Only if my charming enemy abused my facility, and was ready to escape me, I restrained her by the same fear whose happy effects I had already made proof of. Well, without my taking any other exertion, the tender mistress, forgetting her oaths, yielded at first and ended up by consenting; not but that after the first moment reproaches and tears returned in concert; I do not know whether they were true or feigned; but, as always happens, they ceased as soon as I busied myself with giving reason for others. In short, from frailty to reproaches and from reproaches to frailty, we did not separate until we were satisfied with each other and had both agreed on the rendezvous for this evening.

I did not go back to my room until dawn. And I was worn out with fatigue and lack of sleep; however I sacrificed both to the desire of being at breakfast in the morning; I have a passion for observing behaviours the morning after. You can have no idea of what this was. There was embarrassment in her countenance! Difficulty in walking! Eyes continually lowered, and so large and so tired! That round face had grown so much longer! Nothing could be more amusing. And for the first time, her mother (alarmed by this extreme change), showed quite a tender interest in her! And Madame de Tourvel too was very attentive about her! Oh! Her attentions are only lent; a day will come when they can be returned to her and that day is not far off. Goodbye, my fair friend.

FROM THE CHÂTEAU DE . . . , IST OF OCTOBER, 17—

Cécile Volanges to the Marquise de Merteuil

AH HEAVEN! MADAME, how distressed I am! How miserable I am! Who will console me in my grief? Who will advise me in my present state of embarrassment? This Monsieur de Valmont . . . and Danceny! No, the idea of Danceny fills me with despair . . . How can I relate it to you? How can I tell you? . . . I do not know what to do. Yet my heart is full . . . I must speak to someone and you are the only person in whom I can, in whom I dare confide. You are so kind to me! But do not be so now; I am not worthy of it; how shall I put it? I do not desire your kindness. Everyone here has showed an interest in me today; they all increased my pain. I felt so much that I did not deserve it! Scold me, rather; scold me well, for I deserve it; but afterwards save me; if you do not have the kindness to advise me I shall die of grief.

You must know then . . . my hand trembles, as you see, I can hardly write, my face feels on fire . . . Ah! it is indeed the red of shame. Well, I will endure it; it will be the first punishment for my fault. Yes, I will tell you everything.

You must know then that Monsieur de Valmont, who hitherto had been handing me Monsieur Danceny's letters, suddenly found that it was too difficult and wanted to have the key of my room. I can assure you I did not want to do it; but he went to the extent of writing to Danceny and Danceny wanted it too; and it hurts me so much when I refuse him anything, especially since my absence which makes him so unhappy, that I ended by consenting to it. I did not foresee the misfortune which would occur from it.

Yesterday Monsieur de Valmont made use of this key to come into my room when I was asleep; I expected it so little that he frightened me very much when he woke me up; but as he spoke to me at once, I recognized him and did not scream; and then my first idea was that he had perhaps come to bring me a letter from Danceny. It was far from that. A moment afterwards he wanted to kiss me; and while I defended myself, as was natural, he did what I would not have him do for anything in the world ... but, he wanted a kiss first. I had to, for what could I do? I had tried to call, but I could not and then he told me that if somebody came he could throw all the blame on me; and indeed that was very easy on account of the key. After it he did not withdraw at all. He wanted a second; and I don't know what there was about this one but it completely disturbed me; and after, it was still worse than before. Oh! This is very wrong. Afterwards ... you will exempt me from telling you the rest; but I am as unhappy as one can be.

What I blame myself the most for, and yet must speak to you about, is that I am afraid I did not defend myself as much as I could have; I do not know how this could have happened; assuredly I do not love Monsieur de Valmont, on the contrary; and there were moments when it was as if I loved him ... You may well suppose that did not prevent me from continuing to say no to him; but I felt I was not doing what I said; and it was as if in spite of myself; and then I was very much upset! If it is always as difficult as that to defend oneself, one must need a lot of practice! It is true that Monsieur de Valmont has a way of talking that one does not know how to answer; and will you believe it? when he went away it was as if I was sorry, and I was weak enough to consent that he should come again this evening; that troubles me even more than all the rest.

Oh! In spite of this, I promise you I shall prevent him from coming. He had scarcely gone when I felt how wrong I had been to promise it him. And I cried all the rest of the time. Above all Danceny grieved me! Every time I thought of him my tears increased until they stifled me, and still I thought of him ... and even now you see what happens; my paper is all wet. No, I shall never be consoled were it only for his sake ... At last I could cry no more, and yet I could not sleep a minute. This morning when I got up and looked at myself in the mirror, it frightened me to see how changed I was.

Mamma noticed it as soon as she saw me and asked me what was the matter. I began to cry at once. I thought she was going to scold me, and perhaps that would have hurt me less; but, no, she spoke gently to me! I did not deserve it. She told me not to grieve like that! She did not know the reason for my grief. That I should make myself ill. There are moments when I wish I were dead. I could not endure it. I threw myself into her arms, saying: 'Ah Mamma! your little girl is very unhappy!' Mamma could not prevent herself from crying a little and that only increased my grief; fortunately she did not ask me why I was so unhappy, for I should not have known what to say to her.

I beg you, Madame, to write to me as soon as you can and tell me what I ought to do, for I have not the courage to think of anything and can do nothing but grieve. Please send me your letter by Monsieur de Valmont; but pray, if you write to him at the same time, do not mention to him what I have told you.

I have the honour to be, Madame, always with great friendship, your most humble and most obedient servant ...

I dare not sign this letter.

FROM THE CHÂTEAU DE . . . , IST OF OCTOBER, 17—

71

GIOVANNI BOCCACCIO

from:
DECAMERON

Translated by J. G. Nichols

Masetto of Lamporecchio pretends to be dumb and becomes a gardener at a convent where all the nuns vie to lie with him.

DEAR LADIES, THERE are plenty of men and women who are so stupid they really believe that, once a young woman has taken the veil and put on a nun's habit, she ceases to be a woman and does not experience any feminine desires, as though simply becoming a nun had turned her to stone. And if they chance to hear anything that goes against that belief, they are as upset as if a great evil had been committed against nature: they do not think of how they are themselves, and how the freedom to do what they like cannot satisfy them, and they do not consider the powerful effect which leisure and solitude can have. Again, there are plenty of people who really believe that the hoe and the spade and poor food and discomfort take the lust away entirely from workers on the land and coarsen their intellect and understanding. But, since the Queen has commanded me to speak, I intend to make clear to you, with a little tale on the theme she has proposed, just how wrong all those people are.

In our region there was once, and still is, a nunnery celebrated for its sanctity. (I shall not name it, in order not to detract from its good repute.) Not long ago, when it contained only eight nuns and their abbess, all of them young, there was a good little fellow there who looked after their beautiful garden. He was not happy with his wages and so, having settled his account with the nuns' steward, he returned to his native village of Lamporecchio. Among those who welcomed him home there was a young workman, called Masetto, who was strong and well built and, for a countryman, good-looking. He asked the ex-gardener, Nuto, where he had been for such a long time, and Nuto told him. Then Masetto asked him what his duties were as a servant in the nunnery.

Nuto answered: 'I used to work in the large beautiful garden there, and I also went to the coppice to gather wood, and I fetched water and did jobs like that; but the nuns gave me such poor wages that I could hardly keep myself in shoes. Besides, they were all young, and in my opinion they all had the Devil in them, because it was impossible to do anything to please them. In fact, when I was working sometimes in the garden, one would say: "Put this here," and another: "Put that there," and still another would snatch the hoe out of my hands and say: "This isn't right," and altogether they made such difficulties that I would leave what I was doing and get out of the garden. And so, what with one thing and another, I had no wish to stay there any longer, and I came home. Their steward, as I was coming away, did ask me if I knew anyone who could do the work and, if I did, to send him to him, and I promised I would – but I won't seek anyone out or send anyone, unless there's someone to whom God has given very broad shoulders.'

Masetto, as he listened to Nuto, felt such a strong desire to be with these nuns that it became an obsession: he thought from what Nuto had said that he would be able to achieve what he desired. He realized, however, that he would not be successful if he mentioned anything about it to Nuto, so he simply said: 'Yes, you did well to get away from there! It has a terrible effect on a man to live with women! You'd do better living with a crowd of devils: nine times out of ten they don't know their own minds.'

But once their conversation was over Masetto started considering how he could get to live with them. He knew he could cope well with the duties which Nuto had mentioned; he was sure he would not lose his job on that account, but he feared he would not be employed because he was too young and handsome. And so, having considered a number of ideas, he thought: 'The place is a long way from here, and nobody knows me there; if I pretend to be dumb, I shall certainly be employed.'

In the guise of a poor man, shouldering an axe and without telling anyone where he was going, but with this idea firmly in mind, he set off for the nunnery. When he arrived there, he happened to come across the steward in the courtyard, and he made signs to him, as dumb people do, to ask for food for the love of God, and to signify that he was willing to chop whatever wood was needed. The steward gladly gave him something to eat, and then took him to a heap of logs which Nuto had not been able to split, but all of which Masetto, with his great strength, split in next to no time. Then the steward, who had to go to the copse, took him with him and there set him to cutting wood. Then he showed him an ass and gave him to understand by signs that he was to take the wood back to the convent. Masetto performed all these tasks so well that the steward kept him there several days doing what was needed, with the result that one day the abbess saw him and asked the steward about him.

He told her: 'Madam, this is a poor deaf and dumb fellow who arrived here some days ago begging; I gave him something to eat, and got him working on some jobs which needed doing. If he is capable of working in the garden and wishes to stay here, then I believe he would give us good service, because we do need a gardener, and he is strong and would do whatever was needed. And besides, you wouldn't need to worry about him teasing these young ladies of yours.'

To this the abbess replied: 'How right you are! Find out if he is a good gardener, and make every effort to keep him here. Give him a pair of shoes and an old cloak, and flatter him, make much of him and give him plenty to eat.'

The steward said he would. Now Masetto was not far away and, as he went through the motions of sweeping the court-yard, he heard every word that was said, and he thought happily: 'If you put me into that garden, I'll work in it as no one has ever worked before.'

Once the steward had seen that he really did know how to work in the garden, he made signs to ask Masetto if he wished to stay there, and Masetto made signs in reply that he would do whatever the steward wanted. So the steward took him on, and put him to work in the garden, after show-ing him what needed doing. Then the steward went away to attend to other matters, and left him there. And as he worked there day after day, the nuns began to be a nuisance and to make fun of him, as people often do with deaf mutes, and said the most shocking things to him, not realizing that he could understand them – and the abbess, perhaps imagining that he had lost his tail as well as his tongue, hardly bothered about this at all.

Now it happened one day that, as he was resting after a spell of hard work, two young nuns who were walking through the garden approached him, while he was pretend-ing to be asleep, and started gazing at him. One of them, who was bolder than the other, said to her companion: 'If I thought that you would keep it secret, I'd tell you some-thing I've often thought about, something which might be of interest to you too.'

The other answered: 'You can speak safely: I won't tell a soul.'

At that point the bold nun said: 'I don't know if you've ever thought how strictly we are guarded here, and how no man dares to enter except the steward, who is old, and this deaf mute. Now, I've often heard it said by ladies who were visiting us that all the pleasures in the world are nothing to that pleasure which women can have with a man. And so I've often had it in mind to find out with this deaf mute whether that's true or not, since I can't do it with anyone else. And he's the best person in the world to do it with since, even if he wanted to, he couldn't tell anyone about it afterwards. You can see yourself what a stupid fellow he is, with a better body than a mind. I'd like to know how this strikes you.'

'Oh dear!' said the other nun. 'What are you saying? Don't you know that we've promised our virginity to God?'

The first nun answered: 'Oh, people make Him lots of promises every day which they never keep! We did promise to preserve our virginity, but others can be found to preserve theirs for Him.'

Then her friend objected: 'But what would we do if we became pregnant?'

The answer was: 'You're crossing your bridges before you come to them. If that happens, well then we'll have to think about it. There are probably a thousand ways of making sure no one gets to know, provided we both keep our own counsel.'

When she heard this, the other nun, who was even more keen than her companion to find out what kind of creature a man was, said: 'All right. How shall we manage this?'

Her friend said: 'As you can see, it will soon be nones. I think all the sisters, apart from the two of us, are about to go to sleep. Let's look through the garden to make sure no one's there, and then all we have to do is take him by the hand

79

and lead him to this shack where he shelters from the rain. Then one can go inside with him, while the other stands on guard outside. He's stupid, and he'll do whatever we want.'

Masetto heard the whole conversation, and he was quite ready to obey, waiting only for one of them to come and take him. When the two nuns had looked all round and made certain that no one could see them, the one who had started the discussion came over to him and roused him. He sprang to his feet, and she took him coaxingly by the hand and, while he giggled like an imbecile, led him to the shack, where Masetto did not need much encouragement to do what she wanted. Then she, as a good friend, having had what she wanted, gave place to the other, and Masetto, still acting like a ninny, did what she wanted. Before the nuns left that place, both of them had had more than one experience of the dumb man's riding ability. And afterwards, when they discussed it, they agreed that that experience was just as sweet as they had heard it was, or even sweeter. From then on they seized any opportunity to amuse themselves with the dumb fellow.

One day a fellow sister happened to notice, from a window in her cell, what was happening, and she brought it to the attention of two others. At first they were going to tell the abbess about it, but then they changed their minds and agreed among themselves to go shares in Masetto's estate. Later, the other three nuns became shareholders also, at different times and in various circumstances. Finally the abbess, who still knew nothing of all this, when she was walking one day through the garden, quite alone, in the heat of the day, came across Masetto. The little work which he was able to do during the day, being worn out by galloping throughout the night, had left him stretched out asleep in the shade of an almond tree. The wind had blown back the clothes covering him, and left him stark naked. When the abbess saw this, and saw that she was alone, she fell prey to the same appetite as her young nuns. She roused him and took him to her room where she kept him for several days, while the nuns lamented that the gardener did not come to tend the garden, and she experienced again and again that pleasure which she had been accustomed to deprecate.

Ultimately, what with her sending him back to his own room, and then very often wanting him back again in hers, and besides that wanting more than her fair share of him, Masetto could no longer satisfy so many women. He realized that his dumbness, if he persisted in it, would impair his health – and so one night when he was with the abbess, he loosened his tongue and said: 'Madam, I have heard that one cock can cope well with ten hens, but that ten men can hardly satisfy one woman – and I have to serve nine. Now, there is no way I can last out like this; in fact with what I have done up to now, I am reduced to such a state that I can't do anything at all. Therefore you must either let me go or find some other way of coping with the situation.'

The abbess was amazed to hear someone speak when she had always thought he could not, and she said: 'What's going on? I thought you were dumb?'

'Madam,' said Masetto, 'I was dumb, but I was not born so. In fact, an illness took away my tongue, and tonight for the first time I feel that it is restored to me, for which I thank God from the heart.'

The abbess believed him and asked him what he meant about having nine to serve. Masetto told her the truth, and when she heard it the abbess realized that all the other nuns were shrewder than she was. She was discreet however and, rather than letting Masetto go, she thought of coming to some agreement with her sisters, so that Masetto might not give the convent a bad reputation. After discussing what they had all been doing, they decided, with Masetto's approval, that the people round about should be led to believe that, through their prayers and the merits of their titular saint, Masetto, after having being dumb so long, had had his speech restored. They now made Masetto their steward, in place of their old steward who had recently died, and divided up his work in such a way that he was able to cope with it. In the course of his work he did father a fair number of little monks and nuns, but it was all managed so discreetly that nothing was known of this until after the abbess's death, and by that time Masetto was already getting old and keen to return home as a rich man, and, once his wish was known, it was readily granted.

And so Masetto, now that he was old, and a father, and a wealthy man, and relieved of the trouble of feeding his children or contributing to their upkeep, having known how to make good use of his youth, returned to where he had come from, shouldering an axe and affirming that that was how Christ treated those who put horns on His crown.

ELIZABETH SPELLER

THOUGHT
WAVES

LATE ON A hot night. So late that even in June the velvet of dark is caught between the large white houses by the canal. A smell of jasmine, of privet, the roar of cars on their distant arc around the city.

On the top floor, two men sit in a large room: coffered ceilings, maps, books, eighteenth-century porcelain, a Bechstein and a minstrel's gallery. Schubert *Lieder* balanced on the night, glasses – several glasses – of brandy, the sash windows hauled open and the one low light behind a chair casting their features in relief.

'Do you ever see that dark girl? Zena? Was that it? Do you still . . . see her?' The older man smiles as he raises his eyebrows to his friend.

'Zinnia. It was Zinnia,' the figure in the deep chair replies. 'Still is Zinnia, actually.'

'So Jane doesn't mind . . . I mean, she knows, I assume?'

'Yes and no. You know. But would you like to see her – Zinnia, I mean?' The younger man, not young, but younger, asks. 'Look, I have her photograph.'

He pulls out a book – one of his more successful novels – from the tall cases; the picture is hidden within its pages.

The grey-haired man looks down, tips the picture towards the light, is surprised. The woman is naked, reclining like Maya, on large pillows, one knee up, one arm behind her head, her eyes looking directly at the photographer, between her legs dusk, her dark nipples disproportionately large for her small breasts.

'Lucky man.'

He gazes, embarrassment and arousal struggling within him. He drinks deeply from his glass.

'Do you see her often? I mean, it must be difficult.'

'It is difficult,' the writer smiles ruefully. 'She loves me, passionately. I desire her. And she lives in France much of the time. And there's Jane. But there are ways. And she is very compliant. That's love, you see. She'll do anything for me; it's terrifying in some ways. Should I set her free? I often mean to but I never quite do.'

His friend looks puzzled. The writer fills his glass.

'Would you like me to show you? Not photographs, I mean, but how it works?'

At a nod, he picks up a telephone and touches keys in the semi-darkness. The older man can just hear it ringing. It rings and rings. Finally an answer.

'It's me.' The writer smiles, whether for his friend or his lover or himself, who can tell?

'Yes. I am. Of course. And you?'

'Where are you? In bed. Yes, it's late. I know.'

'So, what are you wearing?'

'Of course. It's hot. No, I knew. Do you miss me?'

Is he acting? The one-sided conversation seems unreal.

'Zinnia ... I want you to do something for me. I'm here thinking of you. Missing you. You know what would make me happy.'

'Close your eyes. Now touch your breast. Yes. For me. For me, darling girl.'

It is silent in the darkness. Is he being teased? The older man is appalled and captivated.

'Put your finger in your mouth, sweetheart, now wet your nipple for me ... Stroke it, stroke it for me. Is it hard? Tell me, darling? How does it feel?'

86

'Now, take your nipple between your thumb and fore-finger . . . Squeeze it.'

'Now, the other one. Hurt it a little. Oh, I like that.' He exhales.

'Now, you know what I want you to do, don't you, sweet-heart? Tell me, are you ready for me? Are you wet? Open your legs, darling. Open them wide for me. As if I were there. Touch yourself. Gently. Gently. Stroke yourself for me.'

He cradles the telephone to his neck like a lover. He looks up at his friend and a smile, sensuous but perhaps mocking, hovers and is gone.

'How does it feel, Zinnia? Tell me. Is it opening for me? Is your clitoris hard? Run your finger over it; is it slippery? Yes, darling, go on.'

He reaches forward and presses the handset, and suddenly, shocking yet wonderful, the woman's voice is broadcast to the room. Her breath uneven, vibrating very slightly.

'Oh.' A ragged sigh. 'Oh, I love you.' Her words drawn out, soft in the near darkness. 'And it feels so good.'

The older man cannot look at the younger. He shifts in his chair but he listens on.

'Zinnia . . . now I want you to open yourself and slip your finger in. Are you really wet, darling? Tell me . . . are your lips swollen for me?'

'Oh yes.' The woman's voice sounds eager. 'Yes, yes, I'm doing that now, as you tell me, now, now and . . . Oh, I want you . . . My fingers, no, my whole palm is wet.'

The loudspeaker throws her sighs around the shadows.

'Darling, put your finger in your mouth. Suck. Does it taste good, darling? Let me hear you do it.'

Unmistakably in the darkness, faint but magical, there are the sounds of wetness; the woman sucks and she gives a soft groan.

'Now two – no –' the writer looks up at his friend '– three fingers.'

'You can, of course you can. I've given you more than that. Much more.' His voice is persuasive.

The woman murmurs assent.

'Push, darling, push them all in for me. Now out, now in again. Is that lovely, sweetheart? How does it make you feel?'

'Uh. Oh, it's wonderful. Oh, I love you so much. Always. Please . . .' Her voice sounds young.

They are all three in the night with the woman's breathing, deep and hoarse, and the grey-haired man is afraid that his own must be audible. He tries not to breathe with her. The writer seems not aroused but something else, something darker, less tangible. He smiles on.

'Zinnia, darling. Stroke yourself, long strokes, are you ready for me? Would you take me inside you?'

'Yes.' The clarity of sound is so good and the room high above the city so silent that they hear her swallow, a tiny grunt . . . she moves in the bed . . . she is in bed, the older man feels sure . . . the rustle of covers. There is another long, long sigh.

'Darling –' The writer has lowered his own voice now and leans forward, curling the phone in his hand. 'You know what I want, don't you?'

'Yes,' she whispers. 'Just like usual.' He looks up, challenges his friend with a stare. He cups the receiver with his hand. 'Shall we go on?' he asks him. 'Finish it . . . or . . .?'

The older man finds himself blushing and yet wanting her to be encouraged, not deterred. He stays silent. Does his head nod imperceptibly? He fears that it betrays him.

The writer turns his mouth to the phone. 'I want you to find something, darling, something . . . anything . . . whatever you like.'

They hear the woman move. For a few seconds her breathing dies down as she moves away. Then, although she says nothing, she is close again. Breathing. Aroused. Unknown, yet utterly exposed. The older man has never known such intimacy. There is heat and night and her.

'Have you found something, darling?' The writer's voice is low, but level. 'Lie back, bring your knees up the way I like it. Now push it into you. Go on ... all the way ... up to the hilt.'

For a moment, nothing but the lurching power of imagination. Then she catches her breath and it seems to last for ever.

'Yes. Oh yes.'

'Is it inside you? Is it filling you?' the younger man asks his lover. 'Now move it in and out slowly. Let me hear you, let me hear it.'

The woman calls out endearments; her moans are regular and faster.

The two men listen. She needs no instructions now, although from time to time she mutters something almost incomprehensible, then darling then please, then oh Jesus Jesus.

'Go on, go on,' the writer urges. 'Hard, do it hard. For me, sweetheart, I'm with you, it's just us, so show me, do it for me.'

The woman makes little noises in the back of her throat. The older man's erection aches and somewhere in his heart there is pain. For the obedience? For the deceit? He does not know. The photograph lies on the table beside him, just within the pool of light. There she lies naked, exposed, vulnerable.

'Oh God, I'm ... It's so lovely, uh uh uh ... I'm going to come, oh, I'm coming, I'm coming.' Her words tumble, echo, caught up in her falling breath.

'Darling, darling.' She cries out so loud that the great room is full of her, and then she seems to be weeping.

'Oh, I love you, I love you so much.' And her breath, her voice, her climax subside. The writer waits.

'You're so good, Zinnia, so good. My darling girl. My only love. Sleep now.'

'I love you.' The faintest fading whisper a long, long way away in the darkness.

The writer puts down the phone. He looks, almost challengingly, at his older friend.

'Did you enjoy that? She loves doing it ... loves me ... She was made for pleasure, so why shouldn't it be shared? No one else need know.'

The grey-haired man, his arousal still unassuaged, meets the eyes of his friend, now a stranger, and knows he sees his need.

In a small flat some miles away, the curtains billow. Zinnia, damp with sweat, bends back, sleepily, greedily. The man underneath her, spent but still slightly erect, looks up at her face.

'That,' he says, 'that was, well, extraordinary. How the hell I kept quiet when you came, when I came, doing it, knowing he was listening, and getting off on it, having to be so quiet. But God, how erotic. And you like an eel all over the place.' He laughs, lifts her off him.

'Find something ... anything you like, eh? And you did. And you did. But did you ever feel anything for him? Did you really do it for real for him?'

Zinnia smiles her slippery mermaid smile, her skin shines in the lamplight. For once she is completely satisfied.

NICHOLSON BAKER

from:
THE FERMATA

I AM GOING to call my autobiography *The Fermata*, even though 'fermata' is only one of the main names I have for the Fold. 'Fold' is, obviously, another. Every so often, usually in the fall (perhaps mundanely because my hormone-flows are at their highest then), I discover that I have the power to drop into the Fold. A Fold-drop is a period of time of variable length during which I am alive and ambulatory and thinking and looking, while the rest of the world is stopped, or paused. Over the years, I have had to come up with various techniques to trigger the pause, some of which have made use of rocker-switches, rubber bands, sewing needles, fingernail clippers, and other hardware, some of which have not. The power seems ultimately to come from within me, grandiose as that sounds, but as I invoke it I have to believe that it is external for it to work properly. I don't inquire into origins very often, fearing that too close a scrutiny will damage whatever interior states have given rise to it, since it is the most important ongoing adventure of my life.

I'm in the Fold right now, as a matter of fact. I want first to type out my name – it's Arnold Strine. I prefer Arno to the full Arnold. Putting my own name down is loin-girding somehow – it helps me go ahead with this. I'm thirty-five. I'm seated in an office chair whose four wide black casters roll silently over the carpeting, on the sixth floor of the MassBank building in downtown Boston. I'm looking up at a woman named Joyce, whose clothes I have rearranged somewhat, although I have not actually removed any of them. I'm looking directly at her, but she doesn't know this. While I look I'm using a Casio CW-16 portable electronic typewriter, which is powered by four D batteries, to record what I see and think. Before I snapped my fingers to stop the flow of time in the universe, Joyce was walking across the carpeting in a gray-blue knit dress, and I was sitting behind a desk twenty or thirty feet away, transcribing a tape. I could see her hipbones under her dress, and I immediately knew it was the time to Snap in. Her pocketbook is still over her shoulder. Her pubic hair is very black and nice to look at – there is lots and lots of it. If I didn't already know her name, I would probably now open her purse and find out her name, because it helps to know the name of a woman I undress. There is moreover something very exciting, almost moving, about taking a peek at a woman's driver's license without her knowing – studying the picture and wondering whether it was one that pleased her or made her unhappy when she was first given it at the DMV.

But I do know this woman's name. I've typed some of her tapes. The language of her dictations is looser than some of the other loan officers' – she will occasionally use a phrase like 'spruce up' or 'polish off' or 'kick in' that you very seldom come across in the credit updates of large regional banks. One of her more recent dictations ended with something like 'Kyle Roller indicated that he had been dealing with the subject since 1989. Volume since that time has been $80,000. He emphatically stated that their service was substandard. He indicated that he has put further business with them on hold because they had "lied like hell" to him. He indicated he did not want his name mentioned back to the Pauley brothers. This information was returned to Joyce Collier on –' and then she said the date. As prose it is not Penelope

Fitzgerald, perhaps, but you crave any tremor of life in these reports, and I will admit that I felt an arrow go through me when I heard her say 'lied like hell.'

Last week, Joyce was wearing this very same gray-blue hipbone-flaunting dress one day. She dropped off a tape for me to do and told me that she liked my glasses, and I've been nuts about her since. I blushed and thanked her and told her I liked her scarf, which really was a very likable scarf. It had all sorts of golds and blacks and yellows in it, and Cyrillic letters seemed to be part of the design. She said, 'Well thank you, I like it, too,' and she surprised me (surprised us both possibly) by untying it from her neck and pulling it slowly through her fingers. I asked whether those were indeed Cyrillic letters I saw before me, and she said that they were, pleased at my attentiveness, but she said that she had asked a friend of hers who knew Russian what they spelled, and he had told her that they meant nothing, they were just a jumble of letters. 'Even better,' I said, somewhat idiotically, anxious to show how completely uninterested I was in her mention of a male friend. 'The designer picked the letters for their formal beauty – he didn't try to pretend he knew the language by using a real word.' The moment threatened to become more flirtatious than either of us wanted. I hurried us past it by asking her how soon she needed her tape done. (I'm a temp, by the way.) 'No big rush,' she said. She retied her scarf, and we smiled quite warmly at each other again before she went off. I was happy all that day just because she had told me she liked my glasses.

Joyce is probably not going to play a large part in this account of my life. I have fallen in love with women many, many times, maybe a hundred or a hundred and fifty times; I've taken off women's clothes many times, too: there is nothing particularly unusual about this occasion within which

95

I am currently parked. The only unusual thing about it is that this time I'm writing about it. I know there are thousands of women in the world I could potentially feel love for as I do feel it now for Joyce – she just happens to work at this office in the domestic-credit department of MassBank where I happen to be a temp for a few weeks. But that is the strange thing about what you are expected to do in life – you are supposed to forget that there are hundreds of cities, each one of them full of women, and that it is most unlikely that you have found the perfect one for you. You are just supposed to pick the best one out of the ones you know and can attract, and in fact you do this happily – you feel that the love you direct toward the one you do choose is not arbitrarily bestowed.

And it *was* brave and friendly of Joyce to compliment me that way about my glasses. I always melt instantly when I'm praised for features about which I have private doubts. I first got glasses in the summer after fourth grade. (Incidentally, fourth grade is also the year I first dropped into the Fold – my temporal powers have always been linked in a way I don't pretend to understand with my sense of sight.) I wore them steadily until about two years ago, when I decided that I should at least try contact lenses. Maybe everything would be different if I got contacts. So I did get them, and I enjoyed the rituals of caring for them – caring for this pair of demanding twins that had to be bathed and changed constantly. I liked squirting the salt water on them, and holding one of them in an aqueous bead on the tip of my finger and admiring its Saarinenesque upcurve, and when I folded it in half and rubbed its slightly slimy surface against itself to break up the protein deposits, I often remembered the satisfactions of making omelets in Teflon fry-pans. But though as a hobby they were rewarding, though I was as excited in opening the

96

centrifugal spin-cleaning machine I ordered for them as I would have been if I had bought an automatic bread baker or a new kind of sexual utensil, they interfered with my appreciation of the world. I could see things through them, but I wasn't *pleased* to look at things. The bandwidth of my optical processors was being flooded with 'there is an intruder on your eyeball' messages, so that a lot of the incidental visual haul from my retina was simply not able to get through. I wasn't enjoying the sights you were obviously meant to enjoy, as when you walked around a park on a windy day watching people's briefcases get blown around on their arms.

At first I thought it was worth losing the beauty of the world in order to look better to the world: I really was more handsome without glasses – the dashing scar on my left eyebrow, where I cut myself on a scrap of aluminum, was more evident. A girl I knew (and whose clothes I removed) in high school used to sing '*Il faut souffrir pour être belle*' in a soft voice to a tune of her own devising, and I took that overheard precept seriously; I was willing to understand it not just in the narrow sense of painful hair-brushing or (say) eyebrow-tweezing or liposuction, but in some broader sense that suffering makes for beauty in art, that the artist has to suffer griefs and privations in order to deliver beauty to his or her public, all that well-ventilated junk. So I continued to wear contacts even when each blink was a dry torment. But then I noticed that my *typing* was suffering, too – and there, since I am a temp and typing is my livelihood, I really had to draw the line. Especially when I typed numbers, my error rate was way up. (Once I spent two weeks doing nothing but typing six-digit numbers.) People began bringing back financial charts that I had done with mistyped numbers circled in red, asking, 'Are you all right today, Arno?' Contact lenses also,

I noticed, made me feel, as loud continuous factory noise also will, ten feet farther away from anyone else around me. They were isolating me, heightening rather than helping rid me of my – well, I suppose it is proper to call it my loneliness. I missed the sharp corners of my glasses, which had helped me dig my way out into sociability; they had been part of what I felt was my characteristic expression.

When I started today, I had no intention of getting into all this about eyeglasses. But it is germane. I love looking at women. I love being able to see them clearly. I particularly like being in the position I am in this very second, which is not looking at Joyce, but rather thinking about the amazing fact that I *can* look up from this page at any time and stare at any part of her that calls out to me for as long as I want without troubling or embarrassing her. Joyce doesn't wear glasses, but my ex-girlfriend Rhody did – and somewhere along the line I realized that if I liked glasses on women, which I do very much, maybe women would tolerate glasses on me. On naked women glasses work for me the way spike heels or a snake tattoo or an ankle bracelet or a fake beauty spot work for some men – they make the nudity pop out at me; they make the woman seem more naked than she would have seemed if she were completely naked. Also, I want to be very sure that she can see every inch of my richard with utter clarity, and if she is wearing glasses I know that she can if she wants to.

The deciding moment really came when I spent the night with a woman, an office manager, who, I *think* anyway, had sex with me sooner than she wanted to simply to distract me from noticing the fact that her contacts were bothering her. It was very late, but I think she wanted to talk for a while longer, and yet (this is my theory) she hurried to the sex because the extreme intimacy, to her way of thinking, of

98

appearing before me in her glasses was only possible after the less extreme intimacy of fucking me. Several times as we talked I was on the point of saying, since her eyes did look quite unhappily pink, 'You want to take out your contacts? I'll take out mine.' But I didn't, because I thought it might have a condescending sort of 'I know everything about you, baby, your bloodshot eyes give you away' quality. Probably I should have. A few days after that, though, I resumed wearing my glasses to work. My error rate dropped right back down. I was instantly happier. In particular, I recognized the crucial importance of hinges to my pleasure in life. When I open my glasses in the morning before taking a shower and going to work, I am like an excited tourist who has just risen from his hotel bed on the first day of a vacation: I've just flung open a set of double French doors leading out onto a sunlit balcony with a view of the entire whatever – shipping corridor, bay, valley, parking lot. (How can people not like views over motel parking lots in the early morning? The new subtler car colors, the blue-greens and warmer grays, and the sense that all those drivers are leveled in the democracy of sleep and that the glass and hoods out there are cold and even dewy, make for one of the more inspiring visions that life can offer before nine o'clock.) Or maybe French-door hinges are not entirely it. Maybe I think that the hinges of my glasses are a woman's hip-sockets: her long graceful legs open and straddle my head all day. I asked Rhody once whether she liked the tickling of my glasses-frames on the inside of her thighs. She said, 'Usually your glasses are off by then, aren't they?' I admitted that was true. She said she didn't like it when I wore my glasses because she wanted my sense of her open vadge to be more Sisley than Richard Estes. 'But I do sometimes like feeling your ears high on my thighs,' she conceded. 'And if I clamp your ears hard with my thighs I can make more noise without feeling I'm getting out of hand.' Rhody was a good, good person, and I probably should not have tried to allude even obliquely to my Fold experiences to her, since she found what little I told her of Fermation repellent; her knowledge of it contributed to our breakup.

Well! I think I have established that there *is* an emotional history to my wearing of glasses. So in saying that she liked them, tall Joyce – who as I sit typing this towers above me now in a state of semi-nudity – was definitely saying the right thing if she was interested in getting to my heart, which she probably wasn't. You have to be extremely careful about complimenting a thirty-five-year-old male temp who has achieved nothing in his life. 'Hi, I'm the temp!' That's usually what I say to receptionists on my first day of an assignment; that's the word I use, because it's the word everyone uses, though it was a long time before I stopped thinking that it was a horrible abbreviation, worse than 'Frisco.' I have been a temp for over ten years, ever since I quit graduate school. The reason I have done nothing with my life is simply that my power to enter the Fold (or 'hit the clutch' or 'find the Cleft' or 'take a personal day' or 'instigate an Estoppel') comes and goes. I value the ability, which I suspect is not widespread, but because I don't have it consistently, because it fades without warning and doesn't return until months or years later, I've gotten hooked into a sort of damaging boom-and-bust Kondratieff cycle. When I've lost the power, I simply exist, I do the minimum I have to do to make a living, because I know that in a sense everything I want to accomplish (and I *am* a person with ambitions) is infinitely postponable.

As a rough estimate, I think I have probably spent only a total of two years of personal time in the Fold, if you lump the individual minutes or hours together, maybe even less;

but they have been some of the best, most alive times I've had. My life reminds me of the capital-gains tax problem, as I once read about it in an op-ed piece: if legislators keep changing, or even promising to change, the capital-gains percentages, repealing and reinstating the tax, the rational investor will begin to base his investment decisions not on the existing tax laws, but on his certainty of change, which mischannels (the person who wrote the op-ed piece convincingly argued) in some destructive way the circulation of capital. So too with me during those periods when I wait for the return of my ability to stop time: I think, Why should I read Ernest Renan or learn matrix algebra now, since when I'm able to Drop again, I'll be able to spend private hours, or even years, satisfying any fleeting intellectual curiosity while the whole world waits for me? I can always catch up. That's the problem.

People are somewhat puzzled by me when I first show up at their office – What is this unyoung man, this thirty-five-year-old man, doing temping? Maybe he has a criminal past, or maybe he's lost a decade to drugs, or: Maybe He's an Artist? But after a day or two, they adjust, since I am a fairly efficient and good-natured typist, familiar with most of the commonly used kinds of software (and some of the forgotten kinds too, like nroff, Lanier, and NBI, and the good old dedicated DEC systems with the gold key), and I am unusually good at reading difficult handwriting and supplying punctuation for dictators who in their creative excitement forget. Once in a great while I use my Fold-powers to amaze everyone with my apparent typing speed, transcribing a two-hour tape in one hour and that kind of thing. But I'm careful not to amaze too often and become a temp legend, since this is my great secret and I don't want to imperil it – this is the one thing that makes my life worth living. When some of the more intelligent people in a given office ask little prob-ingly polite questions to try to figure me out, I often lie and tell them that I'm a writer. It is almost funny to see how relieved they are to have a way of explaining my lowly work status to themselves. Nor is it so much of a lie, because if I had not wasted so much of my life waiting for the next Fermata-phase to come along I would very likely have written some sort of a book by now. And I have written a few shorter things.

I'm typing this on a portable electronic typewriter because I don't want to risk putting any of it on the bank's LAN. Local area networks behave erratically in the Fold. When my carpal-tunnel problem gets bad, I use a manual for my private writing; it seems to help. But I don't have to: batteries and electricity *do* function in the Fold – in fact, all the laws of physics still obtain, as far as I can tell, but only to the extent that I reawaken them. The best way to describe it is that right now, because I have snapped my fingers, every event everywhere is in a state of gel-like suspension. I can move, and the air molecules part to let me through, but they do it resistingly, reluctantly, and the farther that objects are from me, the more thoroughly they are paused. If someone was riding a motorcycle down a hill before I stopped time 'half an hour' ago the rider will remain motionless on his vehicle unless I walk up to him and give him a push – in which case he will fall down, but somewhat more slowly than if he fell in an unpaused universe. He won't take off down the hill at the speed he was riding, he will just tip over. I used to be tempted to fly small airplanes in the Fold, but I'm not that stupid. Flight, though, is definitely possible, as is the pausing of time on an airplane flight. The world stays halted exactly as it is except where I mess with it, and for the most part I try to be as unobtrusive as possible – as unobtrusive as my lusts let me be. This typewriter, for instance, puts what

I type on the page because the act of pressing a letter makes cause and effect function locally. A circuit is completed, a little electricity dribbles from the batteries, etc. I honestly don't know how far outward my personal distortion of the temporary timelessness that I create measurably spreads. I do know that during a Fermata a woman's skin feels soft where it is soft, warm when it is warm – her sweat feels warm when it is warm. It's a sort of reverse Midas touch that I have while in the Fold – the world is inert and statuesque until I touch it and make it live ordinarily.

I had this idea of writing my life story while within a typical chronanistic experience just yesterday. It's almost incredible to think that I've been Dropping since fourth grade and yet I've never made the effort to write about it right while it was going on. I kept an abbreviated log for a while in high school and college – date and time of Drop, what I did, how long in personal minutes or hours or days it took (for a watch usually starts up again in the Fold if I shake it, so I can easily measure how long I have been out), whether I learned anything new or not, and so on. You would think, if a person really could stop the world and get off, as I can, that it would occur to him fairly early on to stop the world in order to record with some care what it felt like to stop the world and get off, for the benefit of the curious. But I now see, even this far into my first autobiographical Fermata, why I never did it before. Sad to say, it is just as hard to write during a Fermation as it is in real time. You still must dole out all the things you have to say one by one, when what you want of course is to say them all at once. But I am going to give it a try. I am thirty-five now, and I have done quite a lot of things, mostly bad, with the Fold's help (including, incidentally, reciting Dylan Thomas's 'Poem on His Birthday' apparently from memory at the final session of a class in modern lyric poetry in college: it is a longish poem, and whenever nervousness made me forget a line, I just paused the world by pressing the switch of my Time Perverter – which is what I called the modified garage-door opener that I used in those days – and refreshed my memory by looking at a copy of the text that I had in my notebook, and no one was the wiser) – and if I don't write some of these private adventures down now, I know I'm going to regret it.

Just now I spun around once in my chair in order to surprise myself again with the sight of Joyce's pubic hair. It really is amazing to me that I can do this, even after all these years. She was walking about thirty feet from my desk, across an empty stretch of space, carrying some papers, on her way to someone's cube, and my gaze just launched toward her, diving cleanly, without ripples, through the glasses that she had complimented, taking heart from having to pass through the optical influence of something she had noticed and liked. It was as if I traveled along the arc of my sight and reached her visually. (There is definitely something to those medieval theories of sight that had the eye sending out rays.) And just as my sighted self reached her, she stopped walking for a second, to check something on one of the papers she held, and when she looked down I was struck by the simple fact that today her hair is *braided*.

It is arranged in what I think is called a French braid. Each of the solid clumps of her hair feeds into the overall solidity of the braid, and the whole structure is plaited as part of her head, like a set of glossy external vertebrae. I'm impressed that women are able to arrange this sort of complicated figure, without too many stray strands, without help, in the morning, by feel. Women are much more in touch with the backs of themselves than men are: they can reach higher up on their back, and do so daily to unfasten bras; they can clip and braid their hair; they can keep their rearward blouse-tails smoothly tucked into their skirts. They give thought to how the edges of their underpants look through their pocket-less pants from the back. ('Panties' is a word to be avoided, I feel.) But French braids, in which three sporting dolphins dip smoothly under one another and surface in a continuous elegant entrainment, are the most beautiful and impressive results of this sense of dorsal space. As soon as I saw Joyce's braid I knew that it was time to stop time. I needed to feel her solid braid, and her head beneath it, in my palm.

So, just as she started walking again, I snapped my fingers. This is my latest method of entering the Fold, and one of the simpler I have been able to develop (much more straight-forward than my earlier mathematical-formula technique, or the sewn calluses, for instance, both of which I will get into later). She didn't hear the snap, only I did – the universe halts at some indeterminate point just before my middle finger swats against the base of my thumb. I got out my Casio type-writer and scooted over here to her on my chair. (I didn't scoot backwards, I scooted frontwards, which isn't easy to do over carpeting, because it is hard to get the proper traction. I wanted to keep my eyes on her.) She was in mid-stride. I reached forward and put my hands on her hipbones. It felt as if there were cashmere or something fancy in the wool, and it was good to feel her hipbones through that soft material, and to see my hands angling to follow the incurve of her waist, which the dress had to an extent hidden. Some-times when I first touch a woman in the Fold I tense up my arms until they vibrate, so that the shape of whatever is under my palms keeps on being sent through my nerves as new information. I never know exactly what I will do during a Drop. To get her dress out of the way, I lifted its soft hem up over her hips and gathered it into two wingy bunches and tied a big soft knot with them. It had seemed as if she had a tiny potbelly with the dress on (this can be a sexy touch, I think, on some women), but if she had, it disappeared or lost definition as soon as I pulled her pantyhose and under-pants down as far as I could get them, which wasn't that far because her legs were walkingly apart. (Also, before I pulled down her pantyhose, which is a smoky-blue color, I touched an oval of her skin through a run in the darker part high on her thigh.) And then I was given this sight that I have before me now, of her pubic hair.

I'm not normally a pubic-hair obsessive – I really have no ongoing fetishes, I don't think, because each woman is different, and you never know what particular feature or transition between features is going to grab you and say, 'Look at this – you've never thought about exactly this before!' Each woman inspires her own fetishes. And it isn't that Joyce has some ludicrous Vagi-fro or massive Koosh-ball explosion of a sex-goatee – in fact her hair isn't thicker really than most. It's just that it covers a wider area, maybe, and its blackness *sparkles*, if you will – its curving border reaches a little higher on her stomach. A little? – what am I saying? It's the size of South America. To think that I could have died and not seen this – that I could have picked a different temp assignment when Jenny, my coordinator, told me my choices a few weeks ago. What is exciting about its extent is maybe that, because it reaches higher than other women's pubic hair, it becomes less and more sexual at the same time – the slang for it, like 'pussy hair' and 'cunt hair' (I flinch at both those words, except when I'm close to coming), doesn't apply because it is no longer, strictly speaking, 'pubic' hair at all – its borders are reaching out into soft abdominal love-areas, so love and sex mix. I wanted to feel it, the dense sisaly lush resilience of it, which makes that whole hippy part of her body look extraordinarily graceful. It is a kind of black cocktail dress under which her clit-heart beats – it has that much *dignity*.

But rather than holding it immediately, I deprived myself of the sight of it for a little while and instead gently placed my hand on her braid, which was cool and thick and smooth and dense, a totally different idea of hair, so different that it is strange to think of the two orders of hair as sharing the same word, but which follows the curve of her head in the same way that her pubic hair follows the curve over her mound-bone, and when I felt the French-braid sensation sinking into the hollow of my palm, which craves sexual shapes and textures, I then went ahead and curled the fingers of my other hand through her devil's food fur, connecting the two kinky handfuls of home-grown protein with my arms, and it felt as if I were hot-wiring a car; my heart's twin carburetors roared into life. That's all I did, then I started typing this before I forgot the feeling. Maybe that's all I will do. That sexy, *sexy* pubic hair! I'm noticing now that its contours are similar to those of a black bicycle seat: a black leather seat on a racing bicycle. Maybe this is why those sad sniffers of comic legend sniff girls' bicycle seats? No, for them it isn't the shape, it's the fact that the seat has been between a girl's legs. They are truly pathetic. I have no sympathy to spare for compulsions other than my own. I would, though, like to rescue the correspondence between pubic hair and narrow black-leather bicycle seats from them.

All right, I think that is enough for now. I've been in the Fold for, let's see, almost four hours and written eight single-spaced pages, and the problem is that if I stay in too long I'll have jet lag tomorrow, since according to my inner clock it will be four hours later than it is. Usually I don't spend nearly this long in a Drop. I am going to put Joyce's clothes back in order and smooth out her dress (I would never have tied a knot in it if she wore a cotton dress, because the wrinkles would show up too much and puzzle her) and I'm going to scoot back to my desk and finish out the day. The good thing is that if she brings me a tape to do later this afternoon, I will be much more relaxed and therefore likable than if I hadn't partially stripped her without her knowledge or consent. I will jest knowingly and winningly with her. I will compliment her on today's scarf – which isn't, honestly, quite as nice as the Cyrillic one. (Maybe when she was getting dressed this morning she put on this knit dress and then remembered that I had admired her scarf, and maybe she thought that wearing it again as well would be too direct a Yes from her; but then again maybe the reason she was wearing the dress this soon again was that she had liked my complimenting her on her scarf and wanted to allude to that compliment indirectly by wearing the same dress with another scarf.) This new one is a Liberty pattern of purply grays and greens, definitely worth smiling at and even acknowledging outright. But I don't want to get into one of those awful running-compliment patterns, where I have to mention her scarves every time she wears one.

The other thing I should say is that under normal circumstances I would probably give serious thought to 'poaching an egg' at this point, but because I have written all this, and because this is, I believe, going to be the very beginning of a sort of autobiography, I can't. What a surprise, though, to find this Casio typewriter acting as chaperon! (Maybe what I will do is go ahead, but not mention it.)

SEXUAL
ALCHEMY

APULEIUS

from:
THE GOLDEN ASS

Translated by Robert Graves

THE TALE OF my wonderful talents spread in all directions, so that my master became famous on my account. People said: 'Think of it! He has an ass whom he treats like a friend and invites to dinner with him. Believe it or not, that ass can wrestle, and actually dance, and understands what people say to him, and uses a language of signs!'

Here I must tell you, rather late in the day, who Thyasus was. He came from Corinth, the capital of the province of Achaia, and having been successively raised to all the junior offices to which his rank and position entitled him he was now to be Lord Chief Justice of Corinth for the next five years. Since convention required him to live up to the dignity of this appointment by staging a public entertainment, he had undertaken to provide a three-day gladiatorial show in evidence of his open-handedness. It was this, indeed, that accounted for his presence in the north: he was trying to please his fellow-citizens by buying up the finest wild animals and hiring the most famous gladiators in all Thessaly. Now, having found all that he needed, he was on the point of returning to Corinth, quite satisfied with his purchases; but instead of riding in one of his own splendid gigs, some covered and some open, which formed the tail of his long retinue, or on one of his valuable Thessalian thorough-bred hunters or pedigreed Gallic cobs, preferred to mount lovingly on my back; saying that he had come to despise all other forms of conveyance. I now sported gilt harness, a red morocco saddle, a purple ass-cloth, a silver bit and little bells that tinkled as I went along. He used to talk to me in the kindest way, telling me for example how delighted he was to own a charger whom he could count as his friend. When we reached the port of Iolcos we embarked with our menagerie and finished our journey by sea, sailing along the coast of Boeotia and Attica until we arrived at Corinth, where a vast crowd poured out to greet us. I think, though, that more people were there to see me than to welcome Thyasus.

So many visitors wanted to watch my performances that my trainer decided to make money out of me. He kept the stable doors shut and charged a high price for admittance, one person at a time. His daily takings were considerable.

Among these visitors was a rich noblewoman. My various tricks enchanted her and at last she conceived the odd desire of getting to know me intimately. In fact, she grew so passionately fond of me that, like Pasiphaë in the legend who fell in love with a bull, she bribed my trainer with a large sum of money to let her spend a night in my company. I am sorry to record that the rascal agreed with no thought for anything but his own pocket.

When I had dined with Thyasus and come back to my stable, I found the noblewoman waiting for me. She had been there some time already. Heavens, what magnificent preparations she had made for her love-affair! Four eunuchs had spread the floor with several plump feather-beds, covered them with a Tyrian purple cloth embroidered in gold, and laid a heap of little pillows at the head end, of the downy sort used by women of fashion. Then, not wishing to postpone their mistress's enjoyment by staying a moment longer than necessary, out they trooped, but left fine, white candles burning to light up the shadowy corners.

She undressed at once, taking everything off, even to the

gauze scarf tied across her beautiful breasts, then stood close to the lamp and rubbed her body all over with oil of balsam from a pewter pot. She then did the same to mine, most generously, but concentrating mostly on my nose. After this she gave me a lingering kiss – not of the mercenary sort that one expects in a brothel, or from a whore picked up in the street or sent along by an agency, but a pure, sincere, really loving kiss. 'Darling,' she cried, 'I love you. You are all I want in this world. I could never live without you.' She added all the other pretty things that women say when they want men to share their own passionate feelings. Then she took me by my head-band and had no difficulty in making me lie down on the bed, reclining on one elbow, because that was one of the tricks I had learned, and she evidently was not expecting me to do anything that I had not done before.

You must understand that she was a beautiful woman and desperately eager for my embraces. Besides, I had been continent for several months and now, with all this fragrant scent in my nostrils and a kegful of Thyasus's best wine inside me, I felt fit for anything. All the same, I was worried, very worried indeed, at the thought of sleeping with so lovely a woman: my great hairy legs and hard hooves pressed against her milk-and-honey skin – her dewy red lips kissed by my huge mouth with its ugly great teeth. Worst of all, how could any woman alive, though exuding lust from her very finger nails, accept the formidable challenge of my thighs? If I proved too much for her, if I seriously injured her – think of it, a noblewoman too – my master would be forced to use me in his promised entertainment as food for his wild beasts. But her burning eyes devoured mine, as she cooed sweetly at me between kisses and finally gasped: 'Ah, ah, I have you safe now, my little dove, my little birdie.' Then I realized how foolish my fears had been. She pressed me closer and closer to her and met my challenge to the full. I tried to back away, but she resisted every attempt to spare her, twining her arms tight around my back, until I wondered whether after all I was capable of serving her as she wished. I began to appreciate the story of Pasiphaë: if she was anything like this woman she had every reason to fix her affections on the bull who fathered the Minotaur on her. My new mistress did not allow me to sleep a wink that night, but as soon as the embarrassing daylight crept into the room she crept out, first pleading with my keeper to let her spend another night with me for the same fee. He was willing enough to agree, partly because she paid handsomely, partly because he wished to give Thyasus a novel peep-show.

He went off at once to Thyasus with a detailed account of the night's events, and was rewarded with a large tip. 'Splendid, splendid!' cried Thyasus. 'That's the very act we need to liven up our show. But what a pity that his sweetheart is a noblewoman: her family would never allow her to perform in public.'

Advertisements circulated in the brothel districts of Corinth failed to find any volunteer to take her place: apparently no woman was abandoned enough to sell what remained of her reputation even for the generous fee that was offered. In the end Thyasus did not have to pay anything: he got hold of a woman who had been sentenced to be thrown to the wild beasts but would, he thought, make a suitable mistress for me. We were to be caged up together in the centre of the packed amphitheatre.

ALIFA RIFAAT

MY WORLD OF
THE UNKNOWN

Translated by Denys Johnson-Davies

THERE ARE MANY mysteries in life, unseen powers in the universe, worlds other than our own, hidden links and radiations that draw creatures together and whose effect is interacting. They may merge or be incompatible, and perhaps the day will come when science will find a method for connecting up these worlds in the same way as it has made it possible to voyage to other planets. Who knows?

Yet one of these other worlds I have explored; I have lived in it and been linked with its creatures through the bond of love. I used to pass with amazing speed between this tangible world of ours and another invisible earth, mixing in the two worlds on one and the same day, as though living it twice over.

When entering into the world of my love, and being summoned and yielding to its call, no one around me would be aware of what was happening to me. All that occurred was that I would be overcome by something resembling a state of languor and would go off into a semi-sleep. Nothing about me would change except that I would become very silent and withdrawn, though I am normally a person who is talkative and eager to go out into the world of people. I would yearn to be on my own, would long for the moment of surrender as I prepared myself for answering the call.

Love had its beginning when an order came through for my husband to be transferred to a quiet country town and, being too busy with his work, delegated to me the task of going to this town to choose suitable accommodation prior to his taking up the new appointment. He cabled one of his subordinates named Kamil and asked him to meet me at the station and to assist me.

I took the early morning train. The images of a dream I had had that night came to me as I looked out at the vast fields and gauged the distances between the towns through which the train passed and reckoned how far it was between the new town in which we were fated to live and beloved Cairo.

The images of the dream kept reappearing to me, forcing themselves upon my mind: images of a small white house surrounded by a garden with bushes bearing yellow flowers, a house lying on the edge of a broad canal in which were swans and tall sailing boats. I kept on wondering at my dream and trying to analyse it. Perhaps it was some secret wish I had had, or maybe the echo of some image that my unconscious had stored up and was chewing over.

As the train arrived at its destination, I awoke from my thoughts. I found Kamil awaiting me. We set out in his car, passing through the local souk. I gazed at the mounds of fruit with delight, chatting away happily with Kamil. When we emerged from the souk we found ourselves on the bank of the Mansoura canal, a canal on which swans swam and sailing boats moved to and fro. I kept staring at them with uneasy longing. Kamil directed the driver to the residential buildings the governorate had put up for housing government employees. While gazing at the opposite bank a large boat with a great fluttering sail glided past. Behind it could be seen a white house that had a garden with trees with yellow flowers and that lay on its own amidst vast fields. I shouted out in confusion, overcome by the feeling that I had been here before.

'Go to that house,' I called to the driver. Kamil leapt up, objecting vehemently: 'No, no – no one lives in that house. The best thing is to go to the employees' buildings.'

I shouted insistently, like someone hypnotized: 'I must have a look at that house.' 'All right,' he said. 'You won't like it, though – it's old and needs repairing.' Giving in to my wish, he ordered the driver to make his way there.

At the garden door we found a young woman, spare and of fair complexion. A fat child with ragged clothes encircled her neck with his burly legs. In a strange silence, she stood as though nailed to the ground, barring the door with her hands and looking at us with doltish inquiry.

I took a sweet from my bag and handed it to the boy. He snatched it eagerly, tightening his grip on her neck with his podgy, mud-bespattered feet so that her face became flushed from his high-spirited embrace. A half-smile showed on her tightly closed lips. Taking courage, I addressed her in a friendly tone: 'I'd like to see over this house.' She braced her hands resolutely against the door. 'No,' she said quite simply. I turned helplessly to Kamil, who went up to her and pushed her violently in the chest so that she staggered back. 'Don't you realize,' he shouted at her, 'that this is the director's wife? Off with you!'

Lowering her head so that the child all but slipped from her, she walked off dejectedly to the canal bank where she lay down on the ground, put the child on her lap, and rested her head in her hands in silent submission.

Moved by pity, I remonstrated: 'There's no reason to be so rough, Mr Kamil. Who is the woman?' 'Some mad woman,' he said with a shrug of his shoulders, 'who's a stranger to the town. Out of kindness the owner of this house put her in charge of it until someone should come along to live in it.'

With increased interest I said: 'Will he be asking a high rent for it?' 'Not at all,' he said with an enigmatic smile. 'He'd welcome anyone taking it over. There are no restrictions and the rent is modest – no more than four pounds.'

I was beside myself with joy. Who in these days can find somewhere to live for such an amount? I rushed through the door into the house with Kamil behind me and went over the rooms: five spacious rooms with wooden floors, with a pleasant hall, modern lavatory, and a beautifully roomy kitchen with a large veranda overlooking vast pistachio-green fields of generously watered rice. A breeze, limpid and cool, blew, playing with the tips of the crop and making the delicate leaves move in continuous dancing waves.

I went back to the first room with its spacious balcony overlooking the road and revealing the other bank of the canal where, along its strand, extended the houses of the town. Kamil pointed out to me a building facing the house on the other side. 'That's where we work,' he said, 'and behind it is where the children's schools are.'

'Thanks be to God,' I said joyfully. 'It means that everything is within easy reach of this house – and the souk's near by too.' 'Yes,' he said, 'and the fishermen will knock at your door to show you the fresh fish they've caught in their nets. But the house needs painting and redoing, also there are all sorts of rumours about it – the people around here believe in djinn and spirits.'

'This house is going to be my home,' I said with determination. 'Its low rent will make up for whatever we may have to spend on redoing it. You'll see what this house will look like when I get the garden arranged. As for the story about djinn and spirits, just leave them to us – we're more spirited than them.'

We laughed at my joke as we left the house. On my way

to the station we agreed about the repairs that needed doing to the house. Directly I reached Cairo I cabled my husband to send the furniture from the town we had been living in, specifying a suitable date to fit in with the completion of the repairs and the house being ready for occupation.

On the date fixed I once again set off and found that all my wishes had been carried out and that the house was pleasantly spruce with its rooms painted a cheerful orange tinge, the floors well polished and the garden tidied up and made into small flowerbeds.

I took possession of the keys and Kamil went off to attend to his business, having put a chair on the front balcony for me to sit on while I awaited the arrival of the furniture van. I stretched out contentedly in the chair and gazed at the two banks with their towering trees like two rows of guards between which passed the boats with their lofty sails, while around them glided a male swan heading a flotilla of females. Halfway across the canal he turned and flirted with them, one after the other, like a sultan amidst his harem.

Relaxed, I closed my eyes. I projected myself into the future and pictured to myself the enjoyment I would have in this house after it had been put in order and the garden fixed up. I awoke to the touch of clammy fingers shaking me by the shoulders.

I started and found myself staring at the fair-complexioned woman with her child squatting on her shoulders as she stood erect in front of me staring at me in silence. 'What do you want?' I said to her sharply. 'How did you get in?' 'I got in with this,' she said simply, revealing a key between her fingers.

I snatched the key from her hand as I loudly rebuked her: 'Give it here. We have rented the house and you have no right to come into it like this.' 'I have a lot of other keys,' she answered briefly. 'And what,' I said to her, 'do you want of this house?' 'I want to stay on in it and for you to go,' she said. I laughed in amazement at her words as I asked myself: Is she really mad? Finally I said impatiently: 'Listen here, I'm not leaving here and you're not entering this house unless I wish it. My husband is coming with the children, and the furniture is on the way. He'll be arriving in a little while and we'll be living here for such period of time as my husband is required to work in this town.'

She looked at me in a daze. For a long time she was silent, then she said: 'All right, your husband will stay with me and you can go.' Despite my utter astonishment I felt pity for her. 'I'll allow you to stay on with us for the little boy's sake,' I said to her gently, 'until you find yourself another place. If you'd like to help me with the housework I'll pay you what you ask.'

Shaking her head, she said with strange emphasis: 'I'm not a servant. I'm Aneesa.' 'You're not staying here,' I said to her coldly, rising to my feet. Collecting all my courage and emulating Kamil's determination when he rebuked her, I began pushing her in the chest as I caught hold of the young boy's hand, 'Get out of here and don't come near this house,' I shouted at her. 'Let me have all the keys. I'll not let go of your child till you've given them all to me.'

With a set face that did not flicker she put her hand to her bosom and took out a ring on which were several keys, which she dropped into my hand. I released my grip on the young boy. Supporting him on her shoulders, she started to leave. Regretting my harshness, I took out several piastres from my bag and placed them in the boy's hand. With the same silence and stiffness she wrested the piastres from the boy's hand and gave them back to me. Then she went straight out. Bolting the door this time, I sat down, tense and upset, to wait.

My husband arrived, then the furniture, and for several days I occupied myself with putting the house in order. My husband was busy with his work and the children occupied themselves with making new friends and I completely forgot about Aneesa, that is until my husband returned one night wringing his hands with fury: 'This woman Aneesa, can you imagine that since we came to live in this house she's been hanging around it every night. Tonight she was so crazy she blocked my way and suggested I should send you off so that she might live with me. The woman's gone completely off her head about this house and I'm afraid she might do something to the children or assault you.'

Joking with him and masking the jealousy that raged within me, I said: 'And what is there for you to get angry about? She's a fair and attractive enough woman – a blessing brought to your very doorstep!' With a sneer he took up the telephone, muttering: 'May God look after her!'

He contacted the police and asked them to come and take her away. When I heard the sound of the police van coming I ran to the window and saw them taking her off. The poor woman did not resist, did not object, but submitted with a gentle sadness that as usual with her aroused one's pity. Yet, when she saw me standing in tears and watching her, she turned to me and, pointing to the wall of the house, called out: 'I'll leave her to you.' 'Who?' I shouted. 'Who, Aneesa?' Once again pointing at the bottom of the house, she said: 'Her.'

The van took her off and I spent a sleepless night. No sooner did day come than I hurried to the garden to examine my plants and to walk round the house and carefully inspect its walls. All I found were some cracks, the house being old, and laughed at the frivolous thought that came to me: Could, for example, there be jewels buried here, as told in fairy tales?

Who could 'she' be? What was the secret of this house? Who was Aneesa and was she really mad? Where were she and her son living? So great did my concern for Aneesa become that I began pressing my husband with questions until he brought me news of her. The police had learnt that she was the wife of a well-to-do teacher living in a nearby town. One night he had caught her in an act of infidelity, and in fear she had fled with her son and had settled here, no one knowing why she had betaken herself to this particular house. However, the owner of the house had been good enough to allow her to put up in it until someone should come to live in it, while some kind person had intervened on her behalf to have her name included among those receiving monthly allowances from the Ministry of Social Affairs. There were many rumours that cast doubt upon her conduct: people passing by her house at night would hear her conversing with unknown persons. Her madness took the form of a predilection for silence and isolation from people during the daytime as she wandered about in a dream world. After the police had persuaded them to take her in to safeguard the good repute of her family, she was returned to her relatives.

The days passed and the story of Aneesa was lost in oblivion. Winter came and with it heavy downpours of rain. The vegetation in my garden flourished though the castor-oil plants withered and their yellow flowers fell. I came to find pleasure in sitting out on the kitchen balcony looking at my flowers and vegetables and enjoying the belts of sunbeams that lay between the clouds and lavished my balcony with warmth and light.

One sunny morning my attention was drawn to the limb of a nearby tree whose branches curved up gracefully despite its having dried up and its dark bark being cracked. My gaze was attracted by something twisting and turning along the tip of a branch: bands of yellow and others of red, intermingled with bands of black, were creeping forward. It was a long, smooth tube, at its end a small striped head with two bright, wary eyes.

The snake curled round on itself in spiral rings, then tautened its body and moved forward. The sight gripped me; I felt terror turning my blood cold and freezing my limbs.

My senses were numbed, my soul intoxicated with a strange elation at the exciting beauty of the snake. I was rooted to the spot, wavering between two thoughts that contended in my mind at one and the same time: should I snatch up some implement from the kitchen and kill the snake, or should I enjoy the rare moment of beauty that had been afforded me?

As though the snake had read what was passing through my mind, it raised its head, tilting it to right and left in thrilling coquetry. Then, by means of two tiny fangs like pearls, and a golden tongue like a twig of *arak* wood, it smiled at me and fastened its eyes on mine in one fleeting, commanding glance. The thought of killing left me. I felt a current, a radiation from its eyes that penetrated to my heart ordering me to stay where I was. A warning against continuing to sit out there in front of it surged inside me, but my attraction to it paralysed my limbs and I did not move. I kept on watching it, utterly entranced and captivated. Like a bashful virgin being lavished with compliments, it tried to conceal its pride in its beauty, and, having made certain of captivating its lover, the snake coyly twisted round and gently, gracefully glided away until swallowed up by a crack in the wall. Could the snake be the 'she' that Aneesa had referred to on the day of her departure?

At last I rose from my place, overwhelmed by the feeling that I was on the brink of a new world, a new destiny, or rather, if you wish, the threshold of a new love. I threw myself on to the bed in a dreamlike state, unaware of the passage of time. No sooner, though, did I hear my husband's voice and the children with their clatter as they returned at noon than I regained my sense of being a human being, wary and frightened about itself, determined about the existence and continuance of its species. Without intending to I called out: 'A snake – there's a snake in the house.'

My husband took up the telephone and some men came and searched the house. I pointed out to them the crack into which the snake had disappeared, though racked with a feeling of remorse at being guilty of betrayal. For here I was denouncing the beloved, inviting people against it after it had felt safe with me.

The men found no trace of the snake. They burned some wormwood and fumigated the hole but without result. Then my husband summoned Sheikh Farid, Sheikh of the Rifa'iyya order in the town, who went on chanting verses from the Qur'an as he tapped the ground with his stick. He then asked to speak to me alone and said:

'Madam, the sovereign of the house has sought you out and what you saw is no snake, rather it is one of the monarchs of the earth – may God make your words pleasant to them – who has appeared to you in the form of a snake. Here in this house there are many holes of snakes, but they are of the non-poisonous kind. They inhabit houses and go and come as they please. What you saw, though, is something else.'

'I don't believe a word of it,' I said, stupefied. 'This is nonsense. I know that the djinn are creatures that actually exist, but they are not in touch with our world, there is no contact between them and the world of humans.'

With an enigmatic smile he said: 'My child, the Prophet went out to them and read the Qur'an to them in their country. Some of them are virtuous and some of them are Muslims, and how do you know there is no contact between us and them? Let your prayer be "O Lord, increase me in knowledge" and do not be nervous. Your purity of spirit, your translucence of soul have opened to you doors that will take you to other worlds known only to their Creator. Do not be afraid. Even if you should find her one night sleeping in your bed, do not be alarmed but talk to her with all politeness and friendliness.'

'That's enough of all that, Sheikh Farid. Thank you,' I said, alarmed, and he left us.

We went on discussing the matter. 'Let's be practical,' suggested my husband, 'and stop all the cracks at the bottom of the outside walls and put wire mesh over the windows, also paint wormwood all round the garden fence.'

We set about putting into effect what we had agreed. I, though, no longer dared to go out on to the balconies. I neglected my garden and stopped wandering about in it. Generally I would spend my free time in bed. I changed to being someone who liked to sit around lazily and was disinclined to mix with people; those diversions and recreations that previously used to tempt me no longer gave me any pleasure. All I wanted was to stretch myself out and drowse. In bewilderment I asked myself: Could it be that I was in love? But how could I love a snake? Or could she really be one of the daughters of the monarchs of the djinn? I would awake from my musings to find that I had been wandering in my thoughts and recalling to mind how magnificent she was. And what is the secret of her beauty? I would ask myself.

Was it that I was fascinated by her multi-coloured, supple body? Or was it that I had been dazzled by that intelligent, commanding way she had of looking at me? Or could it be the sleek way she had of gliding along, so excitingly dangerous, that had captivated me?

Excitingly dangerous! No doubt it was this excitement that had stirred my feelings and awakened my love, for did they not make films to excite and frighten? There was no doubt but that the secret of my passion for her, my preoccupation with her, was due to the excitement that had aroused, through intense fear, desire within myself; an excitement that was sufficiently strong to drive the blood hotly through my veins whenever the memory of her came to me, thrusting the blood in bursts that made my heart beat wildly, my limbs limp. And so, throwing myself down in a pleasurable state of torpor, my craving for her would be awakened and I would wish for her coil-like touch, her graceful gliding motion.

And yet I fell to wondering how union could come about, how craving be quenched, the delights of the body be realized, between a woman and a snake. And did she, I wondered, love me and want me as I loved her? An idea would obtrude itself upon me sometimes: did Cleopatra, the very legend of love, have sexual intercourse with her serpent after having given up sleeping with men, having wearied of amorous adventures with them so that her sated instincts were no longer moved other than by the excitement of fear, her senses no longer aroused other than by bites from a snake? And the last of her lovers had been a viper that had destroyed her.

I came to live in a state of continuous torment, for a strange feeling of longing scorched my body and rent my senses, while my circumstances obliged me to carry out the duties and responsibilities that had been placed on me as the wife of a man who occupied an important position in the small town, he and his family being objects of attention and his house a Kaaba for those seeking favours; also as a mother who must look after her children and concern herself with every detail of their lives so as to exercise control over them; there was also the house and its chores, this house that was inhabited by the mysterious lover who lived in a world other than mine. How, I wondered, was union between us to be achieved? Was wishing for this love a sin or was there nothing to reproach myself about?

And as my self-questioning increased so did my yearning, my curiosity, my desire. Was the snake from the world of reptiles or from the djinn? When would the meeting be? Was she, I wondered, aware of me and would she return out of pity for my consuming passion? One stormy morning with the rain pouring down so hard that I could hear the drops rattling on the window-pane, I lit the stove and lay down in bed between the covers seeking refuge from an agonizing trembling that racked my yearning body which, ablaze with unquenchable desire, called out for relief.

I heard a faint rustling sound coming from the corner of the wall right beside my bed. I looked down and kept my eyes fixed on one of the holes in the wall, which I found was slowly, very slowly, expanding. Closing my eyes, my heart raced with joy and my body throbbed with mounting desire as there dawned in me the hope of an encounter. I lay back in sub-mission to what was to be. No longer did I care whether love was coming from the world of reptiles or from that of the djinn, sovereigns of the world. Even were this love to mean my destruction, my desire for it was greater.

I heard a hissing noise that drew nearer, then it changed to a gentle whispering in my ear, calling to me: 'I am love, O enchantress. I showed you my home in your sleep; I called you to my kingdom when your soul was dozing on the horizon of dreams, so come, my sweet beloved, come and let us explore the depths of the azure sea of pleasure. There, in the chamber of coral, amidst cool, shady rocks where reigns deep, restful silence lies our bed, lined with soft, bright green damask, inlaid with pearls newly wrenched from their shells. Come, let me sleep with you as I have slept with beautiful women and have given them bliss. Come, let me prise out your pearl from its shell that I may polish it and bring forth its splendour. Come to where no one will find us, where no one will see us, for the eyes of swimming creatures are innocent and will not heed what we do nor understand what we say. Down there lies repose, lies a cure for all your yearnings and ills. Come, without fear or dread, for no creature will reach us in our hidden world, and only the eye of God alone will see us; He alone will know what we are about and He will watch over us.'

I began to be intoxicated by the soft musical whisperings. I felt her cool and soft and smooth, her coldness producing a painful convulsion in my body and hurting me to the point of terror. I felt her as she slipped between the covers, then her two tiny fangs, like two pearls, began to caress my body; arriving at my thighs, the golden tongue, like an *arak* twig, inserted its pronged tip between them and began sipping and exhaling; sipping the poisons of my desire and exhaling the nectar of my ecstasy, till my whole body tingled and started to shake in sharp, painful, rapturous spasms – and all the while the tenderest of words were whispered to me as I confided to her all my longings.

At last the cool touch withdrew, leaving me exhausted. I went into a deep slumber to awake at noon full of energy, all of me a joyful burgeoning to life. Curiosity and a desire to know who it was seized me again. I looked at the corner of the wall and found that the hole was wide open. Once again I was overcome by fear. I pointed out the crack to my husband, unable to utter, although terror had once again awakened in me passionate desire. My husband filled up the crack with cement and went to sleep.

Morning came and everyone went out. I finished my housework and began roaming around the rooms in boredom, battling against the desire to surrender myself to sleep. I sat in the hallway and suddenly she appeared before me, gentle as an angel, white as day, softly undulating and flexing herself, calling to me in her bewitching whisper: 'Bride of mine, I called you and brought you to my home. I have wedded you, so there is no sin in our love, nothing to reproach yourself about. I am the guardian of the house, and I hold sway over the snakes and vipers that inhabit it, so come and I shall show you where they live. Have no fear so long as we are together. You and I are in accord. Bring a container with water and I shall place my fingers over your hand and we shall recite together some verses from the Qur'an, then we shall sprinkle it in the places from which they emerge and shall thus close the doors on them, and it shall be a pact between us that your hands will not do harm to them.'

'Then you are one of the monarchs of the djinn?' I asked eagerly. 'Why do you not bring me treasures and riches as we hear about in fables when a human takes as sister her companion among the djinn?'

She laughed at my words, shaking her golden hair that was like dazzling threads of light. She whispered to me, coquettishly: 'How greedy is mankind! Are not the pleasures of the body enough? Were I to come to you with wealth we would both die consumed by fire.'

'No, no,' I called out in alarm. 'God forbid that I should ask for unlawful wealth. I merely asked it of you as a test, that it might be positive proof that I am not imagining things and living in dreams.'

She said: 'And do intelligent humans have to have something tangible as evidence? By God, do you not believe in His ability to create worlds and living beings? Do you not know that you have an existence in worlds other than that of matter and the transitory? Fine, since you ask for proof, come close to me and my caresses will put vitality back into your limbs. You will retain your youth. I shall give you abiding youth and the delights of love – and they are more precious than wealth in the world of man. How many fortunes have women spent in quest of them? As for me I shall feed from the poisons of your desire, the exhalations of your burning passion, for that is my nourishment and through it I live.'

'I thought that your union with me was for love, not for nourishment and the perpetuation of youth and vigour,' I said in amazement.

'And is sex anything but food for the body and an interaction in union and love?' she said. 'Is it not this that makes human beings happy and is the secret of feeling joy and elation?'

She stretched out her radiant hand to my body, passing over it like the sun's rays and discharging into it warmth and a sensation of languor.

'I am ill,' I said. 'I am ill. I am ill,' I kept on repeating. When he heard me my husband brought the doctor, who said: 'High blood pressure, heart trouble, nervous depression.' Having prescribed various medicaments he left. The stupidity of doctors! My doctor did not know that he was describing the symptoms of love, did not even know it was from love I was suffering. Yet I knew my illness and the secret of my cure. I showed my husband the enlarged hole in the wall and once again he stopped it up. We then carried the bed to another corner.

After some days had passed I found another hole alongside my bed. My beloved came and whispered to me: 'Why are you so coy and flee from me, my bride? Is it fear of your being rebuffed or is it from aversion? Are you not happy with our being together? Why do you want for us to be apart?'

'I am in agony,' I whispered back. 'Your love is so intense and the desire to enjoy you so consuming. I am frightened I shall feel that I am tumbling down into a bottomless pit and being destroyed.'

'My beloved,' she said. 'I shall only appear to you in beauty's most immaculate form.'

'But it is natural for you to be a man,' I said in a precipitate outburst, 'seeing that you are so determined to have a love affair with me.'

'Perfect beauty is to be found only in woman,' she said, 'so yield to me and I shall let you taste undreamed of happiness; I shall guide you to worlds possessed of such beauty as you have never imagined.'

She stretched out her fingers to caress me, while her delicate mouth sucked in the poisons of my desire and exhaled the nectar of my ecstasy, carrying me off into a trance of delicious happiness.

After that we began the most pleasurable of love affairs, wandering together in worlds and living on horizons of dazzling beauty, a world fashioned of jewels, a world whose every moment was radiant with light and formed a thousand shapes, a thousand colours.

As for the opening in the wall, I no longer took any notice. I no longer complained of feeling ill, in fact there burned within me abounding vitality. Sometimes I would bring a handful of wormwood and, by way of jest, would stop up the crack, just as the beloved teases her lover and closes the window in his face that, ablaze with desire for her, he may hasten to the door. After that I would sit for a long time and enjoy watching the wormwood powder being scattered in spiral rings by unseen puffs of wind. Then I would throw myself down on the bed and wait.

For months I immersed myself in my world, no longer calculating time or counting the days, until one morning my husband went out on the balcony lying behind our favoured wall alongside the bed. After a while I heard him utter a cry of alarm. We all hurried out to find him holding a stick, with a black, ugly snake almost two metres long, lying at his feet.

I cried out with a sorrow whose claws clutched at my heart so that it began to beat wildly. With crazed fury I shouted at my husband: 'Why have you broken the pact and killed it? What harm has it done?' How cruel is man! He lets no creature live in peace.

I spent the night sorrowful and apprehensive. My lover came to me and embraced me more passionately then ever. I whispered to her imploringly: 'Be kind, beloved. Are you angry with me or sad because of me?'

'It is farewell,' she said. 'You have broken the pact and have betrayed one of my subjects, so you must both depart from this house, for only love lives in it.'

In the morning I packed up so that we might move to one of the employees' buildings, leaving the house in which I had learnt of love and enjoyed incomparable pleasures.

I still live in memory and in hope. I crave for the house and miss my secret love. Who knows, perhaps one day my beloved will call me. Who really knows?

ANGELICA JACOB

MISHA

IF I HAD TO describe her, I would liken her to a body of water. Something that can be contained, but more often than not slips through your fingers, something in which you can float, but in which you can also drown.

It's late afternoon. The sun is setting and I can hear the distant hum of a motorboat crossing the harbour. Light swills through the window, then Misha opens the door and dumps her bag next to my desk. She walks to the bathroom. I anticipate the sound of the shower, glimpse her undressing as she pads backwards and forwards. She peels off her jumper, lets her skirt drift to the floor.

She tells me that it's been a long day, her shoulders are aching. She stands to the side of my desk, wraps her arms round my waist and kisses my neck. She's had to take a group of tourists to the hot-water springs on the west side of the island. Her skin smells of her work. It's a heavenly mixture of hot salt and sulphur. I smell this scent everywhere; on her clothes, inside our bed, on the cushions that lie scattered over the floor. No bottled perfume smells this sweet or this good, though for some reason, I like it better when she is bleeding. There's something incredibly sexy about the undertow of her body. Her smell changes texture. It's thicker, rougher; a rich compound of seaweed and blood.

Misha twists me round in the chair. She licks her lips, then makes me stand up and unbuckles my belt. The metal rattles and the leather uncurls like a snake. She throws the belt to the floor. I take the hint and we move through to the bathroom.

The mirror is misted and the air wet with steam. Misha steps into the shower and unravels her hair. When we first met, I told her how her hair reminded me of a river. It turned me on in ways I didn't quite understand. For instance, the way in which it hung down and brushed the small of her back. It had a tendency to flow and to stream. Small curls would unspool like thin rivulets and when she swam under water her hair would spread out like a red velvet cloak. It was both soft and alive. I liked to lie on my stomach while she dragged it over my shoulders and whipped me with it, over and over.

I rub Misha's back and lather up some soap. Her skin is hot and slippery. I think of the veins that run up her arms, the way they spread out at the wrist. They're like a river's vast estuary. If I were a boat I would want to sail in these waters. I would pack a compass and map, a supply of fast food, a thermos of whisky, then start by exploring the distant archipelagos and far-flung islands and atolls. I would float down each finger, chug through the aqueous halls of her brain, sail through the aortic channel, discover the caverns inside her heart. The ebb and the flow of each thunderous blood-pulse would push me deeper and deeper inside her. I would cross to the other side of her world, dive into the Dead Sea of her tears, lie on my back and later, much later, take shelter inside her lachrymal bones.

Misha turns round. The shower continues to pummel and pound. She lifts a bottle of oil off the ledge and pours a few drops into her hand. The oil slickens her skin. It's so soft and supple, and I think of a seal pup. She nudges her head against my neck, nuzzles my dry, slightly chapped lips. Her face is calm, almost sleepy. When I kiss her, I taste the remains of the salt. In winter they spread it over the roads. It's supposed to melt down the ice and turn it to slush. One kiss from Misha and my whole body pools over the tiles.

She lifts her leg and wraps it around the top of my thigh. She's a winter landscape. I press my head to her chest, listen to her slow groans that sound as though ice were cracking inside her. Her back is curved and white, granular as sugar, like the sweep of a wind as it blows over the Arctic. She curls her arms and bends further towards me. She knows that I want to make love, but instead sits on the lip of the tub and demands that I start washing her feet.

Misha's toes are ticklish. With their bright silver nails they remind me of minnows. I hook one and Misha squeals with delight. I nibble another and each toe squirms in my lap. When we emerge from the shower, Misha wraps a towel round me and leads me through to the bedroom. We pour two glasses of wine and slip under the cool linen sheets.

Her eyes flicker, her nostrils flare. The air she breathes out is the air I inhale. I run my hands down her sides and we lie face-to-face. Downstairs I can hear the drip of the shower and outside it has started to rain. Our bodies and the sound of the water mix and then merge. A dim half-light leaks through the window, tattooing wet shadows over her spine. Misha whispers strange things into my ear.

Her mouth is a storybook. She tells me tales of fantastic sea-creatures who live twenty leagues under the ocean. She tells me of sailors who murder their loved ones, then cut out their hearts and carry them wherever they go. On an island in the far north, the people use feathers as currency (or so Misha says), while another story involves a man who makes shoes out of the throats of black-headed seagulls.

I turn her on to her belly and trace some words over her skin with my tongue. I write the word 'love'. I write the word 'fuck', then lift my wine from the table and make a lake in the small of her back. I would like to skim stones over the surface. I would like to watch them as they skipped and then sank. Instead, I bend down and brew up a storm. I blow on the wine and it trickles between Misha's buttocks while she squirms with delight. I lap the wine up, and think of a dog crouching down over a puddle, slaking its thirst.

Misha flips over and straddles my belly. She arches her back and all of a sudden I see a salmon leaping into the air. Sunlight flashes over her shoulders. Her body is packed with steel; the shave of her collarbone is silvered and bright. She opens her legs and lets a small sigh escape from her mouth while my eyes slide down her belly and nestle in the friendly cave of her cunt.

Inside Misha is moist. She smells of rock pools and crystallized brine, and I have an overwhelming desire to lean down and kiss her, to feel her lips slowly part. They're soft as anemones, pinker than clams and I want to wade thigh-deep into that water, skinny-dip in the suck of those tides. Misha goes quiet. She's staring at me and I know it's a cliché, but her eyes *do* look like lakes. Imagine a blue stretching into infinity. Imagine a chiffony, sub-aqueous turquoise. Now imagine plunging into that water, the clean cut of the deeps, the glittering spray, the joy of moving in rhythm to the beat of those waves.

I flex my muscles and try to sit up, but instead Misha pushes a finger inside my mouth. She presses the nail into the gum-flesh and I feel like a fish that's been hooked and reeled in. No matter how hard I struggle, no matter which way I twist, I cannot break free. Her arm is a rod; she switches it this way and that. Misha is teasing me and though I hate to admit it, I enjoy being caught.

'I want to make love to you.'

'I know,' she says, then she blinks and rests her head on the pillow. She licks the tips of my fingers and round each of my wrists. She tucks her knees to her chest and curls up like a shrimp.

'Later?' I ask.

'Later,' she echoes.

Sleep is deep. We both drift off quickly. I only wish I could link her dreams to mine. As it is, I wander around like a soul in search of salvation. Nothing inside my dreams compares to her mystery, nothing contains her breadth or capacity. I watch a blue fish eating a cat. I notice an egg swallow a snake. A desert unravels before me; each grain of sand is cut like a diamond. They unfold as I walk over bright yellow dunes. Streams of it blow into my eyes. The sand catches my lashes and all of a sudden I stumble and fall. The sun beats down on my neck and I can feel my skin beginning to burn.

When I wake, it's pitch black, but I can feel Misha's breath on my cheek. Her eyes are rimmed with the richness of sleep. They're swimming with dreams and somewhere within them I see an oasis. It's a lush, green, fertile place and I want to kneel down and drink all of her in. I need to assuage my thirst, to take deep long gulps of her, feel her body slip down my throat. Instead, Misha stands up and begins to get dressed.

We're taking a walk by the harbour. It's eight o'clock and Misha has booked us a table at an exclusive hotel. She strides ahead while I look out towards the long wooden jetty. I stare at the waves, the bright coloured lights that jangle and sway in the breeze. Some water swills over my shoes and there's a tide-line of weed ruffled with seashells. After ten minutes Misha stops and slips her hand into mine. There's an old man sitting outside the Fish House, scaling cod and rock salmon with a broad silver knife. Misha exchanges small pleasantries.

They talk about quotas, about the best way to skin herring and sea bream. A few of the scales catch on her dress and glitter like sequins. Then she tells me that the sand feels thicker than fudge. It's wormed its way into the dips of her knees; it's grinding down the soles of her feet, scratching her ankles and buffing her toenails. The sea flings itself against the high harbour wall and quickly we make our way to the hotel.

Inside, the restaurant is hushed. Waiters glide to and fro. There's the chink of cutlery, the tinkle of cut-crystal glass-ware and when we order our drinks Misha starts talking about something I mentioned two weeks ago. Her mind recalls everything: the gifts I have given her, the trips we have taken, our promises, even our arguments. She's like a reservoir, damming up every last word in case of emergencies; storing up names, places and dates. Nothing is ever wasted on Misha.

She says, 'Remember how you wanted to do something exciting?'

'I think so,' I say.

'Because I've got an idea.' She dives under the table to retrieve her napkin and when she bobs up again I ask what it is.

'Not yet,' she says.

'But soon?'

She smiles. 'You'll have to wait. But I promise it won't be that long.'

Seconds later our waiter returns and we order our food: moules marinière for Misha, seared fillet steak for me. I watch as she drinks, watch as she sips the sparkling water, the deep, blood-red wine. Sometimes I think her throat is a wishing-well. It's so long and deep. I've picked cherries and dropped them into her mouth, wishing to kiss her. I've fed her truffles and oysters, omelettes and sweetmeats, wishing to touch her. The food slips down her throat with the satisfying ease of a coin. In this way Misha is richer than oil. She fizzes like silver.

Our food arrives and with a decorous flick of the wrist Misha scoops the mussels out of their shells, then slips the soft, fishy flesh into her mouth. Her swallow is smooth and sleek. Think of a swan, think of the fish that slip down its throat. She dabs up the juice with a thick sponge of bread and all of a sudden I feel a strong stab of jealousy. *I* want to be the food that she eats. *I* want to mop up the juices and be chewed and consumed.

For dessert we both need something cold.

'Ice-cream?' she whispers.

'Ice-cream,' I echo.

She dips her wafer into the bowl, paddles in the shallows with the tip of her spoon. By the time she's finished her lips are coated in a thick layer of chocolate. I imagine kissing her, the glorious mixture of saliva and sugar, her tongue furred over with cream.

'Let's get out of this place,' she says. 'We'll take a car to our next destination.'

Or to be more precise, we take *Misha's* car. After all, this is her surprise, her way, she says, of showing how much she loves me. I wind down the window and let the air wash over my face. Stars crackle. The sky is a sheet of black metal. The road is studded with cat's-eyes.

'Where are we going?' I say.

'Somewhere exciting. Trust me.' She turns on the radio and for a time we drive to the sound of light-hearted pop songs and jingles. The night flashes past. The clock on the dashboard clicks and then whirrs. We pass a gas station and the occasional farmhouse. We pass a forest of stubbly pine trees. The air grows colder.

Finally, she stops the car and I step out. The first thing I notice is the smell of sulphur. She's brought me up to the pools. I can hear them gurgling, see the mist spiralling out of control. This is prehistory; a snowscape, a land of shimmering glaciers, lava and rock. There are patches of ice, dazzling flashes of steam. It's a world reduced to mineral crystal. Misha stares up and I follow her gaze. Above us the moon hangs like an icicle. Snowflakes glide through the air and catch on her eyelids. Her breath blooms out like a flower.

Misha grins and takes hold of my hand. She leads me around the edge of the pools. There are hundreds and hundreds of these deep, bubbling fissures and we walk for what seems like hours enshrouded in mist. My shirt sticks to the back of my neck. My hair drips with sweat, then Misha steps slightly ahead of me and disappears into the haze.

I can hear her voice, hear her singing. My lover as Siren, luring me towards rocks. 'Over here,' she calls, and I stumble towards the thin, reedy voice. Something warm brushes my hand. It's the foam from the pools. Then Misha calls out again and the echo swirls round and round in the mist. 'Here,' she says. 'Over here.'

When I finally find her, Misha has stripped. She's lying face-up on a slab of lava, her eyes are trained on the stars. She begins to undress me and, button by button, I unfold in her arms. My nerve endings prickle. Her eyes glisten, then she opens her legs and begins to rub herself with her finger. It's a slow movement, calm and deliberate, and my body aches with guilt and desire. Beads of sweat run down my forehead. I watch her hand, watch her finger as it strokes and caresses her flesh and after she comes, she draws this pale, oystery digit over my belly and into my mouth. I envy her hands and she knows it.

'Jealous?' she says.

146

'Very.'

'Exciting enough?'

I nod.

She cradles my head and embraces me with the longest and deepest of kisses. This time her eyes resemble glass-bottomed boats. Beneath the surface I see whole shoals of emotion: love, passion, desire, death. I run my hand down her back, down the ridges of her coralline spine. Her hair sparkles and the steam spits.

Misha motions towards the dark water.

'Come on,' she says. 'Let's go for a swim.'

'Isn't it dangerous? Without any light?'

'It's fine,' she says.

I watch as she dives into the pool and woozily slide in behind her. The warmth is voluptuous. She locks her arms round my waist; the water smells of steam and pure sex. It's pungent. There's the undertow of thick sulphur and the slowly fermenting aroma of mud. Our feet squelch near the sides, but the further we swim, the deeper it is. We cling to each other. We're two lobsters inside a pot. The water is boiling and our skin is bright pink. She digs her fingers into my back. I run my tongue along the line of her breasts. I can feel the rise of each cone-shaped nipple, the golden hoops of her areolae. I push her legs as wide apart as I can; I want her spread-eagled. Only then can I slide into the depths of my fantasies.

'Beyond this point, there be dragons,' she says. The quote is familiar, but I am being swept into uncharted territory. That's what she's saying. This is the end of the world.

Misha grabs hold of my hair, then pulls back on my head so hard that I gasp. I dive deeper. I ride down the waves of her body. My head slips under, my lungs tighten. It's black down here, black with a silty, sub-aqueous silence. Black with sludge and curious soft-bodied creatures. I try to speak, but each word that escapes from my mouth forms a bubble. Another wave, only this time it drags me further away. I bang my head on her shoulder. I flex my muscles, struggle to find a good footing, but the grab of the water is too overpowering. It's sucking me down – wave after glorious wave, and suddenly I know that I'm going to drown.

Misha's eyes are lighter than driftwood.

I call out her name and finally, finally, sink into the depths.

LOVE HURTS

E. M. FORSTER

DR
WOOLACOTT

For this, from stiller seats we came
CYMBELINE V.iv

I

PEOPLE, SEVERAL OF them, crossing the park...

Clesant said to himself, 'There is no reason I should not live for years now that I have given up the violin,' and leant back with the knowledge that he had faced a fact. From where he lay, he could see a little of the garden and a little of the park, a little of the fields and the river, and hear a little of the tennis; a little of everything was what was good for him, and what Dr Woolacott had prescribed. Every few weeks he must expect a relapse, and he would never be able to travel or marry or manage the estates, still there, he didn't want to much, he didn't much want to do anything. An electric bell connected him with the house, the strong beautiful slightly alarming house where his father had died, still there, not so very alarming, not so bad lying out in the tepid sun and watching the colourless shapeless country people...

No, there was no reason he should not live for years.

'In 1990, why even 2000 is possible, I am young,' he thought. Then he frowned, for Dr Woolacott was bound to be dead by 2000, and the treatment might not be continued intelligently. The anxiety made his head ache, the trees and grass turned black or crimson, and he nearly rang his bell.

Soothed by the advancing figures, he desisted. Looking for mushrooms apparently, they soothed him because of their inadequacy. No mushrooms grew in the park. He felt friendly and called out in his gentle voice, 'Come here.'

'Oh aye,' came the answer.

'I'm the squire, I want you a moment, it's all right.'

Set in motion, the answerer climbed over the park fence. Clesant had not intended him to do this, and fearful of being bored said: 'You'll find no mushrooms here, but they'll give you a drink or anything else you fancy up at the house.'

'Sir, the squire, did you say?'

'Yes; I pass for the squire.'

'The one who's sick?'

'Yes, that one.'

'I'm sorry.'

'Thank you, thanks,' said the boy, pleased by the unexpected scrap of sympathy.

'Sir . . .'

'All right, what is it?' he smiled encouragingly.

'Sick of what illness?'

Clesant hesitated. As a rule he resented that question, but this morning it pleased him, it was as if he too had been detected by friendly eyes zigzagging in search of a treasure which did not exist. He replied: 'Of being myself perhaps! Well, what they call functional. Nothing organic. I can't possibly die, but my heart makes my nerves go wrong, my nerves my digestion, then my head aches, so I can't sleep, which affects my heart, and round we go again. However, I'm better this morning.'

'When shall you be well?'

He gave the contemptuous laugh of the chronic invalid. 'Well? That's a very different question. It depends. It depends on a good many things. On how carefully I live. I must avoid

all excitement, I must never get fired, I mustn't be—' He was
going to say 'mustn't be intimate with people', but it was no
use employing expressions which would be meaningless to a
farmworker, and such the man appeared to be, so he changed
it to 'I must do as Dr Woolacott tells me.'

'Oh, Woolacott . . .'

'Of course you know him, everyone round here does,
marvellous doctor.'

'Yes, I know Woolacott.'

Clesant looked up, intrigued by something positive in the
tone of the voice.

'Woolacott, Woolacott, so I must be getting on.' Not quite
as he had come, he vaulted over the park palings, paused,
repeated 'Woolacott' and walked rapidly after his compan-
ions, who had almost disappeared.

A servant now answered the bell. It had failed to ring
the first time, which would have been annoying had the
visitor proved tedious. The little incident was over now, and
nothing else disturbed the peace of the morning. The park,
the garden, the sounds from the tennis, all reassumed their
due proportions, but it seemed to Clesant that they were
pleasanter and more significant than they had been, that the
colours of the grass and the shapes of the trees had beauty,
that the sun wandered with a purpose through the sky, that
the little clouds, wafted by westerly airs, were moving against
the course of doom and fate, and were inviting him to
follow them.

II

Continuance of convalescence . . . tea in the gun-room. The
gun-room, a grand place in the old squire's time, much energy

155

had flowed through it, intellectual and bodily. Now the book-cases were locked, the trophies between them desolate, the tall shallow cupboard designed for fishing-rods and concealed in the wainscoting contained only medicine-bottles and air cushions. Still, it was Clesant's nearest approach to normality, for the rest of his household had tea in the gun-room too. There was innocuous talk as they flitted out and in, pursuing their affairs like birds, and troubling him only with the external glint of their plumage. He knew nothing about them, although they were his guardians and familiars; even their sex left no impression on his mind. Throned on the pedestal of a sofa, he heard them speak of their wishes and plans, and give one another to understand that they had passionate impulses, while he barricaded himself in the circle of his thoughts.

He was thinking about music.

Was it quite out of the question that he should take up the violin again? He felt better, the morning in the garden had started him upon a good road, a refreshing sleep had followed. Now a languorous yearning filled him, which might not the violin satisfy? The effect might be the contrary, the yearning might turn to pain, yet even pain seemed unlikely in this kindly house, this house which had not always been kindly, yet surely this afternoon it was accepting him.

A stranger entered his consciousness – a young man in good if somewhat provincial clothes, with a pleasant and resolute expression upon his face. People always were coming into the house on some business or other; and then going out of it. He stopped in the middle of the room, evidently a little shy. No one spoke to him for the reason that no one remained: they had all gone away while Clesant followed his meditations. Obliged to exert himself for a moment, Clesant said: 'I'm sorry – I expect you're wanting one of the others.'

156

He smiled and twiddled his cap.

'I'm afraid I mustn't entertain you myself. I'm something of an invalid, and this is my first day up. I suffer from one of those wretched functional troubles – fortunately nothing organic.'

Smiling more broadly, he remarked: 'Oh aye.'

Clesant clutched at his heart, jumped up, sat down, burst out laughing. It was that farmworker who had been crossing the park.

'Thought I'd surprise you, thought I'd give you a turn,' he cried gaily. 'I've come for that drink you promised.'

Clesant couldn't speak for laughing, the whole room seemed to join in, it was a tremendous joke.

'I was around in my working-kit when you invited me this morning, so I thought after I'd washed myself up a bit and had a shave my proper course was to call and explain,' he continued more seriously. There was something fresh and rough in his voice which caught at the boy's heart.

'But who on earth are you, who are you working for?'

'For you.'

'Oh nonsense, don't be silly.'

' 'Tisn't nonsense, I'm not silly, I'm one of your farm-hands. Rather an unusual one, if you like. Still, I've been working here for the last three months, ask your bailiff if I haven't. But I say – I've kept thinking about you – how are you?'

'Better – because I saw you this morning!'

'That's fine. Now you've seen me this afternoon you'll be well.'

But this last remark was flippant, and the visitor through making it lost more than the ground he had gained. It reminded Clesant that he had been guilty of laughter and of rapid movements, and he replied in reproving tones: 'To be well and to be better are very different. I'm afraid one can't get well from one's self. Excuse me if we don't talk any more. It's so bad for my heart.' He closed his eyes. He opened them again immediately. He had had, during that instant of twilight, a curious and pleasurable sensation. However, there was the young man still over at the farther side of the room. He was smiling. He was attractive – fresh as a daisy, strong as a horse. His shyness had gone.

'Thanks for that tea, a treat,' he said, lighting a cigarette. 'Now for who I am. I'm a farmer – or rather, going to be a farmer. I'm only an agricultural labourer now – exactly what you took me for this morning. I wasn't dressing up or posing with that broad talk. It's come natural to say "Oh aye", especially when startled.'

'Did I startle you?'

'Yes, you weren't in my mind.'

'I thought you were looking for mushrooms.'

'So I was. We all do when we're shifting across, and when there's a market we sell them. I've been living with that sort all the summer, your regular hands, temporaries like myself, tramps, sharing their work, thinking their thoughts when they have any.' He paused. 'I like them.'

'Do they like you?'

'Oh well . . .' He laughed, drew a ring off his finger, laid it on the palm of his hand, looked at it for a moment, put it on again. All his gestures were definite and a trifle unusual. 'I've no pride anyway, nor any reason to have. I only have my health, and I didn't always have that. I've known what it is to be an invalid, though no one guesses it now.' He looked across gently at Clesant. He seemed to say: 'Come to me, and you shall be as happy as I am and as strong.' He gave a short account of his life. He dealt in facts, very much so when they arrived – and the tale he unfolded was high-spirited and a trifle romantic here and there, but in no way remarkable. Aged twenty-two, he was the son of an engineer at Wolver-hampton, his two brothers were also engineers, but he him-self had always taken after his mother's family, and preferred country life. All his holidays on a farm. The war. After which he took up agriculture seriously, and went through a course of Cirencester. The course terminated last spring, he had done well, his people were about to invest money in him, but he himself felt 'too scientific' after it all. He was deter-mined to 'get down into the manure' and feel people instead of thinking about them. 'Later on it's too late.' So off he went and roughed it, with a few decent clothes in a suitcase, and now and then, just for the fun of the thing, he took them out and dressed up. He described the estate, how decent the bailiff was, how sorry people seemed to be about the squire's illness, how he himself got a certain amount of time off, prac-tically any evening. Extinguishing his cigarette, he put back what was left of it into his case for future use, laid a hand upon either knee, smiled.

There was a silence. Clesant could not think of anything to say, and began to tremble.

'Oh, my name—'

'Oh yes, of course, what's your name?'

'Let me write it down, my address too. Both my Wolver-hampton address I'll give you, also where I'm lodging here so if ever – got a pencil?'

'Yes.'

'Don't get up.'

He came over and sat on the sofa; his weight sent a tremor, the warmth and sweetness of his body began casting nets.

'And now we've no paper.'

'Never mind,' said Clesant, his heart beating violently.

'Talking's better, isn't it?'

159

'Yes.'

'Or even not talking.' His hand came nearer, his eyes danced round the room, which began to fill with golden haze. He beckoned, and Clesant moved into his arms. Clesant had often been proud of his disease but never, never of his body, it had never occurred to him that he could provoke desire. The sudden revelation shattered him, he fell from his pedestal, but not alone, there was someone to cling to, broad shoulders, a sunburnt throat, lips that parted as they touched him to murmur – 'And to hell with Woolacott.'

Woolacott! He had completely forgotten the doctor's existence. Woolacott! The word crashed between them and exploded with a sober light, and he saw in the light of the years that had passed and would come how ridiculously he was behaving. To hell with Woolacott, indeed! What an idea! His charming new friend must be mad. He started, recoiling, and exclaimed: 'Whatever made you say that?'

The other did not reply. He looked rather foolish, and he too recoiled, and leant back in the opposite corner of the sofa, wiping his forehead. At last he said: 'He's not a good doctor.'

'Why, he's our family doctor, he's everyone's doctor round here!'

'I didn't mean to be rude – it slipped out. I just had to say it, it must have sounded curious.'

'Oh, all right then,' said the boy, willing enough to be mollified. But the radiance had passed and no effort of theirs could recall it.

The young man took out his unfinished cigarette, and raised it towards his lips. He was evidently a good deal worried. 'Perhaps I'd better explain what I meant,' he said.

'As you like, it doesn't matter.'

'Got a match?'

'I'm afraid I haven't.'

He went for one to the farther side of the room, and sat down there again. Then he began: 'I'm perfectly straight – I'm not trying to work in some friend of my own as your doctor. I only can't bear to think of this particular one coming to your house – this grand house – you so rich and important at the first sight and yet so awfully undefended and deceived.' His voice faltered. 'No, we won't talk it over. You're right. We've found each other, nothing else matters, it's a chance in a million we've found each other. I'd do anything for you, I'd die if I could for you, and there's this one thing you must do straight away for me: sack Woolacott.'

'Tell me what you've got against him instead of talking sentimentally.'

He hardened at once. 'Sentimental, was I? All right, what I've got against Woolacott is that he never makes anyone well, which seems a defect in a doctor. I may be wrong.'

'Yes, you're wrong,' said Clesant; the mere repetition of the doctor's name was steadying him. 'I've been under him for years.'

'So I should think.'

'Of course, I'm different, I'm not well, it's not natural for me to be well, I'm not a fair test, but other people—'

'Which other people?'

The names of Dr Woolacott's successful cases escaped him for the moment. They filled the centre of his mind, yet the moment he looked at them they disappeared.

'Quite so,' said the other. 'Woolacott,' he kept on saying. 'Woolacott! I've my eye on him. What's life after twenty-five? Impotent, blind, paralytic. What's life before it unless you're fit? Woolacott! Even the poor can't escape. The crying, the limping, the nagging, the medicine-bottles, the running sores – in the cottages too; kind Dr Woolacott won't let them stop ... You think I'm mad, but it's not your own thought you're thinking: Woolacott stuck it ready diseased into your mind.'

Clesant sighed. He looked at the arms now folded hard against each other, and longed to feel them around him. He had only to say, 'Very well, I'll change doctors,' and immediately ... But he never hesitated. Life until 1990 or 2000 retained the prior claim. 'He keeps people alive,' he persisted.

'Alive for what?'

'And there's always the marvellously unselfish work he did during the war.'

'Did he not. I saw him doing it.'

'Oh – it was in France you knew him?'

'Was it not. He was at his marvellously unselfish work night and day, and not a single man he touched ever got well. Woolacott dosed, Woolacott inoculated, Woolacott operated, Woolacott spoke a kind word even, and there they were and here they are.'

'Were you in hospital yourself?'

'Oh aye, a shell. This hand – ring and all mashed and twisted, the head – hair's thick enough on it now, but brain stuck out then, so did my guts, I was a butcher's shop. A perfect case for Woolacott. Up he came with his "Let me patch you up, do let me just patch you up", oh, patience itself and all that, but I took his measure, I was only a boy then, but I refused.'

'Can one refuse in a military hospital?'

'You can refuse anywhere.'

'I hadn't realized you'd been wounded. Are you all right now?'

'Yes, thanks,' and he resumed his grievances. The pleasant purple-grey suit, the big well-made shoes and soft white collar, all suggested a sensible country lad on his holiday, perhaps on courtship – farmhand or farmer, countrified anyway. Yet with them went this wretched war-obsession, this desire to be revenged on a man who had never wronged him and must have forgotten his existence. 'He is stronger than I am,' he said angrily. 'He can fight alone, I can't. My great disadvantage – never could fight alone. I counted on you to help, but you prefer to let me down, you pretended at first you'd join up with me – you're no good.'

'Look here, you'll have to be going. So much talk is fatal for me, I simply mustn't get overtired. I've already far exceeded my allowance, and anyhow I can't enter into this sort of thing. Can you find your own way out, or shall I ring this bell?' For inserted into the fabric of the sofa was an electric bell.

'I'll go. I know where I'm not wanted. Don't you worry, you'll never see me again.' And he slapped his cap on to his head and swung to the door. The normal life of the house entered the gun-room as he opened it – servants, inmates, talking in the passages, in the hall outside. It disconcerted him, he came back with a complete change of manner, and before ever he spoke Clesant had the sense of an incredible catastrophe moving up towards them both.

'Is there another way out?' he inquired anxiously.

'No, of course not. Go out the way you came in.'

'I didn't tell you, but the fact is I'm in trouble.'

'How dare you, I mustn't be upset, this is the kind of thing that makes me ill,' he wailed.

'I can't meet those people – they've heard of something I did out in France.'

'What was it?'

'I can't tell you.'

In the sinister silence, Clesant's heart resumed its violent beating, and though the door was now closed voices could be heard through it. They were coming. The stranger rushed at the windows and tried to climb out. He plunged about, soiling his freshness, and whimpering, 'Hide me.'

'There's nowhere.'

'There must be . . .'

'Only that cupboard,' said Clesant in a voice not his own.

'I can't find it,' he gasped, thumping stupidly on the panelling. 'Do it for me. Open it. They're coming.'

Clesant dragged himself up and across the floor, he opened the cupboard, and the man bundled in and hid, and that was how it ended.

Yes, that's how it ends, that's what comes of being kind to handsome strangers and wanting to touch them. Aware of all his weaknesses, Dr Woolacott had warned him against this one. He crawled back to the sofa, where a pain stabbed him through the heart and another struck between the eyes. He was going to be ill.

The voices came nearer, and with the cunning of a sufferer he decided what he must do. He must betray his late friend and pretend to have trapped him on purpose in the cupboard, cry 'Open it . . .'

The voices entered. They spoke of the sounds of a violin. A violin had apparently been heard playing in the great house for the last half-hour, and no one could find out where it was. Playing all sorts of music, gay, grave and passionate. But never completing a theme. Always breaking off. A beautiful instrument. Yet so unsatisfying . . . leaving the hearers much sadder than if it had never performed. What was the use (someone asked) of music like that? Better silence absolute than this aimless disturbance of our peace. The discussion broke off, his distress had been observed, and like a familiar refrain rose up 'Telephone, nurse, doctor . . .' Yes, it was coming again – the illness, merely functional, the heart had affected the nerves, the muscles, the brain. He groaned, shrieked, but love died last; as he writhed in convulsions he cried: 'Don't go to the cupboard, no one's there.'

So they went to it. And no one was there. It was as it had always been since his father's death – shallow, tidy, a few medicine-bottles on the upper shelf, a few cushions stored on the lower.

III

Collapse . . . He fell back into the apparatus of decay without further disaster, and in a few hours any other machinery for life became unreal. It always was like this, increasingly like this, when he was ill. Discomfort and pain brought their compensation, because they were so superbly organized. His bedroom, the anteroom where the night-nurse sat, the bathroom and tiny kitchen, throbbed like a nerve in the corner of the great house, and elsewhere normal life proceeded, people pursued their avocations in channels which did not disturb him.

Delirium . . . The nurse kept coming in, she performed medical incantations and took notes against the doctor's arrival. She did not make him better, he grew worse, but disease knows its harmonies as well as health, and through its soft advances now rang the promise, 'You shall live to grow old.'

'I did something wrong, tell me, what was it?' It made him happy to abase himself before his disease, nor was this colloquy their first.

'Intimacy,' the disease replied.

'I remember . . . Do not punish me this once, let me live and I will be careful. Oh, save me from him.'

'No – from yourself. Not from him. He does not exist. He is an illusion, whom you created in the garden because you wanted to feel you were attractive.'

'I know I am not attractive, I will never excite myself again, but he does exist, I think.'

'No.'

'He may be death, but he does exist.'

'No. He never came into the gun-room. You only wished that he would. He never sat down on the sofa by your side and made love. You handed a pencil, but he never took it, you fell into his arms, but they were not there, it has all been a daydream of the kind forbidden. And when the others came in and opened the cupboard: your muscular and intelligent farmhand, your saviour from Wolverhampton in his Sunday suit – was he there?'

'No, he was not,' the boy sobbed.

'No, he was not,' came an echo, 'but perhaps I am here.'

The disease began to crouch and gurgle. There was the sound of a struggle, a spewing sound, a fall. Clesant, not greatly frightened, sat up and peered into the chaos. The nightmare passed, he felt better. Something survived from it, an echo that said 'Here, here'. And, he not dissenting, bare feet seemed to walk to the little table by his side, and hollow, filled with the dark, a shell of nakedness bent towards him and sighed 'Here'.

Clesant declined to reply.

'Here is the end, unless you . . .' Then silence. Then, as if emitted by a machine, the syllables 'Oh aye'.

Clesant, after thought, put out his hand and touched the bell.

'I put her to sleep as I passed her, this is my hour, I can do that much . . .' He seemed to gather strength from any recognition of his presence, and to say, 'Tell my story for me, explain how I got here, pour life into me and I shall live as before when our bodies touched.' He sighed. 'Come home with me now, perhaps it is a farm. I have just enough power. Come away with me for an evening to my earthly lodging, easily managed by a ... the ... such a visit would be love. Ah, that was the word – love – why they pursued me and still know I am in the house; love was the word they cannot endure, I have remembered it at last.'

Then Clesant spoke, sighing in his turn. 'I don't even know what is real, so how can I know what is love? Unless it is excitement, and of that I am afraid. Do not love me, whatever you are; at all events this is my life and no one shall disturb it; a little sleep followed by a little pain.'

And his speech evoked strength. More powerfully the other answered now, giving instances and arguments, throwing into sentences the glow they had borne during daylight. Clesant was drawn into a struggle, but whether to reach or elude the hovering presence he did not know. There was always a barrier either way, always his own nature. He began calling for people to come, and the adversary, waxing lovely and powerful, struck them dead before they could waken and help. His household perished, the whole earth was thinning, one instant more, and he would be alone with his ghost – and then through the walls of the house he saw the lights of a car rushing across the park.

It was Dr Woolacott at last.

Instantly the spell broke, the dead revived, and went downstairs to receive life's universal lord; and he – he was left with a human being who had somehow trespassed and been caught, and blundered over the furniture in the dark, bruising his defenceless body, and whispering, 'Hide me.'

And Clesant took pity on him again, and lifted the clothes of the bed, and they hid.

Voices approached, a great company, Dr Woolacott leading his army. They touched, their limbs intertwined, they gripped and grew mad with delight, yet through it all sounded the tramp of that army.

'They are coming.'

'They will part us.'

'Clesant, shall I take you away from all this?'

'Have you still the power?'

'Yes, until Woolacott sees me.'

'Oh, what is your name?'

'I have none.'

'Where is your home?'

'Woolacott calls it the grave.'

'Shall I be with you in it?'

'I can promise you that. We shall be together for ever and ever, we shall never be ill, and never grow old.'

'Take me.'

They entwined more closely, their lips touched never to part, and then something gashed him where life had concentrated, and Dr Woolacott, arriving too late, found him dead on the floor.

The doctor examined the room carefully. It presented its usual appearance, yet it reminded him of another place. Dimly, from France, came the vision of a hospital ward, dimly the sound of his own voice saying to a mutilated recruit, 'Do let me patch you up, oh but you must just let me patch you up . . .'

PAULINE RÉAGE

from:
THE STORY OF O

'PLEASE STAY A MOMENT, please, and tell me—' But O's words were cut off by the opening of the door: it was her lover, and he was not alone.

It was René, dressed the way he was when he got up from bed and lit his first cigarette of the day; he was in striped pyjamas and a blue wool bathrobe: the one with the quilted silk lining they'd chosen together the year before. And his slippers were shabby, truly moth-eaten, he needed a new pair. The two women disappeared without a sound save for the rustling of silk when they lifted their skirts (all the skirts trailed somewhat); the clogs couldn't be heard upon the carpeting. O, who was sitting rather precariously half on and half off the bed, one leg hanging over the edge, the other tucked up towards her body, didn't budge, although the cup suddenly began to shake in her hand and she lost hold of her croissant. 'Pick it up,' René said. That was the first thing he'd said. She posed the cup on the table, retrieved the partly chewed croissant, and laid it by the cup. A large croissant-crumb remained on the floor, touching O's naked foot. In his turn, René stooped down and picked it up. Then he sat down next to O, bent her backward and kissed her. She asked him if he loved her. 'Ah, yes! I do love you,' he answered, then got up, stood her up too, and gently pressed his cool palms, then his lips, to her welts, to all her welts. Since the other man had come in with her lover, O wasn't sure whether or not she was allowed to look at him; he had turned his back for an instant and was smoking near the door. What came next could not have been an encouragement to her. 'Let's have a look at you, come here,' her lover said and, having steered her to the foot of the bed, remarked to his companion that he had been altogether correct, expressed his thanks, adding that it seemed only fair that he, the stranger, be the first to try her out if he were so inclined. The stranger, whom she still dared not look at, after he had glided his hands over her breasts and down her buttocks, then asked her to spread her legs. 'Do as you're told,' said René, against whose chest her back was leaning and who was holding her erect; and his right hand was caressing one of her breasts, his left held her shoulder. The stranger had seated himself on the edge of the bed, by means of the hairs growing on them had taken hold of and gradually opened the labia guarding the entrance to her crack. René nudged her forward in an effort to facilitate the task, but no, that wasn't quite it, then he understood what the other was after and slipped his right arm around her waist, thus improving his grip. Under this caress, which she had never hitherto accepted without a struggle and without an overpowering feeling of shame, from which she would escape as quickly as she could, so quickly that it scarcely had the opportunity to register its effects, and which seemed a sacrilege to her, because it seemed to her sacrilegious that her lover be on his knees when she ought to be on hers – of a sudden she sensed that she was not going to escape this caress, not this time, and she saw herself doomed. For she moaned when that strange mouth pushed aside the fold of flesh whence the inner corolla emerges, moaned when those strange lips abruptly set her afire then retreated to let a strange tongue's hot tip burn her still more; she moaned louder when strange lips seized her anew; she sensed the hidden point harden and protrude to be taken between strange teeth and tongue in a long sucking bite that held her and held her still; she reeled, lost her footing, and found herself upon her back, René's mouth upon her mouth; his two hands pinned her shoulders to the mattress whilst two other hands gripping her calves were opening and flexing her legs. Her own hands – they were behind and under her back (for at the same moment he had thrust her towards the stranger René had bound her wrists by joining the two wrist-bands' catches) – her hands were brushed by the sex of the man who was rubbing himself in the crease between her buttocks; that sex now rose and shot swiftly to the depths of the hole in her belly. In answer to that first blow she emitted a cry as when under the lash, acknowledged each succeeding blow with a cry, and her lover bit her mouth. It was as though snatched forcefully away that the man quit her, hurled backwards as though thunderstruck, and from his throat there also came a cry. René detached O's hands, eased her along the bed, and tucked her away under the blanket. The stranger got up and the two men went towards the door. In a flash, O saw herself immolated, annihilated, cursed. She had groaned under the stranger's mouth as never she had under René's, cried before the onslaught of the stranger's member as never her lover had made her cry. She was profaned and guilty. If he were to abandon her, it would be rightfully. But no: the door swung to again, he was still there, was staying with her, he walked towards her, lay full length down beside her, beneath the fur blanket, slipped himself into her wet and burning belly and, holding her thus embraced, said to her: 'I love you. After I've also given you to the valets, I'll come some night and lash you till the blood flows.'

The sunshine had dissipated the mists, its rays flooded the room. But it wasn't until the midday bell rang that they woke.

O did not know what to do. Her lover was there, just as near, just as defencelessly, as sweetly abandoned as in the bed of the low-ceilinged room where almost every night ever since they'd been living together he'd come to sleep beside her. It was a big four-poster of mahogany, but without the canopy, and the posts at the head were taller than the two at the feet. He would always sleep to her left and, when he'd awake, would always reach a hand towards her legs. That was why she never wore anything but nightgowns, or, if pyjamas, never the pyjama-bottoms. And he too; she took that hand and kissed it, not daring to ask him anything. But he spoke. He told her, and as he spoke he slipped two fingers between her neck and the collar, he told her that he intended that from now on she be held in common by him and by others of his choosing and by still others whom he didn't know who were affiliated with the society that owned the château, she'd be subject to general use, as she'd been the evening before. He told her that she belonged, and was ultimately answerable to him, only to him, even if she were to receive orders from others than he, no matter whether he were there or absent, for by way of principle he concurred in no matter what she might be required to do or might be inflicted upon her, and that it was he who possessed and enjoyed her through the agency of those into whose hands he surrendered her, and this was so from the mere fact that she was surrendered to them by him, she was the gift, he the donor. She was to show obedience to them all, and greet them with the same respectfulness she greeted him, as so many images of him. Thus would he possess her as a god possessed his creatures whereupon he lays hands guised as some monster or bird, as some invisible spirit or as ecstasy itself. He did not want to, he was not going to leave her. The more he subjected her to, the more important to him she would become. The fact he gave her to others was proof thereof, proof in his eyes, it ought to be proof also in hers, that she belonged to him. He gave her so as to have her immediately back, and recovered her enriched a hundredfold in his eyes, as is an ordinary object that has served some divine purpose and thereby become infused with sanctity. For a long time he had desired to prostitute her, and it was gladly he now discovered that the pleasure he reaped from it was greater than he had even dared hope, and increased his attachment to her as it did hers to him, and that attachment would be the greater, the more her prostitution would humiliate and soil and ruin her. Since she loved him, she had no choice but to love the treatment she got from him. O listened and trembled from happiness; since he loved her, she trembled, consentingly. In all likelihood he discerned her consent, for he continued: 'It's because it's so easy for you to consent that I want from you something you can't possibly consent to, even if you say yes in advance, even if you say yes now and suppose that you are actually capable of submitting to it. You won't be able to prevent yourself from saying no when the time comes. When the time comes, it won't matter what you say, you'll be made to submit, not only for the sake of the incomparable pleasure I or others will find in your submission, but so that you will be aware of what has been done to you.' O was about to reply that she was his slave and dwelt joyfully in bondage; but he halted her: 'Yesterday you were told that, so long as you are in this château, you're neither to look a man in the face nor speak to him. Nor must you look at me or speak to me any more. You're simply to be still and to obey. I love you. Get up. From now on, while you're here, you'll not open your mouth again in the presence of a man, except to scream or to bestow caresses.' So O got up. René remained stretched out on the bed. She bathed, did her hair; upon contact with her bruised buttocks the tepid water made her shiver, she had to sponge herself but not rub to avoid reviving the fiery pain. She painted her mouth, but not her eyes, powdered herself and, still naked, but with her eyes lowered, came back into the cell. René was looking at Jeanne, who had entered and who was standing quietly by the head of the bed, she too with lowered eyes, she, too, mute. He told her to dress O. Jeanne took the green satin bodice, the white petticoat, the gown, the green clogs and, having hooked O's bodice in front, began to lace it up tight in back.

The bodice was stoutly whaleboned, long and rigid, something from the days when wasp-waists were in fashion, and was fitted with gussets upon which the breasts lay. The tighter it was drawn, the more prominently O's breasts rose, pushed up by the supporting gussets, and the more sharply upward her nipples were tilted. At the same time, as her waist was constricted, her womb and buttocks were made to swell out. The odd thing is that this veritable cuirass was exceedingly comfortable and, up to a certain point, relaxing. In it, one felt very upright, but, without one being able to tell just how or why unless it was by contrast, it increased one's consciousness of the freedom or rather the availability of the parts it left unencompassed. The wide skirt and the neckline, sweeping down from her shoulders to below and the whole width of her breasts, looked on the girl clad in it, not so much like an article of clothing, a protective device, but like a provocative one, a mechanism for display. When Jeanne had tied a bow in the laces and knotted it for good measure, O took her gown from the bed. It was in one piece, the petticoat tacked inside the skirt like an interchangeable lining, and the bodice, cross-laced in front and secured in back by a second series of laces, was thus, depending on how tightly it was done up, able to reproduce more or less exactly the subtler lines of the bust. Jeanne had laced it very tight, and O caught a glimpse of herself through the open door to the bathroom, her slender torso rising like a flower from the mass of green satin billowing out from her hips as if she were wearing a hoop-skirt. The two

176

women were standing side by side. Jeanne reached to correct a pleat in the sleeve of the green gown, and her breasts stirred beneath her gauze kerchief, breasts whose nipples were long, whose halos were brown. Her gown was of yellow faille. René, who had approached the two women, said to O: 'Look.' And to Jeanne: 'Lift your dress.' With both hands she lifted the stiff crackling silk and the linen lining it to reveal a golden belly, honey-smooth thighs and knees, and a black, closed triangle. René put forth his hand and probed it slowly, with his other hand exciting the nipple of one breast, till it grew hard and yet darker. 'That's so you can see,' he told O. O saw. She saw his ironic but concentrated face, his intent eyes scanning Jeanne's half-opened mouth and the back-bent throat girdled by the leather collar. What pleasure could she, O, give him, that this woman or some other could not give him too? 'Hadn't you thought of that?' he asked. No, she'd not thought of that. She had slumped against the wall between the two doors; her spine was straight, her arms trailed limply. There was no further need for ordering her to silence. How could she have spoken? He may perhaps have been moved by her despair, for he relinquished Jeanne to take O in his arms, hugging her to him, calling her his love and his life, saying again and again that he loved her. The hand with which he was caressing her throat and neck was moist with the wetness and smell of Jeanne. And then? And then the despair in whose tide she had been drowning ebbed away: he loved her, ah yes, he did love her. He did indeed have the right to take pleasure with Jeanne, to seek it with others, he loved her. 'I love you,' she whispered in his ear, 'I love you,' in so soft a whisper he could just barely hear.

'I love you.'

It wasn't until he saw the sweetness flow back into her and the brightness into her eyes that he took leave of her, happy.

EDITH TEMPLETON

from:
GORDON

HE HAD TOLD me to meet him at Shepherds two days later, at six in the afternoon.

I put on a red cotton dress with white dots and white zig-zag braiding outlining the seams. It was akin to a kitchen-maid's frock. I looked in it a 'slip of a girl', and as near as I could get to looking like a floozie. It was made from the same pattern as my elegant, well-bred silk dress of the other day, but because of the humble material it had this entirely different character. I had yet a third dress made of that same pattern. It was of thin dark blue wool, with long sleeves; I had worn it for my interview in the War Office when applying for a job, and I imagined that it made me look serious, studious, and reliable.

On this afternoon I had chosen the red cotton on purpose. I hoped it would imply how little I wished to please him. I believed I did not care whether I pleased him or not. Yet I fiercely resented how he had treated me in the garden that night, and I hoped to hurt him by showing my indifference. It need hardly be said that I arrived, purposely, a quarter of an hour after the appointed time.

He was standing at the same spot where I had had my first glimpse of him, with his back against the flower-strewn panel of the sedan chair.

He was in uniform, in battle dress and beret, with the insignia of a major. It did not suit him. The coarse material of the baggy tunic made him appear shorter and slighter than he was; the beret hid the devilishly attractive hairline; the khaki turned his pallor to sallowness.

'I'm afraid I'm late,' I said, determined to point out my insulting tardiness, in case he might not have noticed it.

He said, 'You mean you are late because you are afraid.'

For an instant I looked at him. Then I cast my eyes to the ground.

'I've put on my uniform for the last time today,' he remarked, 'as a swan song.' His voice became wheezing, quaking, trembling with the emotions of a very old man: 'As a heartfelt tribute to all the dear brave boys who gave their lives and their all to the cause of the fatherland,' and then, as I was giggling, he resumed in his ordinary tone, 'Let's get out of here.'

Again he took me by the wrist; this time I did not resent it. Outside, he halted, raised my hand and held it away from him at a distance, shifting it slightly, so that the light struck a sparkle from my wedding ring.

He said, 'This thin band of gold does not seem to weigh heavily on that little hand of yours.'

'No,' I said.

He lowered my hand and fell in step beside me, still holding my wrist.

'When did you walk out on your husband?' he asked.

'How do you know I walked out on him?'

'You are very good at walking out on people altogether, I should imagine,' he said.

'I don't know,' I said, 'I've never thought about it.'

'It was merely an idle observation of mine,' he remarked. 'You needn't think about it. When did you walk out on him?'

'Three years ago.' I was certain he was going to question me about the reasons for my having left my husband, and

I was determined not to tell him. I was therefore astonished when his next question was of an entirely different nature.

'How old was he then?' he asked.

'Twenty-seven,' I said.

'So he was not old and beautiful, was he?' he remarked with a satisfied smile.

'Don't be so idiotic,' I said. 'What's that got to do with it?'

'How should I know?' he said, still smiling. 'You should know. But as you don't seem to like the idea, don't give it another thought.'

'You are really quite idiotic,' I said. 'It's like the man who was given the secret of how to make gold out of stone, with all the right rules and regulations; but while he was to do it, he must not for a second ever think of white elephants. And of course he couldn't stop himself thinking of white elephants. So why do you tell me, don't think about it? Because now I will.'

'Of course you will,' he said; 'but it won't get you anywhere.'

'Where should it get me? I don't understand you,' I said.

'You don't have to understand me, my poor child,' he said.

'You are talking nothing but rot,' I said haughtily. I was elated because I was able to be as rude to him as I liked. I had never enjoyed such freedom before. I was drunk with my own impertinence. 'Just because you say something non-sensical you imagine it's going to sound clever. It's like the poetry of T. S. Eliot. Nobody understands him and every-body says it's clever. And don't call me "my poor child". I hate it.'

We had been walking along Piccadilly, and now he came to a halt in front of an antique shop. 'Here,' he said, 'this will soothe you. And now, tell me why I shouldn't call you "my poor child".'

'Because it's so sad,' I said. 'There is a poem by Goethe – "Mignon's Song". And it's in it. *Und alle Bilder stehn und sehn Dich an, was hat man Dir, Du armes Kind getan?* I always feel like weeping when I read it. Of course you wouldn't know it.'

'I did know it,' he said. 'Tell me the whole, roughly. How does it go?'

'She wants him to go with her to Italy,' I said.

'Who is he?' he asked.

'Her father,' I said, and added hastily, 'No, sorry. I've messed it up. It's not quite clear who he is. Because in the first verse she calls him her lover. That's with the oranges and lemons. In the second verse she calls him her father. That's where the bit with the statues and the pictures comes in, and that sadness with the "my poor child, what have they done to you?"... It's heartbreaking. That's why I don't like it,' and I turned from the shop-window and raised my eyes to him.

'Go on,' he said. There was again on his countenance that cold, fascinated attention, the look of lying in wait.

I grew flustered. 'Then it gets wild and gruesome. High crags and dragons and rushing floods. You have to go over them and through them, if you want to get to Italy.'

'And what does she call him in this verse?' he asked.

'She calls him "my protector",' I said. I added, 'You don't know much, do you?' and gave him an arrogant look.

He did not seem to notice it. 'It's excellent,' he remarked; 'it's most interesting.'

'Of course it's excellent,' I said; 'it's Goethe. Goethe always is.'

'I was not thinking of Goethe, my poor child,' he said. 'I was thinking of you. You have a lovely brain.'

I was astonished by his compliment, though not pleased. It was not the kind of praise I wanted. Besides, it was not true. Anyone could have given a crude rehash of 'Mignon's Song'.

'You are very easy to please,' I said as we continued on our way. Yet, somehow, his 'You have a lovely brain' had appeased me and I had stopped resenting his calling me 'my poor child'.

We had drinks in a pub in Shaftesbury Avenue. He took a double whisky and I had a sweet sherry which, to my relief, he ordered without comment.

'I'll take you to a Chinese restaurant now,' he said.

'Oh, I know an awfully good one,' I cried.

'That's not the one I mean,' he said.

'How do you know the one I mean is not the one you mean?' I asked.

'Because you mean another one,' he said.

'Well, what's yours called?' I asked.

'Bellevue,' he said.

'You are cretinous,' I said; 'that's not Chinese.'

'Oh, but definitely,' he said, 'Bellevue is Chinese for chopsticks.'

He took me to a place in Wardour Street, and I was glad it was not the one in Shaftesbury Avenue which had been in my mind. It would, I felt, have spoilt my dinner if we had gone there; and it would not have been a case of 'chasing one's memories', as he had expressed it the other day, it would have been a case of my memories chasing me. Never mind, I said to myself; it would all come right, now that I was back in London. And in the meantime, what did I care? He ordered the dishes without asking for my approval, but I did not resent it. On the contrary, it pleased me, though I would have taken exception to it with anyone else.

He just isn't my type, I told myself, that's why I don't care. And he is looking his worst today, in uniform.

At one point, while he was talking, there was a drop of gravy trickling down his chin; I gloated over it and did not tell him about it; I was quite disappointed when he wiped it off with his napkin a second later. I would have dearly liked to see him ridiculed and humiliated. I knew he would be taking me to where he lived as a matter of course and that I would go with him. But I had the idea that it did not matter as long as I did not care for him, and that if I managed to convey to him that he was unattractive to me, I would have achieved my aim.

After dinner we took a bus from Regent Street. It was not a number going to South Kensington or anywhere near it. I supposed he was taking me to another club. We got out in Portman Square, crossed over and halted in front of a tall old house, very well kept up and with an impressive black-painted door. He let himself in with his own key.

'This way,' he said, and unlocked a door a few steps down the entrance hall. 'Just this for the time being. I moved into here yesterday. I must now seriously look round for a place in Harley Street. Come in.'

We entered a little hall and he led me into a fair-sized room. It was furnished in blond wood, in a bastard style of bow legs and crests of carved posies and knotted ribbon, faintly suggestive of Louis Quinze, with a moss-green fitted carpet and cream-washed walls. There was a quilted, buttoned settee covered in dark green wool to match the seats of the chairs. A desk stood near the window. The divan bed was made up, with the green brocade cover folded over the foot end and, without glancing at them, I knew that the curtains would be of the same brocade.

It was a decent, sub-luxurious room in an expensive neighbourhood, conforming exactly to its type, down to the colour scheme of blond cream and green, complete with the copper ashtrays, the pressed-glass vases imitating crystal, and the print of a sailing ship on stiff white-capped late-eighteenth-century waves. I knew that the bathroom off the hall would have tiles without a single crack in them, the wash-hand basin would be spacious and oval, the bath would be encased in panels of black glass, and the floor would be of black white-veined marble.

At a glance, I saw that there was nothing in the room belonging to him, and I was glad of it. I have always had a poor opinion of people who tell me they can transform the despair of a rented furnished bed-sitting room into a place of homely cosiness with a jug filled with flowers, an embroidered cloth, and a few pictures.

I was just then living in a room, too, much smaller, shabbier and poorer than the one we were in, in the attic of a boarding-house, with the bathroom and the lavatory three flights below on the ground floor, and I had not tried to 'transform' it with those touches of 'personal magic'. I am an extremist. If I cannot have everything, I want nothing. Besides, at that time, I was content. I did not have the yearning for a home of my own which is supposed to claw at every woman's heart.

'I've got nothing to drink,' he said.

'That's all right,' I said, 'I wouldn't want a drink, anyway.'

He began to pace the room. 'When you go to the bathroom,' he said, 'be careful. The basin might come crashing down on you. I'll have a new one put in tomorrow.'

'I will be careful,' I said, sitting down on the settee.

'I had a girl here last night,' he said, 'and I threw her out. She went into the bathroom, knocked a jar from the shelf and cracked the basin.'

'How do you mean?' I asked. 'You threw her out because of it?'

'Yes,' he said, moving about, opening drawers in the chest and shutting them.

'But why?' I asked. 'You really threw her out because of it? She didn't do it on purpose.'

'I know,' he said. 'But it was done on purpose just the same. It was an act of spite against me. I can't be bothered with that sort of thing. Not from her, anyway. I couldn't be bothered with her altogether.'

I remained silent. I asked myself if I was glad that a rival had been removed. I was not. I did not care either way.

'Get undressed and go to bed,' he said without turning round, still busy with the chest of drawers.

I went over to a chair near the divan and slipped out of my dress, and while I did so, he left the room. Perhaps he did it on purpose, to spare any feelings of modesty I might have had; but I rather thought not. I took off my underwear and lay down on the bed. I turned on my side with my face to the wall and with my legs crossed and curled up, determined not to be agreeable in any way.

I had never behaved like this with a man before. I believed that once one went as far as to consent one should go through with it as nicely as one could, whether one enjoyed it or not, and that it would have been bad manners to do otherwise.

But with him everything had been out of the usual, starting from the first moment at Shepherds, and as he was the only man who ever had taken me without my consent, I felt free to behave as badly as I wanted to. I was rude to him in my talk; why should I not carry it through in bed as well?

He came over to me, and I bent my arms over my face and clenched my crossed legs still more tightly. I expected he would lift my arms from my face and kiss me, and melt my resistance in this manner, and I was determined to avoid it.

But he slid his hands round my hips and under them, and raised them and turned me over, so that in a flash I was on my back, and with his hard bony knees he pressed into the

188

soft inner part of my thighs, and as I gave way under the pain, he forced them apart and took possession of me in the easy, casual way he had done before.

But this lasted only for a few moments. Then he drove himself more deeply through me, and still more, and still more deeply, reaching depths which I had not known were inside me to be touched. It hurt and it was overwhelmingly outrageous, and I moved and tossed about, and tightened my inside muscles against him, to prevent myself from being invaded, but he seemed to be quite unaware of my distress and went on with a slow, steady, relentless determination, fastening me to him more tightly with each move.

I knew I could not fight him and I knew I could not get away and that I had to accept him. My arms fell from my face and I glanced at him for a short while. He was gazing into space. He did not see me looking at him. His sombre face was quite far away and above me, his brows were drawn together, and there was a bitter crease tightening either side of his mouth. I closed my eyes, and while I suffered the ever-returning knocks of pain inside me, I put my arms down by my sides, with my palms upwards, and wished he would, at least, place his hands in mine. He did not.

When he came down on top of me with the full length and weight of his body, but still not clasping or embracing me, I thought this would bring him to the end at last. I was mistaken. But he moved inside me differently now, without hurting me, more carefully, as though probing. As I relaxed with relief, he suddenly stabbed me with such sharp insistence that I cried out. It was really a repetition of the scene in the garden near the gate, when I had wanted to free my wrist and he had forced me to submit, and then, when I had surrendered, had refused to reward me.

And with unflagging thoroughness he went on. I became

nearly senseless. Sometimes I heard myself gasping or screaming, but as I had ceased to have thoughts and almost ceased to have emotions, I did not realize any more why I gasped or why I screamed. And he went on. There is a saying, 'No hour strikes for him who is happy,' and this was true in my case as well, though I was beyond happiness or sadness. I could not imagine that he would come to an end. I was not even aware of myself any more; there was just enough left of me to be aware of him, only of him, and all the time. And he went on.

I did not realize at what point he reached the climax of possessing me. His breathing remained as soundless as it had been, but there was a change in the pressure of his body and then a stillness; I was too exhausted to understand what it meant. I did not know when he left me. I felt light and floating in the stillness as though the bed-sheet were a sheet of silent water, till I felt his fingers underneath my head at the nape of my neck.

I opened my eyes and saw him sitting on the edge of the bed clad in a dressing gown. I closed my eyes again and turned my face away from him and felt that he was pulling the pins out of my plaits and heard the clatter as he placed them on the bedside table.

I was wearing my hair, which was well over waist-length, like a tiara formed of two plaits. It was the traditional Gretchen style, so called after the heroine in Goethe's *Faust*, a coiffure never encountered in the circles I moved in, and commonly associated with the country girls of the Alpine regions.

Apart from its being unfashionable, it did not suit me. I was not a Gretchen. I was not fair and clear-eyed, I had no round pink face and no snub nose. I was neither demure nor naïve nor shy. And yet, I did have the one essential Gretchen quality, only I did not know it then; it was still hidden, but he must have discerned it at once.

Gretchen is seduced by Faust with Mephisto's help, has a child, goes mad, drowns the child, kills her mother, is responsible for her brother's death, is cast into prison, and is executed. I do not mean to say that anything of this was in store for me. I only mean that he must have guessed in me the same willingness to go under, to play Gretchen to a Mephisto-driven Faust.

The clatter ceased. He said: 'All these dreadful weapons, these pins and daggers, you carry in your hair. You put them in on purpose, to injure me. You'd love to injure me, wouldn't you?'

I did not reply.

He tugged at one of my plaits and loosened it and laid the unwound strands over my shoulder.

'And yet, I am so kind to you,' he said. 'Here I am, even undoing your hair. So very kind. Just like a kind father.'

I sat up and said heatedly, 'Yes, you are quite right. I'd love to injure you.'

He looked at me with a delighted smile. 'You react so beautifully, it's a joy,' he said; 'just one simple, common, ordinary word, and you are up in arms.'

'Which word? How do you mean?' I asked.

'I'll tell you another time,' he said. 'I don't want to have you upset. I must humour you now, you are still weak. Come, lie down again, and we'll have a nice, quiet talk. Only nice, pleasant things.'

I lay down again.

He started to unwind and spread out my second plait.

'Why do you wear your hair so long?' he asked.

'I've always wanted it long,' I said, 'but my mother – oh, who cares.'

'But your mother what?'

'She never let me have long hair. I always had to have it cut short and tied to one side with a satin bow. So terribly childish.'

'But you were a child at the time, weren't you?' he said. 'So, why should you have minded so much that it was childish?'

He said it in a soothing, consoling tone of voice, as though merely in order to keep the conversation going, for the purpose of 'I must humour you now,' and I, lying with my eyes closed, said wearily, 'Yes, of course, I was a child. You are amazingly stupid with your remarks,' and I started to laugh.

'What made you laugh now?' he asked.

'I thought of something,' I said, 'a line of a poem by Kaestner. In German. You wouldn't understand.'

'I do understand some German,' he said, 'tell me.'

I said, 'It's, *ich wurde einst als Kind geboren und lebte dennoch weiter*. And in case you don't get it, it means, once upon a time I was born a child. And despite this, I went on living.'

'It's very clever,' he said, 'but you are side-tracking me. Why didn't your mother let you have long hair?'

'I thought you'd forgotten by now,' I said.

'Oh, no,' he said, 'and why did you want to have long hair?'

'I wanted to have it because she had it, too, when she was small. So why couldn't I, if she could? It wasn't fair. And there was one day of the year when my mother was allowed to wear her hair long and open down her back. That was on the emperor's birthday. She had it all. And when I was born, in 1918, the old Emperor Franz-Josef was dead and there was the break-up of the empire and we lived in a republic with a president, and of course, he wouldn't dare to have a birthday. She had had everything and I had nothing. Neither the emperor nor the long hair.'

'But that's all so long ago,' he said. 'Why do you still think it is so nice to have long hair?'

'Because of the Empress Elisabeth,' I said, 'the empress of Austria. She wore her hair in a crown of plaits, much higher than mine, and she was the most beautiful woman of her day. Even the Empress Eugénie was a rag compared to her.'

He said, 'And you think of yourself as the Empress Elisabeth. And you'd like to open your hair for the emperor. No man sees a woman with her hair open except when he goes to bed with her. You didn't want to open your hair for me. I had to do it myself. You want to keep it for the emperor.'

I opened my eyes. He seemed amused. I turned my face to the wall.

'Don't be so idiotic,' I said, 'it's a beastly habit you've got. First one tells you something perfectly decent and ordinary and you twist it till it sounds indecent and extraordinary.'

'Just what I thought,' he said. 'I knew straightaway we'd get a lot of pleasure out of your long hair. We'll go on about this long hair.'

'For how long?' I asked. 'For the next half hour?'

'Oh, no,' he said, 'for longer.'

'For two hours?' I asked.

'Oh, no,' he said. 'Longer.'

I turned round and sat up. 'For how long, then?'

'At least six weeks,' he remarked, 'I should say.'

'For six weeks?' I asked, 'talk about nothing but my long hair?'

'Yes,' he said.

'You are pulling my leg!' I exclaimed.

'I am quite serious, my poor child, I assure you,' he said.

'And it won't bore you?' I asked.

'No,' he said.

'But what is there to talk about?'

193

'You'd be surprised,' he said; 'but you'll go to sleep now. Come on, get up, and go to the bathroom first.'

I felt myself go hot and blush. I was greatly embarrassed. I remained as I was, sitting on my heels, with the top sheet clutched to my throat.

He was looking at me gravely and intently. 'And I don't mean you should go and wash,' he said. 'Tell me how you say it.'

'Spend a penny,' I said.

'No, spend a penny is not right,' he said, 'because that's English, and English isn't your mother-tongue. How did you say it in your nursery days?'

'Loo-loo,' I said, laughing to cover my embarrassment.

'That's better,' he said. 'Go and loo-loo.'

'That's not the right way to say it,' I remarked, feeling delightfully superior. 'You don't loo-loo. You make it.' And then, as he was still watching me seriously and intently, I fell back into my embarrassment. 'Anyway,' I said, 'I don't want to. I don't feel like it. Leave me alone.'

'I'm going to have so much trouble with you,' he said. 'Come on, now. You haven't been for hours. You are like a little girl of five; one has to think of everything for you.'

My uneasiness and shame left me and I was flooded by relief and gratitude, as though I had been liberated from a burden which had been weighing on me for a long time. No man ever – for that matter, nobody ever – since my childhood days had told me to go and make loo-loo, or whatever one might call it. It was an absurd situation which should have made me indignant; yet, I liked it.

I put my legs over the edge of the bed and hesitated. I looked at him to see if he was not jeering at me, after all. He was not. He was still watching me intently.

'Stand up slowly,' he said; 'you are still weak. Shall I come with you?'

'Don't be so ridiculous,' I said, laughing.

'Oh, dear, oh, dear,' he said, 'I'm always so unlucky with women.'

I took a few steps across the room, when he said, 'Steady. You are not the Empress Elisabeth, you are not at your coronation now,' and he went up to me and detached my clasped hands from my breast, against which I was still clutching the sheet, took the sheet and flung it on the bed.

'You are a bit dazed, aren't you?' he said.

'Yes,' I said.

I went to the bathroom, and when I had finished, I wiped myself with the paper and found that I was sore and swollen between my thighs; the edges of my lips were bruised, as they had been after I was deflowered.

I'll never tell him, I thought. I shan't give him that pleasure. And I don't even know his name. I'll never see him again. He is a beast.

But with my indignation there flowed a satisfaction, like the mingling of wine with water, that he had not only held me in his power and inflicted pain on me but had left the painful traces of his possessing me on my body. I wish I could have been deflowered by him, I thought, instead of that fool ox of a man at that time, and, taking one more piece of paper, I wiped myself once more and looked to see if there was any blood on it. My virginity had been lost in a small pool of blood. There was not a trace of blood on the paper now, and I regretted it.

LEOPOLD VON
SACHER-MASOCH

from:
VENUS IN FURS

Translated by Joachim Neugroschel

WE WERE SITTING on Wanda's small balcony in the warm, fragrant summer night, a twofold roof above us: first the green ceiling of vines, then the canopy of the sky, which was sown with countless scars. From the park came a soft and plaintive caterwauling, and I was perched on a footstool at the feet of my Goddess, talking about my childhood.

'And by then all these singular tendencies had already crystallized in you?' asked Wanda.

'Yes indeed. I can't remember ever not having them. Even in my cradle, as my mother subsequently told me, I was *supra-sensual.* I rejected the healthy breasts of the wet nurse, and they had to feed me goat's milk. When I was a little boy, I had an enigmatic fear of women, but that was actually an intense interest in them. I was frightened by the gray vault, the penumbra of a church, and I panicked before the glittering altars and images of saints. On the other hand, I would secretly steal over – as if to a forbidden joy – to a plaster Venus that stood in my father's small library. I would kneel down and recite to her the prayers that had been inculcated in me, the Lord's Prayer, the Hail Mary, and the Credo.

'One night I left my bed in order to visit her. The sickle moon illuminated the way and shed a cold, wan, blue light on the Goddess. I threw myself down before her and kissed her cold feet as I had seen our farmers do when they kissed the feet of the dead Savior.

'I was seized with an uncontrollable yearning.

'I rose and embraced the beautiful cold body and kissed the cold lips. Now I was overcome by a profound terror and I fled. And in my dreams the Goddess stood in front of my bed and threatened me with her raised arm.

'I was sent to school at an early age, and so I shortly began Gymnasium, where I passionately seized upon everything that the ancient world promised to reveal to me. I was soon more familiar with the gods of Greece than with the religion of Jesus. Together with Paris I gave Venus the fateful apple, I saw Troy burn, and I followed Odysseus on his wanderings. The primal images of all beautiful things sank deep into my soul, and so at a time when other boys act crude and obscene, I displayed an insuperable abhorrence for all that was vile, common, and unsightly.

'And the thing that struck the maturing adolescent as particularly vile and unsightly was the love for women as it was first shown to him in its full vulgarity. I avoided any contact with the fair sex – in short, I was insanely suprasensual.

'When I was about fourteen, my mother hired a charming chambermaid, young, pretty, with a curvaceous figure. One day, while I was studying my Tacitus and enthusing about the virtues of the ancient Germanic tribes, the maid was sweeping my room. Suddenly she stopped, leaned toward me, broom in hand, and two full, fresh, delicious lips touched mine. The kiss of the amorous little cat sent shivers up and down my spine, but I brandished my *Germania* like a shield against the seductress and indignantly stormed out of the room.'

Wanda burst into loud laughter. 'You are truly one of a kind, but do go on.'

'Another episode from that period is unforgettable,' I continued. 'Countess Sobol, a distant aunt of mine, was visiting my parents. She was a beautiful, majestic woman with a charming smile; but I hated her, for the family regarded her as a Messalina, and my behavior toward her was as bad, nasty, and awkward as could be.

'One day my parents went to the district seat. My aunt decided to make use of their absence and take me to task. Unexpectedly she entered in her fur-lined kazabaika, followed by the cook, the kitchen maid, and the little cat that I had spurned. Wasting no time, they grabbed me and, overcoming my violent resistance, they bound me hand and foot. Next, with a wicked smile my aunt rolled up her sleeves and began laying into me with a heavy switch. She hit me so hard that she drew blood, and for all my heroic valor I finally screamed and wept and begged for mercy. She then had me untied, but I was forced to kneel down, thank her for the punishment, and kiss her hand.

'Now just look at the suprasensual fool! The switch held by the beautiful, voluptuous woman, who looked like an angry monarch in her fur jacket, first aroused my desire for women, and from then on my aunt seemed like the most attractive woman on God's earth.

'My Catonian severity, my timidity with women, were simply nothing but the most sublime sense of beauty; sensuality now became a sort of culture in my imagination, and I swore not to squander its holy sensations on an ordinary creature but to save them for an ideal woman – if possible, the Goddess of Love herself.

'I was very young when I began studying at the university in the capital, where my aunt resided. My room resembled that of Dr Faustus. Everything was cluttered and chaotic: towering shelves crammed with books I had gotten dirt-cheap after haggling with a Jewish dealer in Zarvanica, globes, atlases, phials, celestial charts, skulls, animal skeletons, busts of great men. At any moment Mephistopheles as an itinerant Scholastic might have stepped forth from behind the large green stove.

'I studied everything higgledy-piggledy, unsystematically, promiscuously: chemistry, alchemy, literature, astronomy, philosophy, law, anatomy, and history. I read Homer, Virgil, Ossian, Schiller, Goethe, Shakespeare, Cervantes, Voltaire, Molière, the Koran, the Cosmos, Casanova's memoirs. I grew more and more confused, eccentric, and suprasensual every day. In my mind I always pictured a beautiful female ideal; and now and then, amid my skeletons and my leather-bound tomes, she would appear like a vision, reclining on roses, surrounded by cupids. Sometimes she wore Olympian attire and had the severe white face of the plaster Venus, sometimes she had the voluptuous brow braids, the laughing blue eyes, and the ermine-trimmed, red velvet kazabaika of my beautiful aunt.

'One morning, when she again emerged in full, laughing grace from the golden mists of my imagination, I went to see Countess Sobol, who gave me a friendly, indeed hearty welcome, receiving me with a kiss that made all my senses reel. She must have been close to forty by now, but like most of those die-hard demimondaines she was still desirable. She always wore a fur-lined jacket, this one in green velvet with brown stone marten; but none of the severity that had once delighted me was discernible in her.

'Quite the contrary: she felt so little cruelty toward me that without further ado she gave me permission to worship her.

'She had all too soon discovered my suprasensual foolishness and innocence and she enjoyed making me happy. And I – I was truly as blissful as a young god. What pleasure it was for me to kneel down and be allowed to kiss her hands, which had once chastised me. Ah! What wonderful hands!

So beautifully shaped, so fine and full and white, and with such darling dimples! I was actually in love only with those hands. I played with them, let them rise and sink in the dark fur, I held them up against a flame and could not see enough of them.'

Wanda involuntarily looked at her hands. I noticed it and couldn't help smiling.

'You can tell from the following facts how greatly dominated I was by the suprasensual: in regard to my aunt, I was in love only with the cruel switching I had received from her; and in regard to a young actress I courted some two years later, I was in love only with her roles. I next had a crush on a very respectable lady who feigned an unapproachable virtue but eventually betrayed me with a wealthy Jew. You see: because I was deceived and made a fool of by a woman who shammed the most rigorous principles, the most ideal feelings, I now ardently hate those kinds of poetic and sentimental virtues. Give me a woman who's honest enough to tell me: "I'm a Pompadour, a Lucretia Borgia," and I'll worship her.'

Wanda stood up and opened the window.

'You have a peculiar way of inflaming the imagination, exciting all nerves, making the pulse beat faster. You provide vice with an aureole so long as it's honest. Your ideal is a bold and brilliant courtesan. Oh, you're the kind of man who can thoroughly corrupt a woman!'

In the middle of the night there was a knock on my pane. I got up, opened the window, and recoiled. There stood Venus in furs, just as she had appeared to me the first time.

'Your stories aroused me,' she said, 'I'm tossing and turning and I can't sleep. Come and just keep me company.'

'Right away.'

When I entered her room, Wanda was huddling at the hearth, where she had fanned up a small fire.

'Autumn is setting in,' she began, 'the nights are already quite cold. I'm afraid it may displease you, but I can't toss off my fur until the room is warm enough.'

'Displease – you scamp! ... You do know, Madam ...' I threw my arm around her and kissed her.

'Of course I know, but how did you develop this passion for fur?'

'It's innate,' I answered. 'I already showed it as a child. Incidentally, fur excites all high-strung people – an effect that is consistent with both universal and natural laws. It is a physical stimulus, which is just as strangely tingling and which no one can entirely resist. Science has recently demonstrated a kinship between electricity and warmth – in any case, their effects on the human organism are related. The tropics produce more passionate people, a heated atmosphere causes excitement. The same holds for electricity. Hence the bewitchingly beneficial influence that cats exert on highly sensitive and intelligent people; this has made these long-tailed graces of the animal kingdom, these sweet, spark-spraying electric batteries the darlings of a Mohammed, a Cardinal Richelieu, a Crébillon, a Rousseau, or a Wieland.'

'So a woman wearing fur,' cried Wanda, 'is nothing but a big cat, a charged electric battery?'

'Certainly,' I replied, 'and that's how I account for the symbolic meaning that fur took on as an attribute of power and beauty. It was in those terms that earlier monarchs and ruling aristocracies laid exclusive claim to fur in their clothing hierarchies, and great painters laid exclusive claim to it for the queens of beauty. Thus Raphael found no more delightful frame than fur for the divine curves of Fornarina, and Titian for the rosy body of his beloved.'

'Thank you for the learned erotic treatise,' said Wanda, 'but you haven't told me everything. You associate something very singular with fur.'

'Indeed I do,' I cried. 'I've already told you repeatedly that suffering has a strange appeal for me, that nothing can so readily fan my passion as the tyranny, the cruelty, and, above all, the infidelity of a beautiful woman. Nor can I imagine her without fur – this woman, this strange ideal derived from the aesthetics of ugliness: a Nero's soul in a Phryne's body.'

'I understand,' Wanda threw in. 'There's something domineering, imposing about a woman in fur.'

'It's not just that,' I went on. 'You know, Madam, that I'm "suprasensual," that everything is rooted more in my imagination and nourished by it. I was precocious and overwrought when I got hold of *The Legends of the Martyrs* at the age of ten. I remember reading with a horror that was actually delight: the way the martyrs languished in dungeons, were roasted on grills, were shot through by arrows, boiled in pitch, thrown to wild beasts, nailed to crosses, and they suffered the most dreadful fates with something like joy. From then on, agony, gruesome torture seemed like a pleasure, especially when inflicted by a beautiful woman, since for me all that was poetic and demonic had always been concentrated in women. Indeed I practiced a downright cult.

'I saw sensuality as sacred, indeed the only sacredness, I saw woman and her beauty as divine since her calling is the most important task of existence: the propagation of the species. I saw woman as the personification of nature, as *Isis*, and man as her priest, her slave; and I pictured her treating him as cruelly as Nature, who, when she no longer needs something that has served her, tosses it away, while her abuse, indeed her killing it, are its lascivious bliss.

'I envied King Gunther whom powerful Brunhilde tied

up on their wedding night; the poor troubadour whom his capricious mistress sewed up in wolf skins and then hunted like a wild prey. I envied Sir Ctirad, whom Sharka the bold Amazon cunningly snared in the forest near Prague, dragged back to Castle Divin, and then, after whiling away some time with him, she had him broken on the wheel—'

'Disgusting!' cried Wanda. 'I only wish you would fall into the hands of a member of that savage sisterhood. The poetry would vanish once you were in a wolf skin, under the teeth of hounds, or on the wheel.'

'Do you believe that? I don't.'

'You've taken leave of your senses. You're really not very bright.'

'Perhaps. But let me go on. I greedily devoured stories about the most abominable cruelties and I especially loved pictures, engravings that showed them. And I saw all the bloody tyrants who ever sat on a throne, the inquisitors who tortured, roasted, slaughtered the heretics, all those women whom the pages of history have depicted as lascivious, beautiful, and violent, such as Libussa, Lucretia Borgia, Agnes of Hungary, Queen Margot, Isabeau, Sultana Roxolane, the Russian tsarinas of the eighteenth century – I saw them all in furs or in robes trimmed with ermine.'

'And so now fur arouses your bizarre fantasies,' cried Wanda, and she began coquettishly draping herself in her splendid fur mantle, so that the dark, shiny sables flashed delightfully around her breasts, her arms. 'Well, how do you feel now? Are you already half broken on the wheel?'

Her green, piercing eyes rested on me with a strange, scornful relish as I, overcome with passion, threw myself down before her and flung my arms around her.

'Yes – you've aroused my most cherished fantasy,' I cried, 'which has been dormant long enough.'

'And that would be?' She placed her hand on the back of my neck.

Under that small, warm hand, under her gaze, which fell upon me, tenderly inquisitive, through half-closed eyelids, I was seized with a sweet intoxication.

'*To be the slave of a woman, a beautiful woman, whom I love, whom I worship—!*'

'And who mistreats you for it,' Wanda broke in, laughing.

'Yes, who ties me up and whips me, who kicks me when she belongs to another man.'

'And who, after driving you insane with jealousy and forcing you to face your successful rival, goes so far in her exuberance that she turns you over to him and abandons you to his brutality. Why not? Do you like the final tableau any less?'

I gave Wanda a terrified look. 'You're exceeding my dreams.'

'Yes, we women are inventive,' she said. 'Be careful. When you find your ideal, she might easily treat you more cruelly than you like.'

'I'm afraid I've already found my ideal!' I cried and pressed my hot face into her lap.

'Not me certainly?' cried Wanda, hurling away the fur, striding about the room, and laughing. She was still laughing as I went downstairs; and while I stood musing in the courtyard, I could still hear her malevolent and hilarious laughter.

MOMENTS OF
ECSTASY

GUY DE MAUPASSANT

IDYLL

Translated by Roger Colet

THE TRAIN HAD just left Genoa on its way to Marseilles, and was following the long curves of the rocky coast, gliding like an iron snake between the sea and the mountains, creeping over the beaches of yellow sand edged with silver by the little waves, and plunging abruptly into the black-mouthed tunnels like an animal into its lair.

In the last carriage a stout woman and a young man sat facing each other, not saying a word, but glancing at each other now and then. She was about twenty-five, and sat next to the door, looking out at the scenery. She was a heavily built peasant woman from Piedmont, with dark eyes, a full bosom and fat cheeks. She had pushed several parcels under the wooden seat and was holding a basket on her knees.

The young man was about twenty. He was thin and sunburnt, with the dark complexion which comes from working in the fields in the blazing sun. Beside him, tied up in a kerchief, were his entire possessions: a pair of shoes, a shirt, a pair of breeches and a jacket. Under the seat he had hidden a pick and shovel tied together with a piece of rope. He was going to France to look for work.

The sun, rising in the sky, poured a rain of fire on to the coast. It was towards the end of May, and delightful odours were wafted into the railway carriages through the open windows. The orange-trees and lemon-trees were in flower, exhaling into the peaceful sky their sweet, heavy, disturbing scents, mingling them with the perfume of the roses which grew in profusion everywhere along the track, in the gardens of the rich, at the doors of tumbledown cottages, and in the open country too.

Roses are so very much at home along this coast! They fill the whole region with their light yet powerful fragrance and turn the very air into a delicacy, something tastier than wine and no less intoxicating.

The train was travelling slowly, as if to linger in this luxuriant garden. It kept stopping continually at little stations, in front of a few white houses, then set off again at a leisurely pace, after emitting a long whistle. Nobody ever got on. It was as if the whole world was dozing gently, reluctant to travel anywhere on that hot spring morning.

Every now and then the plump woman shut her eyes, only to open them suddenly whenever she felt her basket slipping off her lap. She would catch hold of it, look out of the window for a few minutes, then doze off again. Beads of sweat covered her forehead and she was breathing with difficulty, as if she were suffering from a painful constriction.

The young man had let his head fall forward on his chest and was sleeping the sound sleep of the countryman.

All of a sudden, as the train was leaving a little station, the peasant woman seemed to wake up; and, opening her basket, she took out a hunk of bread, some hard-boiled eggs, a flask of wine and some fine red plums. Then she started eating.

The man too had woken up suddenly and watched her eat, following every morsel as it travelled from her knees to her lips. He sat there hollow-cheeked, his arms folded, his eyes set, his lips pressed together.

The woman ate like a glutton, taking a swig of wine every now and then to wash down the eggs, and stopping occasionally to get her breath back.

Everything disappeared, the bread, the eggs, the plums, the

wine. As soon as she had finished her meal the man closed his eyes again. Then, feeling a little uncomfortable, she loosened her bodice, and the man suddenly looked at her again.

She took no notice but went on unbuttoning her dress. The pressure of her bosom stretched the material so that as the opening grew larger it revealed, between her breasts, a little white linen and a little flesh.

When she felt more comfortable the peasant woman said in Italian: 'It's so hot you can hardly breathe.'

The young man replied in the same language and with the same pronunciation: 'It's fine weather for travelling.'

'Do you come from Piedmont?' she asked.

'I'm from Asti.'

'And I'm from Casale.'

They were neighbours. They started chatting together.

They exchanged the long commonplace remarks which working people repeat over and over again and which are all-sufficient for their slow-moving and limited minds. They spoke of their homes and found that they had a number of common acquaintances. They quoted names, becoming friendlier every time they discovered another person they both knew. Rapid, hurried words with sonorous endings and the Italian intonation poured from their lips.

Then they talked about themselves. She was married and already had three children whom she had left with her sister, for she had found a situation as a wet-nurse, a good situation with a French lady in Marseilles.

He for his part was looking for work. He had been told that he would find some in Marseilles too, for they were doing a lot of building there.

Then they fell silent.

The heat was becoming terrible, beating down on the roofs of the railway carriages. A cloud of dust rose in the air behind the train and came in through the windows; and the scent of the roses and orange-trees had become stronger, heavier and more penetrating.

The two travellers fell asleep once more.

They opened their eyes again almost at the same time. The sun was sinking towards the sea, pouring its light over the blue waters. It was cooler and the air seemed lighter.

The wet-nurse was panting for breath. Her dress was open, her cheeks looked flabby, and her eyes were dull.

'I haven't given milk since yesterday,' she said disconsolately. 'I feel as if I'm going to faint.'

He made no reply, not knowing what to say. She went on: 'When a woman's got as much milk as me, she's got to give it three times a day or she feels real bad. It's like a weight on my heart, it is; a weight that stops me breathing and makes me feel all limp. It's a terrible thing, having as much milk as that.'

'Yes,' he said. 'It must be very hard on you.'

She did indeed look quite ill, as if she were about to faint.

'I've only got to press on them,' she murmured, 'and the milk comes out like a fountain. It's a queer sight, and no mistake. You wouldn't believe it. At Casale all the neighbours used to come to watch.'

'Really?' he said.

'Yes, really. I wouldn't mind showing you, but it wouldn't do me any good. You can't make enough come out that way.'

And she fell silent.

The train stopped at a halt. Standing by a gate was a woman holding a crying infant in her arms. She was thin and dressed in rags.

'There's another woman I could help. And the baby could help me too. Look here, I'm not well off, seeing as I'm leaving my home and family and my last little darling to go into service; but all the same, I'd willingly give five francs to have that baby for ten minutes so I could feed it. That would calm it down and me too. I think I'd feel a new woman.'

She fell silent once more. Then she passed her hot hand several times over her forehead, which was dripping with sweat, and groaned: 'I can't stand it any more. I feel as if I'm going to die.'

And with an unconscious gesture she opened her dress all the way.

The right breast appeared, huge and taut, with its brown nipple; and the poor woman moaned: 'Oh, dear! Oh, dear! What am I going to do?'

The train had moved off again and was continuing its journey amid the flowers which were giving off the penetrating fragrance they exhale on warm evenings. Now and then a fishing boat came in sight which seemed to be asleep on the blue sea, with its motionless white sail reflected in the water as if another boat were there upside down.

The young man, looking very embarrassed, stammered:

'But . . . Madame . . . I might be able . . . be able to help you.'

In a tired voice she replied: 'Yes, if you like. You'd be doing me a good turn, you would that. I can't stand it any more, really I can't.'

He knelt down in front of her, and she bent forward, pushing the dark tip of her breast towards his mouth as if he were a baby. In the movement she made to hold out her breast with both hands towards the man a drop of milk appeared on the nipple. He licked it up eagerly, gripped the heavy breast between his lips as if it had been a fruit, and began sucking regularly and greedily.

He had put his arms around the woman's waist to press her close to him; and he drunk slowly and steadily, with a movement of the neck like that of a baby.

Suddenly she said: 'That's enough for that one. Now take the other.'

And he obediently moved to the other breast.

She had placed both hands on the young man's back and was now breathing deeply and happily, enjoying the scent of the flowers mingled with the gusts of air blown into the carriages by the movement of the train.

'It smells nice round here,' she said.

He made no reply, but went on drinking at the fountain of her breast, closing his eyes as if to enjoy it better.

But then she gently pushed him away.

'That's enough, I feel better now. That's put new life into me.'

He had stood up, wiping his mouth with the back of his hand.

Pushing her breasts back inside her dress, she said: 'That was a real good turn you did me, Monsieur. Thank you very much.'

And he replied gratefully: 'It's me as has to thank you, Madame. I hadn't had a thing to eat for two days.'

EDITH WHARTON

MY LITTLE GIRL

THE ROOM WAS warm, and softly lit by one or two pink-shaded lamps. A little fire sparkled on the hearth, and a lustrous black bearskin rug, on which a few purple velvet cushions had been flung, was spread out before it.

'And now, darling,' Mr Palmato said, drawing her to the deep divan, 'let me show you what only you and I have the right to show each other.' He caught her wrists as he spoke, and looking straight into her eyes, repeated in a penetrating whisper: 'Only you and I.' But his touch had never been tenderer. Already she felt every fibre vibrating under it, as of old, only now with the more passionate eagerness bred of privation, and of the dull misery of her marriage. She let herself sink backward among the pillows, and already Mr Palmato was on his knees at her side, his face close to hers. Again her burning lips were parted by his tongue, and she felt it insinuate itself between her teeth, and plunge into the depths of her mouth in a long searching caress, while at the same moment his hands softly parted the thin folds of her wrapper.

One by one they gained her bosom, and she felt her two breasts pointing up to them, the nipples hard as coral, but sensitive as lips to his approaching touch. And now his warm palms were holding each breast as in a cup, clasping it, modelling it, softly kneading it, as he whispered to her, 'like the bread of the angels'.

An instant more, and his tongue had left her fainting

mouth, and was twisting like a soft pink snake about each breast in turn, passing from one to the other till his lips closed on the nipples, sucking them with a tender gluttony.

Then suddenly he drew back her wrapper entirely, whispered: 'I want you all, so that my eyes can see all that my lips can't cover,' and in a moment she was free, lying before him in her fresh young nakedness, and feeling that indeed his eyes were covering it with fiery kisses. But Mr Palmato was never idle, and while this sensation flashed through her one of his arms had slipped under her back and wound itself around her so that his hand again enclosed her left breast. At the same moment the other hand softly separated her legs, and began to slip up the old path it had so often travelled in darkness. But now it was light, she was uncovered, and looking downward, beyond his dark silver-sprinkled head, she could see her own parted knees, and outstretched ankles and feet. Suddenly she remembered Austin's rough advances, and shuddered.

The mounting hand paused, the dark head was instantly raised. 'What is it, my own?'

'I was – remembering – last week—' she faltered, below her breath.

'Yes, darling. That experience is a cruel one – but it has to come once in all women's lives. Now we shall reap its fruit.'

But she hardly heard him, for the old swooning sweetness was creeping over her. As his hand stole higher she felt the secret bud of her body swelling, yearning, quivering hotly to burst into bloom. Ah, here was his subtle forefinger pressing it, forcing its tight petals softly apart, and laying on their sensitive edges a circular touch so soft and yet so fiery that already lightnings of heat shot from that palpitating centre all over her surrendered body, to the tips of her fingers, and the ends of her loosened hair.

The sensation was so exquisite that she could have asked

to have it indefinitely prolonged; but suddenly his head bent lower, and with a deeper thrill she felt his lips pressed upon that quivering invisible bud, and then the delicate firm thrust of his tongue, so full and yet so infinitely subtle, pressing apart the close petals, and forcing itself in deeper and deeper through the passage that glowed and seemed to become illumined at its approach . . .

'Ah—' she gasped, pressing her hands against her sharp nipples, and flinging her legs apart.

Instantly one of her hands was caught, and while Mr Palmato, rising, bent over her, his lips on hers again, she felt his fingers pressing into her hand that strong fiery muscle that they used, in their old joke, to call his third hand.

'My little girl,' he breathed, sinking down beside her, his muscular trunk bare, and the third hand quivering and thrusting upward between them, a drop of moisture pearling at its tip.

She instantly understood the reminder that his words conveyed, letting herself downward along the divan until her head was in a line with his middle she flung herself upon the swelling member, and began to caress it insinuatingly with her tongue. It was the first time she had ever seen it actually exposed to her eyes, and her heart swelled excitedly: to have her touch confirmed by sight enriched the sensation that was communicating itself through her ardent twisting tongue. With panting breath she wound her caress deeper and deeper into the thick firm folds, till at length the member, thrusting her lips open, held her gasping, as if at its mercy; then, in a trice, it was withdrawn, her knees were pressed apart, and she saw it before her, above her, like a crimson flash, and at last, sinking backward into new abysses of bliss, felt it descend on her, press open the secret gates, and plunge into the deepest depths of her thirsting body . . .

ANAÏS NIN

MARCEL

MARCEL CAME TO the houseboat, his blue eyes full of surprise and wonder, full of reflections like the river. Hungry eyes, avid, naked. Over the innocent, absorbing glance fell savage eyebrows, wild like a bushman's. The wildness was attenuated by the luminous brow and the silkiness of the hair. The skin was fragile too, the nose and mouth vulnerable, transparent, but again the peasant hands, like the eyebrows, asserted his strength.

In his talk it was the madness that predominated, his compulsion to analyze. Everything which befell him, everything which came into his hands, every hour of the day, was constantly commented upon, ripped apart. He could not kiss, desire, possess, enjoy, without immediate examination. He planned his moves beforehand with the help of astrology; he often met with the marvelous; he had a gift for evoking it. But no sooner had the marvelous befallen him than he grasped it with the violence of a man who was not sure of having seen it, lived it; and who longed to make it real.

I liked his pregnable self, sensitive and porous, just before he talked, when he seemed a very soft animal, or a very sensual one, when his malady was not perceptible. He seemed then without wounds, walking about with a heavy bag full of discoveries, notes, programs, new books, new talismans, new perfumes, photographs. He seemed then to be floating like the houseboat without moorings. He wandered, tramped, explored, visited the insane, cast horoscopes, gathered esoteric knowledge, collected plants, stones.

'There is a perfection in everything that cannot be owned,' he said. 'I see it in fragments of cut marble, I see it in worn pieces of wood. There is a perfection in a woman's body that can never be possessed, known completely, even in intercourse.'

He wore the flowing tie of the Bohemians of a hundred years ago, the cap of an apache, the striped trousers of the French bourgeois. Or he wore a black coat like a monk's, the bow tie of the cheap actor of the provinces, or the scarf of the pimp, wrapped around the throat, a scarf of yellow or bull's-blood red. Or he wore a suit given to him by a businessman, with the tie flaunted by the Parisian gangster or the hat worn on Sunday by the father of eleven children. He appeared in the black shirt of a conspirator, in the checkered shirt of a peasant from Bourgogne, in a workman's suit of blue corduroy with wide baggy trousers. At times he let his beard grow and looked like Christ. At other times he shaved himself and looked like a Hungarian violinist from a traveling fair.

I never knew in what disguise he was coming to see me. If he had an identity, it was the identity of changing, of being anything; it was the identity of the actor for whom there is a continual drama.

He had said to me, 'I will come some day.'

Now he lay on the bed looking at the painted ceiling of the houseboat. He felt the cover of the bed with his hands. He looked out the window at the river.

'I like to come here, to the barge,' he said. 'It lulls me. The river is like a drug. What I suffer from seems unreal when I come here.'

It was raining on the roof of the houseboat. At five o'clock Paris always has a current of eroticism in the air. Is it because it is the hour when lovers meet, the five to seven of all French novels? Never at night, it would seem, for all the women are married and free only at 'tea time', the great alibi. At five I always felt shivers of sensuality, shared with the sensual Paris. As soon as the light faded, it seemed to me that every woman I saw was running to meet her lover, that every man was running to meet his mistress.

When he leaves me, Marcel kisses me on the cheek. His beard touches me like a caress. This kiss on the cheek which is meant to be a brother's is charged with intensity.

We had dinner together. I suggested we go dancing. We went to the Bal Nègre. Immediately Marcel was paralyzed. He was afraid of dancing. He was afraid to touch me. I tried to lure him into the dance, but he would not dance. He was awkward. He was afraid. When he finally held me in his arms he was trembling, and I was enjoying the havoc I caused. I felt a joy at being near to him. I felt a joy in the tall slenderness of his body.

I said, 'Are you sad? Do you want to leave?'

'I'm not sad, but I'm blocked. My whole past seems to stop me. I can't let go. This music is so savage. I feel as if I can inhale but not exhale. I'm just constrained, unnatural.'

I did not ask him to dance any more. I danced with a Negro.

When we left then in the cool night, Marcel was talking about the knots, the fears, the paralysis in him. I felt, the miracle has not happened. I will free him by a miracle, not by words, not directly, not with the words I used for the sick ones. What he suffers I know. I suffered it once. But I know the free Marcel. I want Marcel free.

But when he came to the houseboat and saw Hans there, when he saw Gustavo arriving at midnight and staying on after he left, Marcel got jealous. I saw his blue eyes grow dark. When he kissed me goodnight, he stared at Gustavo with anger.

He said to me, 'Come out with me for a moment.'

I left the houseboat and walked with him along the dark quays. Once we were alone, he leaned over and kissed me passionately, furiously, his full, big mouth drinking mine. I offered my mouth again.

'When will you come to see me?' he asked.

'Tomorrow, Marcel, tomorrow I will come to see you.'

When I arrived at his place he had dressed himself in his Lapland costume to surprise me. It was like a Russian dress, and he wore a fur hat and high black felt boots, which reached almost to his hips.

His room was like a traveler's den, full of objects from all over the world. The walls were covered with red rugs, the bed was covered with animal furs. The place was close, intimate, voluptuous like the rooms of an opium dream. The furs, the deep-red walls, the objects, like the fetishes of an African priest – everything was violently erotic. I wanted to lie naked on the furs, to be taken there lying on this animal smell, caressed by the fur.

I stood there in the red room, and Marcel undressed me. He held my naked waist in his hands. He eagerly explored my body with his hands. He felt the strong fullness of my hips.

'For the first time, a real woman,' he said. 'So many have come here, but for the first time here is a real woman, someone I can worship.'

As I lay on the bed it seemed to me that the smell and feel of the fur and the bestiality of Marcel were combined. Jealousy had broken his timidity. He was like an animal, hungry for every sensation, for every way of knowing me. He kissed me eagerly, he bit my lips. He lay in the animal furs, kissing my breasts, feeling my legs, my sex, my buttocks. Then in the half-light he moved up over me, shoving his penis in my mouth. I felt my teeth catching on it as he pushed it in and out, but he liked it. He was watching and caressing me, his hands all over my body, his fingers everywhere seeking to know me completely, to hold me.

I threw my legs up over his shoulder, high, so that he could plunge into me and see it at the same time. He wanted to see everything. He wanted to see how the penis went in and came out glistening and firm, big. I held myself up on my two fists so as to offer my sex more and more to his thrusts. Then he turned me over and lay over me like a dog, pushing his penis in from behind, with his hands cupping my breasts, caressing me and pushing me at the same time. He was untiring. He would not come. I was waiting to have the orgasm with him, but he postponed and postponed it. He wanted to linger, to feel my body forever, to be endlessly excited. I was growing tired and I cried out, 'Come now, Marcel, come now.' He began then to push violently, moving with me into the wild rising peak of the orgasm, and then I cried out, and he came almost at the same time. We fell back among the furs, released.

We lay in half-darkness, surrounded by strange forms – sleighs, boots, spoons from Russia, crystals, sea shells. There were erotic Chinese pictures on the walls. But everything, even a piece of lava from Krakatoa, even the bottle of sand from the Dead Sea, had a quality of erotic suggestion.

'You have the right rhythm for me,' Marcel said. 'Women are usually too quick for me. I get into a panic about it. They take their pleasure and then I am afraid to go in. They do not give me time to feel them, to know them, to reach them, and I go crazy after they leave thinking about their nakedness and how I have not had my pleasure. But you are slow. You are like me.'

As I dressed we stood by the fireplace, talking. Marcel

slipped his hand under my skirt and began caressing me again. We were suddenly blind again with desire. I stood there with my eyes closed, feeling his hand, moving upon it. He gripped my ass with his hard, peasant grip, and I thought we were going to roll down on the bed again, but instead he said, 'Lift up your dress.'

I leaned against the wall, moving my body up against his. He put his head between my legs, seizing my buttocks in his hands, tonguing my sex, sucking and licking until I was wet again. Then he took his penis out and took me there against the wall. His penis hard and erect like a drill, pushing, pushing, thrusting up into me while I was all wet and dissolved in his passion.

I enjoy making love with Gustavo more than with Marcel, because he has no timidities, no fears, no nervousness. He falls into a dream, we hypnotize each other with caresses. I touch his neck and pass my fingers through his black hair. I caress his belly, his legs, his hips. When I touch his back from neck to buttocks his body begins to shiver with pleasure. Like a woman, he likes caresses. His sex stirs. I don't touch it until it begins to leap. Then he gasps with pleasure. I take it all in my hand, hold it firmly, and press it up and down. Or else I touch the tip of it with my tongue, and then he moves it in and out of my mouth. Sometimes he comes in my mouth and I swallow the sperm. Other times it is he who begins the caresses. My moisture comes easily, his fingers are so warm and knowing. Sometimes I am so excited that I feel the orgasm at the mere touch of his finger. When he feels me throbbing and palpitating, it excites him. He does not wait for the orgasm to finish, he pushes his penis in as if to feel the last contractions of it. His penis fills me completely, it is just made for me, so that he can slide easily.

I close my inner lips around his penis and suck him inwardly. Sometimes the penis is larger than at other times and seems charged with electricity, and then the pleasure is immense, protracted. The orgasm never ends.

Women very often pursue him, but he is like a woman and needs to believe himself in love. Although a beautiful woman can excite him, if he does not feel some kind of love, he is impotent.

It is strange how the character of a person is reflected in the sexual act. If one is nervous, timid, uneasy, fearful, the sexual act is the same. If one is relaxed, the sexual act is enjoyable. Hans's penis never softens, so he takes his time, with a sureness about it. He installs himself inside of his pleasure as he installs himself inside of the present moment, to enjoy calmly, completely, to the last drop. Marcel is more uneasy, restless. I feel even when his penis is hard that he is anxious to show his power and that he is hurrying, driven by fear that his strength will not last.

Last night after reading some of Hans's writing, his sensual scenes, I raised my arms over my head. I felt my satin pants slipping a little at the waist. I felt my belly and sex so alive. In the dark Hans and I threw ourselves into a prolonged orgy. I felt that I was taking all the women he had taken, everything that his fingers had touched, all the tongues, all the sexes he had smelled, every word he had uttered about sex, all this I took inside of me, like an orgy of remembered scenes, a whole world of orgasms and fevers.

Marcel and I were lying together on his couch. In the semi-darkness of the room he was talking about erotic fantasies he had and how difficult it was to satisfy them. He had always wanted a woman to wear a lot of petticoats and he would lie underneath and look. He remembered that is what he did with his first nurse and, pretending to play, had looked up her skirts. This first stirring of the erotic feeling had remained with him.

So I said, 'But I'll do it. Let's do all the things we ever wanted to do or have done to us. We have the whole night. There are so many objects here that we can use. You have costumes too. I'll dress up for you.'

'Oh, will you?' said Marcel. 'I'll do anything you want, anything you ask me to do.'

'First get me the costumes. You have peasant skirts there that I can wear. We will begin with your fantasies. We won't stop until we have realized them all. Now, let me dress.'

I went to the other room, put on various skirts he had brought from Greece and Spain, one on top of another. Marcel was lying on the floor. I came into his room. He was flushed with pleasure when he saw me. I sat on the edge of his bed.

'Now stand up,' said Marcel.

I stood up. He lay on the floor and he looked up between my legs, under the skirts. He spread them a little with his hands. I stood still with my legs apart. Marcel's looking up at me excited me, so that very slowly I began to dance as I had seen the Arab women do, right over Marcel's face, slowly shaking my hips, so that he could see my sex moving between the skirts. I danced and moved and turned, and he kept looking and panting with pleasure. Then he could not contain himself, pulled me down right over his face, and began biting and kissing me. I stopped him after a while: 'Don't make me come, keep it.'

I left him and for his next fantasy I returned naked wearing his black felt boots. Then Marcel wanted me to be cruel. 'Please be cruel,' he begged.

All naked, in the high black boots, I began to order him

234

to do humiliating things. I said, 'Go out and bring me a handsome man. I want him to take me in front of you.'

'That I won't do,' said Marcel.

'I order you to. You said you would do anything I asked you.'

Marcel got up and went downstairs. He came back about half an hour later with a neighbour of his, a very handsome Russian. Marcel was pale; he could see that I liked the Russian. He had told him what we were doing. The Russian looked at me and smiled. I did not need to arouse him. When he walked toward me, he was already roused by the black boots and the nakedness. I not only gave myself to the Russian but I whispered to him, 'Make it last, please make it last.'

Marcel was suffering. I was enjoying the Russian, who was big and powerful and who could hold out for a long time. As Marcel watched us, he took his penis out of his pants, and it was erect. When I felt the orgasm coming in unison with the Russian's, Marcel wanted to put his penis in my mouth but I would not let him. I said, 'You must keep it for later. I have other things to ask you. I won't let you come!' The Russian was taking his pleasure. After the orgasm he stayed inside and wanted more, but I moved away. He said, 'I wish you would let me watch.'

Marcel objected. We let him go. He thanked me, very ironically and feverishly. He would have liked to stay with us.

Marcel fell at my feet. 'That was cruel. You know that I love you. That was very cruel.'

'But it made you passionate, didn't it, it made you passionate.'

'Yes, but it hurt me too, I would not have done that to you.'

'I did not ask you to be cruel to me, did I? When people

are cruel to me it makes me cold, but you wanted it, it excited you.'

'What do you want now?'

'I like to be made love to while looking out of the window,' I said, 'while people are looking at me. I want you to take me from behind, and I want nobody to be able to see what we are doing. I like the secrecy of it.'

I stood by the window. People could look into the room from other houses, and Marcel took me as I stood there. I did not show one sign of excitement, but I was enjoying him. He was panting and could scarcely control himself, as I kept saying, 'Quietly, Marcel, do it quietly so that nobody will know.' People saw us, but they thought we were just standing there looking at the street. But we were enjoying an orgasm, as couples do in doorways and under bridges at night all over Paris.

We were tired. We closed the window. We rested for a little while. We began to talk in the dark, dreaming and remembering.

'A few hours ago, Marcel, I entered the subway at the rush hour, which I rarely do. I was pushed by the waves of people, jammed, and stood there. Suddenly I remembered a subway adventure Alraune told me about, when she was convinced that Hans had taken advantage of the crowdedness to caress a woman. At the very same moment, I felt a hand very lightly touch my dress, as if by accident. My coat was open, my dress thin, and this hand was brushing lightly through my dress just at the tip of my sex. I did not move away. The man in front of me was so tall that I could not see his face. I did not want to look up. I was not sure it was he, I did not want to know who it was. The hand caressed the dress, then very lightly it increased its pressure, feeling for the sex. I made a very slight movement to raise the sex toward the fingers. The fingers became firmer, following the shape of the lips deftly, lightly. I felt a wave of pleasure. As a lurch of the subway pushed us together I pressed against the whole hand, and he made a bolder gesture, gripping the lips of the sex. Now I was frenzied with pleasure, I felt the orgasm approaching, I rubbed against the hand, imperceptibly. The hand seemed to feel what I felt and continued its caress until I came. The orgasm shook my body. The subway stopped and a river of people pushed out. The man disappeared.'

War is declared. Women are weeping in the streets. The very first night there was a black-out. We had seen rehearsals of this, but the real black-out was quite different. The rehearsals had been gay. Now Paris was serious. The streets were absolutely black. Here and there a tiny blue or green or red watch light, small and dim, like the little ikon lights in Russian churches. All the windows were covered with black cloth. The café windows were covered or painted in dark blue. It was a soft September night. Because of the darkness it seemed even softer. There was something very strange in the atmosphere – an expectancy, a suspense.

I walked carefully up the Boulevard Raspail feeling lonely and intending to go to the Dome and talk to someone. I finally reached it. It was overcrowded, half-full of soldiers, half-full of the usual whores and models, but many of the artists were gone. Most of them had been called home, each one to his own country. There were no Americans left, no more Spaniards, no more German refugees sitting about. It was a French atmosphere again. I sat down and was soon joined by Gisele, a young woman I had talked with a few times. She was glad to see me. She said she could not stay at home. Her brother had been called, and the house was sad. Then another friend, Roger, sat at our table. Soon we were five. All of us had come to the café to be with people. All of us felt lonely. The darkness isolated one, it made going out difficult. One was driven indoors — so as not to be alone. We all wanted this. We sat there enjoying the lights, the drinks. The soldiers were animated, everyone was friendly. All the barriers were down. People did not wait for introductions. Everyone was in equal danger and shared the same need of companionship and affection and warmth.

Later I said to Roger, 'Let's go out.' I wanted to be in the dark streets again. We walked slowly, cautiously. We came to an Arabian restaurant that I liked and went in. People were sitting around the very low tables. A fleshy Arabian woman was dancing. Men would give her money and she would place it on her breasts and go on dancing. Tonight the place was full of soldiers, and they were drunk on the heavy Arabian wine. The dancer was drunk, too. She never wore very much, hazy, transparent skirts and a belt, but now the skirt had slit open and when she did her belly dance, it revealed the pubic hair dancing, the massive flesh around it trembling.

One of the officers offered her a ten-franc piece and said, 'Pick it up with your cunt.' Fatima was not at all disturbed. She walked to his table, laid the ten-franc piece on the very edge of it, spread her legs a little and gave a twist like those she did in the dance, so that the lips of her vulva touched the money. At first she could not catch it. While she tried to do this, she made a sucking noise, and the soldiers were laughing and excited by the sight. Finally the lips of the vulva stiffened sufficiently around the piece of money and she picked it up.

The dancing continued. A young Arab boy who played the flute was watching me intently. Roger was sitting next to me dissolved by the dancer, gently smiling. The Arab boy's eyes continued to burn through me. It was like a kiss, a burn on one's flesh. Everybody was drunk and singing and laughing. When I got up, the Arab boy got up too. I was not quite sure of what I was doing. At the entrance there was a dark cubbyhole for coats and hats. The girl who took care of it was sitting with the soldiers. I went in there.

The Arab understood. I waited among the coats. The Arab spread one of them on the floor and pushed me down. In the dim light I could see him taking out a magnificent penis, smooth, beautiful. It was so beautiful that I wanted it in my mouth, but he would not let me have it. He immediately placed it inside my sex. It was so hard and hot. I was afraid we would be caught and I wanted him to hurry. I was so excited that I had come immediately and now he was going on, plunging, and churning. He was untiring.

A half-drunk soldier came out and wanted his coat. We did not move, he grabbed his coat without stepping into the cubbyhole where we lay. He went away. The Arab was slow in coming. He had such a strength in his penis and in his hands and in his tongue. Everything was firm about him. I felt his penis growing larger and hotter, until the edges rubbed so much against the womb that it felt rough, almost like a scraping. He moved in and out at the same even rhythm, never hurrying. I lay back and thought no more of where we were. I thought only of his hard penis moving evenly, moving obsessionally, in and out. Without any warning or change of rhythm, he came, like the spurt of a fountain. Then he did not take his penis out. It remained firm. He wanted me to come again. But people were leaving the restaurant. Fortunately the coats had fallen over us and concealed us. We were in a kind of tent. I did not want to move. The Arab said, 'Will I see you again? You are so soft and beautiful. Will I ever see you again?'

Roger was looking for me. I sat up and arranged myself. The Arab disappeared. More people began to leave. There was an eleven o'clock curfew. People thought I was taking care of the coats. I was no longer drunk. Roger found me. He wanted to take me home. He said, 'I saw the Arab boy staring at you. You must be careful.'

Marcel and I were walking through the darkness, in and out of cafés, pulling aside the heavy black curtains as we entered, which made us both feel as if we were going into some underworld, some city of the demons. Black, like the black underwear of the Parisian whore, the long black stockings of the cancan dancers, the wide black garters of the women especially created to satisfy men's most perverse caprices, the tight little black corsets which set off the breasts and push them up toward men's lips, the black boots of flagellation scenes in French novels. Marcel was shivering with the voluptuousness of it. I asked him, 'Do you think there are places that make one feel like making love?'

'I certainly do,' said Marcel. 'At least, I feel this. Just as you felt like making love on top of my fur bed, I always feel like making love where there are hangings and curtains and materials on the walls, where it is like a womb. I always feel like making love where there is a great deal of red. Also where there are mirrors. But the room which excited me most was one I saw one time near the Boulevard Clichy. As you know, at the corner of this boulevard there is a famous whore with a wooden leg who has many admirers. I was always fascinated with her because I felt that I could never bring myself to make love to her. I was sure that as soon as I saw the wooden leg I would be paralyzed with horror.

'She was a very cheerful young woman, smiling, good-natured. She had dyed her hair blond. But her eyelashes were of deep black and bushy like a man's. She had a soft little bit of hair in her upper lip. She must have been a dark, hairy southern girl before she dyed her hair. Her one good leg was sturdy, firm, her body quite beautiful. But I could not bring myself to ask her. As I looked at her I remembered a painting by Courbet I had seen. It was a painting commissioned by a rich man long ago, who had asked him to paint a woman in the act of sex. Courbet, who was a great realist, painted a woman's sex and nothing else. He left out the head, the arms, the legs. He painted a torso, with a carefully designed sex, in contortions of pleasure, clutching at a penis that came out of a bush of very black hair. That was all. I felt that with this whore it would be the same, one would only think of the sex, try not to look down at her legs or anything else. And perhaps that would be exciting. As I stood in the corner deliberating with myself, another whore came up to me, a very young one. A young whore is rare in Paris. She spoke to the one with the wooden leg. It was beginning to rain. The young one was saying, "I've been walking in the rain for two hours now. My shoes are ruined. And not a single client." I suddenly felt sorry for her. I said, "Will you have a coffee with me?" She accepted joyously. She said, "What are you, a painter?"

'"I'm not a painter," I said, "but I was thinking about a painting I saw."

'"There are wonderful paintings in the Café Wepler," she said. "And look at this one." She took out of her pocketbook what looked like a delicate handkerchief. She held it opened. There was painted on it a big woman's ass, placed so as to reveal the sex fully, and an equally large penis. She tugged at the handkerchief, which was elastic, and it looked as if the ass were moving, the penis too. Then she turned it over, and now the penis was still heaving but it looked as if it had gone inside of the sex. She gave it a certain movement which made the whole picture active. I laughed, but the sight aroused me, so that we never got to the Café Wepler and the girl offered to let me go to her room. It was in a very shabby house of Montmartre, where all the circus and vaudeville people stayed. We had to climb five flights.

'She said, "You'll have to excuse the drabness. I'm just starting in Paris. I've only been here a month. Before that I was working in a house in a small town and it was so boring seeing the same men every week. It was almost like being married! I knew just when they would be coming to see me, the day and hour, regular as clocks. I knew all their habits. There were no more surprises. So I came to Paris."

'As she talked we entered her room. It was very small – just room enough for the big iron bed on which I pushed her and which creaked as if we were already making love like two monkeys. But what I couldn't get used to was that there was no window – absolutely no window. It was like lying in a tomb, a prison, a cell. I can't tell you exactly what it was like. But the feeling it gave me was of security. It was wonderful to be shut in so securely with a young woman. It was almost as wonderful as being already inside her cunt. It was the most marvelous room I ever made love in, so completely shut out of the world, so tight and cozy, and when I got inside of her I felt that the whole rest of the world could vanish for all I cared. There I was, in the best place of all in the world, a womb, warm and soft and shutting me in from everything else, protecting me, hiding me.

'I would like to have lived there with this girl, never to go out again. And I did for two days. For two days and nights we just lay there in her bed and caressed and fell asleep and caressed again and fell asleep, until it was all like a dream. Every time I woke up I was with my penis inside of her, moist, dark, open, and then I would move and then lie quiet, until we got terribly hungry.

'Then I went out, got wine and cold meat and back to bed again. No daylight. We did not know what time of day it was, or whether it was night. We just lay there, feeling with our bodies, one inside of the other almost continuously, talking into each other's ears. Yvonne would say something to make me laugh. I would say, "Yvonne, don't make me laugh so much or it will slip out." My penis would slip out of her when I laughed and I would have to put it back again.

' "Yvonne, are you tired of this?" I asked.

' "Ah, no," said Yvonne, "it is the only time I have ever enjoyed myself. When clients are always in a sort of hurry, you know, it sort of hurts my feelings, so I let them go at it, but I don't take any interest in it. Besides, it's bad for business. It makes you old and tired too quickly if you do. And I always have that feeling that they don't pay enough attention to me, so it makes me draw in, away from them somewhere in myself. You understand that?" '

Then Marcel asked me if he had been a good lover that first time in his place.

'You were a good lover, Marcel. I liked the way you gripped my ass with both hands. You gripped it firmly as if you were going to eat into it. I liked the way you took my sex between your two hands. It was the way you took it, so decisively, with so much maleness. It is a little touch of the caveman you have.'

'Why do women never tell men this? Why do women make such a secret and mystery of it all? They think it destroys their mystery, but it is not true. And here you come out and say just what you felt. It is wonderful.'

'I believe in saying it. There are enough mysteries, and these do not help our enjoyment of each other. Now the war

243

is here and many people will die, knowing nothing because they are tongue-tied about sex. It's ridiculous.'

'I am remembering St Tropez,' said Marcel. 'The most wonderful summer we have had . . .'

As he said this, I saw the place vividly. An artists' colony where society people and actors and actresses went, people with yachts anchored there. The little cafés on the waterfront, the gaiety, the exuberance, the laxity. Everybody in beach costumes. Everybody fraternizing – the yacht people with the artists, the artists with the young postman, the young police-man, the young fisherman, young and dark men of the south.

There was dancing on a patio under the sky. The jazz band came from Martinique and was hotter than the summer night. Marcel and I were sitting in a corner one evening when they announced that they would put all the lights out for five minutes, then for ten, then for fifteen in the middle of each dance.

A man called out, 'Choose your partners carefully for the *quart d'heure de passion*. Choose your partners carefully.'

There was a great flurry and bustle for a moment. Then the dance began, and eventually the lights went out. A few women screamed hysterically. A man's voice said, 'That's an outrage, I won't stand for it.' Someone else screamed, 'Turn on the lights.'

The dance continued in the dark. One felt that bodies were in heat.

Marcel was in ecstasy, holding me as if he would break me, bending over me, his knees between mine, his penis erect. In five minutes people only had time to get a little friction. When the lights went on everybody looked disturbed. A few faces looked apoplectic, others pale. Marcel's hair was tousled. One woman's linen shorts were wrinkled. One man's linen trousers were wrinkled. The atmosphere was sultry,

244

animal, electric. At the same time there was a surface of refinement to be maintained, a form, an elegance. Some people, who were shocked, were leaving. Some waited as if for a storm. Others waited with a light in their eyes.

'Do you think one of them will scream, turn into a beast, lose his control?' I asked.

'I may,' said Marcel.

The second dance began. The lights went out. The voice of the band leader said, 'This is the *quart d'heure de passion.* Messieurs, mesdames, you now have ten minutes of it, and then you will have fifteen.'

There were stifled little screams in the audience, women protesting. Marcel and I were clutched like two tango dancers, and at each moment of the dance I thought I would unleash the orgasm. Then the lights went on, and the disorder and feeling in the place was even greater.

'This will turn into an orgy,' said Marcel.

People sat down with eyes dazed, as if by the lights. Eyes dazed with the turmoil of the blood, the nerves.

One could no longer tell the difference between the whores, the society women, the Bohemians, the town girls. The town girls were beautiful, with the sultry beauty of the south. Every woman was sunburnt and Tahitian, covered with shells and flowers. In the pressure of the dance some of the shells had broken and lay on the dance floor.

Marcel said, 'I don't think I can go through the next dance. I will rape you.' His hand was slipping into my shorts and feeling me. His eyes were burning.

Bodies. Legs, so many legs, all brown and glossy, some hairy as foxes'. One man had such a hairy chest that he wore a net shirt to show it off. He looked like an ape. His arms were long and encircled his dance partner as if he would devour her.

The last dance. The lights went out. One woman let out a little bird cry. Another began to defend herself.

Marcel's head fell on my shoulder and he began to bite my shoulder, hard. We pressed against each other and moved against each other. I closed my eyes. I was reeling with pleasure. I was carried by a wave of desire, which came from all the other dancers, from the night, from the music. I thought I would have the orgasm then. Marcel continued to bite me, and I was afraid we would fall on the floor. But then drunkenness saved us, the drunkenness kept us suspended over the act, enjoying all that lay behind the act.

When the lights went on everybody was drunk, tottering with nervous excitement. Marcel said, 'They like this better than the actual thing. Most of them like this better. It makes it last so long. But I can't stand any more of it. Let them sit there and enjoy the way they feel, they like to be tickled, they like to sit there with their erections and the women all open and moist, but I want to finish it off, I can't wait. Let's go to the beach.'

At the beach the coolness quieted us. We lay on the sand, still hearing the rhythm of the jazz from afar, like a heart thumping, like a penis thumping inside of a woman, and while the waves rolled at our feet, the waves inside of us rolled us over and over each other until we came together, rolling in the sand, to the same thumping of the jazz beats.

Marcel was remembering this, too. He said, 'What a marvelous summer. I think everybody knew it would be the last drop of pleasure.'

SARAH HALL

THE BEAUTIFUL
INDIFFERENCE

HER LOVER HAD missed the train from London and would be arriving late. This was not uncommon after night shift at the hospital. In the hotel room she studied herself in the mirror. The mirror was oval and full-length, in a hinged frame, which could be tilted up or down. She had bought a new dress. The blue was good on her, lighting her face and complementing her eyes. It was fitted through the bodice and waist but slipped to the floor easily when unzipped. He would like it. She finished making up her face, applying a layer of lip gloss, tidying the red spill at the corner of her mouth. Lipstick never lasted long when they were together; he would always kiss her just after she had applied it, as if he liked the smearing, viscous sensation. Sometimes she felt sure it was discomposing her that he enjoyed. She had lost a little weight since their last meeting. This was not deliberate. She'd been travelling a lot and had missed a few meals. The contours of her thighs and shoulders were pleasing. The previous night, after the reading, she had taken codeine and had slept well.

Do you think it's unhealthy?

I didn't say that. Relationships are all defined differently, aren't they? If that's your thing. Anyway. Isn't it what you want, at the moment? Being with him means you can defer all the rest.

This had startled her. The tone. The implication that she

249

was failing to make a sacrifice. Or that she had made a conscious choice.

What do you mean?

With exasperation the friend had turned away from the recalcitrant child, clattering the pot of orange paste and the plastic spoon down on the counter.

Oh, you know. Keep avoiding the hard stuff. Like this. The trouble is you probably don't have long left. Do you? And you act like it's not an issue. But everyone can see it is an issue.

She had noticed a change in the way her female friends responded to the relationship lately. At first they'd been enthusiastic, congratulatory, as if she were doing something avant-garde. She looked wonderful, they told her. She looked radiant. She should just enjoy it. But as the relationship had taken hold, becoming less casual, notes of disapproval had entered the discussion. Was it jealousy? Conservatism? She did not know. Perhaps she did seem ridiculous to them, now that it no longer constituted a fling, a desirability-affirming enterprise. Perhaps she was not entitled to the sex after all. Or the radiance. Men, on the other hand, had been unnerved from the beginning, as if she was not keeping to the natural order of things, as if she was performing an inversion. Or they had commented how lucky her lover was, recalling fondly an affair they themselves had had with an older woman during their youth. How they'd been taught a thing or two. After talking to them she was left with the dual feeling of being both transgressor and specialist. Only her father had been unreservedly for the relationship.

Darling, he had said to her, you should just let yourself feel something. If he makes you happy, be happy.

* * *

She stepped back from the window and looked at herself in the mirror again. The neckline of the dress was quite high. It gave the impression of thickening her collarbones. In the wardrobe hung another dress, belted and with an Edwardian-style bathing stripe, which he had seen before and liked very much. It was more fun, less chic. She reached behind and unfastened the one she was wearing. It drifted over her hips to the floor. She gathered it up and held it at waist height, paralysed for a moment by indecision, by aesthetics. Then she stepped back into it.

She sat on the bed. The book she was reading, or rather the book she had been carrying around for two weeks but not managing to read, was on the side table. She opened it and tried to get through a paragraph or two, but the words floated, the conceptual environment failed. She knew the author reasonably well; they had once shared the same publisher. Usually this motivated her to finish a novel – if only for the sake of etiquette. Often she discarded books. Whenever she made this confession people were astonished. It had come up again at her event last night. A woman on the front row had been appalled during the closing session.

How do we get our children to read more? All they do is play violent video games!

Why should they read? I don't. Given the choice I'd much rather do something else. Including blow things up.

You're joking? You can't really be serious?

Can't I? Why not?

Silence. Murmurs in the crowd. She was not adopting the correct role of advocate.

In truth, she disliked books. She felt a peculiar disquiet when opening the pages. She had felt it since childhood. She did not know why. Something in the act itself, the immersion, the seclusion, was disturbing. Reading was an affirmation of being alone, of being separate, trapped. Books were like oubliettes. Her preference was for company, the tactile world, atoms.

She shut the book. The cover was photographic, part of a female figure, a headless torso and limbs, though the novel itself was about the Second World War. The image was stock, meaningless. Give me a man, she thought. Give me the long cleft in his back. She had a popular science magazine in her bag too, which she had begun to buy in the last few months. But she had already finished the most appealing article about new-generation prosthetics. Soldiers coming home maimed were going to benefit hugely from new bioengineering techniques, according to the piece. The devices were becoming lighter, more flexible, intuitive of the brain's synaptic messages. It was as close to restoration as possible.

It was five thirty. The last she'd heard he had made it to King's Cross but he'd not texted since then to say which train he would be on. They arrived from London at twenty past the hour. The hotel was a ten-minute walk from the station; he had the address and the room number. Either he would be here soon, within a few minutes, or he would be another hour. She'd been primed the whole afternoon and now she felt fraught. She was unsure about the blue dress with its high neckline. She was unsure how it would affect the sex. Her mind felt white, empty of intellectual conversation. She could recall none of the finer points of the article in the magazine, though the subject, the idea of psychology and kinetics, had seemed fascinating. The noise outside was intensifying. Heels striking the pavement. Gales of singing. The thump of music from a pub.

She stood from the bed and looked at herself in the mirror. Her skin was luminous and secretive. She stared. After a minute or so her appearance became unstructured, a collection of shapes and colours. There had been no plan, not for any of this. Perhaps she had planned nothing in her life. And yet here she was, in this room, in this form. Speculatively, side by side in a crowd, she and her lover could be the same age. They had enough in common, and there was enough difference to make the relationship interesting. In practice there was no problem. But perhaps there was a flaw to the whole thing she hadn't seen, or was refusing to see, or which had not yet manifested. Children? Her friends now assumed what her position was.

She put her fingertips to her groin and felt along the ligaments and the gristle at the top of her thighs. The nodes were like unopened buds. She reached behind and unzipped the dress and it slid over her hips to the floor. She felt again, without the fabric barrier. Her body was full of unknowable cartilage, knuckled and furled material. Sometimes, when they lay together, his hands would unconsciously map her contours, pressing the organs and tissues. Or he would find her pulse in alternative places – the vees between her finger bones, the main arteries. He did not seem to realize he was doing this.

She was refastening the dress when the door lock clucked and released and he came into the room.

Hi.

Oh, hi.

He dropped his battered shoulder bag on the floor and came to her and kissed her.

Sorry I'm late.

Don't worry. I've had a good afternoon.

This is a nice hotel.

He greeted her again, softly, then stepped back. He removed his jacket and dropped it onto the bed. He did not look tired from the night shift. He never did. His hair had been cut very short – there were lines along his scalp where the direction of growth altered. The last time she had seen him it had been long and curling around his ears, on the verge of being unkempt, but very attractive. The smell of his wet hair was one of her strongest memories now. Like the feeling of deep humiliation for injuring the junior-school pet rabbit. Like the unhealing gash on her mother's cheek where hospital orderlies had caught her with a metal instrument while wheeling her to the morgue. Bracken burning on the moors.

Excuse me a moment.

He went into the bathroom and there was a trickle of water. In the time she had known him his politeness had never waned. Neither had her enjoyment of it. She glanced at her reflection. The eyes looked dark, shuttered by mascara. The smudged red mouth looked incapable of speech. Something inexact had hold of her. She tried to recall exactly how the nerves at the end of the amputated arm sent signals into the receptors of the bionic limb. How the brain was fluent in the language of electricity.

The shock of the real, she said.

The tap turned off and he came out of the bathroom drying his hands on a towel. He tossed the towel onto the bed, next to his jacket.

Sorry, I didn't hear you. What did you say?

I said, it's strange, each time I see you again. You look different. Altered. You're not like I remember. I have to get used to you.

He smiled. There had always been such invitation between them, always permission. He knew it. And her friends were disquieted.

You too.

Laughter through the open window. A police siren.

It's a little crazy out there.

The weather?

No. After the races.

How was your event? Did they buy books?

Yes. It was fine.

They were at each other's mouths a moment later. She was almost too small for the way he handled her. He liked the blue dress, he told her, it was beautiful, and the stitching, two or three inconsequential stitches, broke, as he lifted it over her head.

They went out and found a restaurant with courtyard dining and took a table. There was no chill in the air. They did not wear jackets, and the other diners, in their shoulder straps and short sleeves, seemed convinced that summer had arrived too. They ordered a bottle of wine. To begin with she was chatty and unlike her earlier indeterminate self. He laughed at her jokes. He asked what she was working on. She spoke briefly about the research and handed the subject to him. He had changed rotation within the last week and was now on the psychiatry ward. It wasn't yet very stimulating.

Aren't there some interesting cases? she asked.

There's a man who thinks he's involved in a conspiracy. It's all to do with a biscuit tin.

Is someone taking his biscuits?

He thinks people are communicating about him through the tin. Paranoid.

He lifted his fork and pressed his thumb against the tines, then looked at the three holes imprinted. He had a strong face. His shirts were never pristine. He seemed unmedical, too earthed. She could not imagine him at work, among the corridors and beds, the metal tables.

I'm going to become deskilled.

Deskilled?

Not performing procedures any more. You get rusty if you don't practise. Lots of ulcers to deal with, though. One woman won't get out of bed. She's too exhausted to speak. Her legs are a mess.

He continued to talk about the patients on the ward. The dementia, the bipolar and dissociative disorders. Those who showed no signs of distress about their symptoms. Freud's legacy. There was a woman who had been sectioned because her house was hazardous. She was hoarding all kinds of things: papers, cartons, tins, her own waste. The place was full to the ceiling and stinking. There were narrow routes through the piles, like a warren. There were rats.

I had an argument with another doctor about her. I'm not sure she should really be there. You can't penalize someone for the way they live. And she's not really a danger to herself, or anyone else. Unless her stuff collapses.

It does seem extreme. My father hoards. His attic is on the point of collapse. In fact it has collapsed. Do you think we all have a glitch? A condition, I mean?

Probably. To some degree.

He had ordered venison. It arrived on a white plate, a tidy maroon-centred shank in a shallow wash of pink. He usually ordered the most interesting meat on the menu – liver, foie gras, hare. She liked to watch him eat. He went very carefully through the dense tissue with his knife and worked across the plate until everything was gone. He would put the knife into his mouth if anything stuck to it. Three or four times during every meal he put the knife there, closing his lips over the blade, slipping it harmlessly along his tongue. The gesture reminded her of television footage of big cats picking up their cubs, lifting the slack bodies harmlessly between their teeth. She was not sure whether these erogenous qualities were noticeable to other people or whether they were simply her invention.

So. What's yours?

My what?

Your condition.

He smiled at her.

I want you all the time. Even right afterwards. I want to break you. It's a sickness.

She laughed.

Sadist.

Under the table, without having to lean too far, he found her leg. He let his hand rest there and with the other he continued to spear his food.

And what's yours?

She had been walking backwards in the pen without looking where she was going. She had crushed the rabbit's paw under her foot by accident. The thing had been pinned. It had twitched and tugged horribly under her shoe. When she'd dragged it from the back of the hutch to investigate the damage its claw had been splayed and bloody. In a remarkable piece of social ostracization, the whole school had ignored her for a week, but she had not been able to accept the punishment. She kept trying to walk or sit with the other children, even as they spoke among themselves about how stupid she was.

Pathological loneliness.

Really? Interesting. I've never heard of that before.

No. It clearly doesn't exist.

Because of what you do? The isolation?

She reached across the table and cut a piece off his meat, from the end of the steak where the exterior was charred and firm.

Oh. Probably because of where I'm from.

I'll have you certified and make a case study.

Great. Call it a syndrome. Give it your name. Do you want to try some risotto?

Do you want me to finish it?

Yes.

You don't eat much.

I get full up quickly.

After paying the bill they left the restaurant and walked a section of the walls. There was an application on his phone that could photograph the night sky and recognize constellations. They tried, but the light pollution was too great, the stars indistinct. They found a club and danced. The music was two decades old, difficult to move to though she knew the songs, and they gave up. They walked back to the hotel. The town had wound out. People were reeling through the streets. They passed a young man with blood running from a wound under his jaw. He was eating chips, impervious to the injury. A girl in a torn blouse was sitting on some church steps vomiting between her legs. Her hair was matted and dripping. A police car sped past almost silently, its rapid blue beam spiralling against the brickwork.

On the ward, she said. The ones who don't care about their illness – why is that?

Hard to say. It's either disease or conversion. It's not well defined.

He pushed her against the wall, slowly, kissed her.

In their room they stripped the heavy coverlet off the bed. The wine had numbed her. There was no pain. Her orgasm was small, towards the base of her spine. He moved her onto all fours. She watched him in the mirror opposite, his head falling forward, and to the side, his brow pleated, his mouth open. He was beautiful to watch. He withdrew and came across her buttocks. The semen was less thick; she felt it trickle as he lifted her up. His chest rose and fell against her back. He kissed her shoulders. He slept first and in the morning she woke and turned on her back and gently pressed against her pubic bone. She reached for more painkillers and the glass of water on the bed stand. She watched light gather in the room. So what if she had fallen behind? So what if she was out of sync? It might end. It might.

In the morning properly they went to the Minster. Another high blue day. The heat was already mature, suggestive of a later season. Men were jumping off a white Bayliner into the river. There were no remaining casualties and the town looked swept of debris. They walked past the riverside swans and geese, ice-cream vendors, picnickers, a funambulist practising between two trees, soft-shoed like a foal.

I read one of your books, he said.

Oh, right. When did that happen?

Recently.

Right. Which one?

There was a discussion. He had thought carefully about what to say. The analysis was astute. She could not tell if anything had altered in his perception of her because of the experience; she thought perhaps it had. Previously, she had doubted whether the work would be to his taste. Now she was not sure whether that mattered. Though he was not being critical, she began to defend the work, to play up its controversy. As if she had meant all along for the book to be problematic. The discussion became a political debate, which was easier. He took hold of her hand.

I'm having a fantastic time. I really like being with you.

She waited for a moment and then returned the compliment. They walked on.

People were sitting and lying on the grass around the

Minster. Inside, most of the building was cordoned off, with a ticket booth controlling entry. They decided not to pay. They could see the colossal stained glass. Veils of coloured light hung over the nave. An official approached them.

First time inside, he asked. Well, it's good you've seen the windows now. They're about to take them down to start cleaning them. Lottery money. It's costing ten million pounds.

The official pointed out a few other noteworthy features inside the cathedral then courteously left them alone and greeted another group. They were both familiar with such places, had a secular interest. Still, the interior was impressive, the size and workmanship. Gold leaf and latticing. Stone tracts and arches, great masonic veins. It had been built without apathy, an estimation of God, Europe's greatest Gothic enterprise. She envied that certainty.

They lay for a time on the grass behind the cathedral, under the branches of a rustling beech, in reticulated sunlight. She lay with her head on his arm. They kissed, murmured to each other. They were lovers. She found herself counting the hours before his train back. After seeing him off she would drive north. Often the hours before parting were more difficult than the parting itself. He would quieten, and she would feel strangely enlivened, sheer, as if walking close to an edge. She watched the beech leaves flicker and interrupt the sky. She remembered then, something from the article about prostheses. That muscle had its own memory system. That consciously thinking about moving the attached arm, or the leg, would not move it. Those with new limbs needed to become unconcerned about articulation. They simply needed to let the body behave. She told him this. He had not read the article. He said that he would.

I had to help amputate a leg, during my surgical rotation. Christ! I can't even imagine doing such a thing.

The vascular surgeon took care of most of it. I just went through the bone. There were problems with the other leg. The patient died.

She lifted her head a fraction and turned to look at him. His eyes were open, staring straight up. She could see through the clear blue yolk of the nearest iris.

That's terrible.

It wasn't really the team's fault. These things happen.

He rolled his head towards her. In the sunlight they looked at each other brightly.

What you do, she said, it's amazing. I couldn't do it.

You'd surprise yourself.

No.

He gathered her in. The heat and smell and closeness of him was peculiarly surrounding, amniotic. Something opened in her belly, like a flower carved from air. She thought about the railway station, with its cyclonic roof, the moment when she would step back, the carriage door would beep and close, and the train would pulse as the engine engaged. Her throat began to constrict. She rose out of his embrace. She reached in her bag for a tablet and swallowed it dry.

I think my hangover's coming back. Might have to fight fire with fire. Drink?

Yeah, great. Let's go to one of the places on the river.

There was a small crowd outside the Minster when they rounded the corner. People were sitting on the steps, queuing outside the stall. At first it looked like a stunt, the horse hammering down the street, the empty carriage swerving behind, and the driver half standing, the reins gripped in his fists. The driver was calling to the horse, whoa, whoa, in a tone of irrefutable stewardship, but something was wrong. She took his arm and pointed. The white shire kicked on, coming towards the crowd, its hooves ringing heavily on the tarmac. It kept coming. The weight of the beast. Its breast working like a machine. Its fore and hind legs riving. Thirty feet from them the horse cut between two bollards and as the carriage hit tore out of its tack. There was the sick sound of brass and wood splintering. The driver flipped from his seat like an unbolted piece and landed lengths ahead. The shire kicked away, its reins trailing, its eye white-cupped and livid. It passed her at the exact moment she thought about stepping out with her arms held up. She felt its wake.

He had already broken from the crowd and was running towards the injured man. He was almost to him when she looked over. She hadn't seen him run before. For every human the action is never as imagined. Then he was kneeling, going to work. His back was to her. She couldn't see what he was doing. Checking the neck perhaps, or the head. The wrists, which had been held out like frail instruments to break the man's fall. His head turned slightly. He was talking as he ministered to the man, asking questions, or issuing instructions. Others began to arrive and cluster round, and her view of him was obscured.

She looked down the street after the horse but it had kept going and was gone. Spectators were walking purposefully towards the scene of the accident. They passed her, their faces set in expressions of shock and disbelief. Still she did not move. She looked after the horse. How real it had seemed, a truly designed thing. Someone would have to catch it before it damaged itself. She took a few steps, as if to follow, then turned and came slowly towards the glut of people. A woman was trying to steward, to move everyone back.

Give him some air. Come on.

Within minutes a medical vehicle arrived and two jacketed paramedics made their way into the fray, one carrying a grey case. The bole of onlookers expanded and thinned. Information was passed between people. She heard talk of the horse having been hit by a taxi, or being spooked by a horn. She saw him. He was standing back, letting the paramedics work. The driver lay on his side, unmoving, then moving economically, but not his lower half. She did not approach. The paramedics stepped in and out, knelt and rose. He was walking towards her when someone in the crowd pointed over and a paramedic called him back. There was a consultation, or he was being thanked. He had been born the year she'd left home. That seemed impossible.

When they regained each other she embraced him. She did not know what else to do. The emotion was like fear, or the abating of fear, and it overtook her and made her grip the back of his shirt. She released him and he gave a brief report. The driver had probably broken a hip. There were bad abrasions. There was no trauma to the head. But he seemed not to care about his injuries. All he had kept asking was whether the horse was hurt.

She drove back across the Pennines. On the moorland the bracken was beginning to regenerate. Tight green spirals were coming up through the sea of dead stalks. The curled fronds looked ovarian. Like the illustration of these organs they had shown her to explain. Now the word and the picture and the bracken were the same somehow. She entered a belt of cloud. The light became more complicated, dense, unfiltered, west coast light. Her phone on the dashboard had chimed and was flashing. He always texted afterwards, to thank her. She would reply similarly. Then they would wait a few days before contacting each other again. She had begun to bleed, lightly. She could feel the intimate transit of fluid. The reassurance this sensation had once provided was fading. There was no meaning to it. She did not want to go back to the house yet and so she took a turning off the main road, south, towards her friend. She could call in without notice. The child meant they were rarely out, and it was not too late. She felt like telling her friend that it was wrong of her to have said the things she had. She was not deferring the hard things in life. Her friend was privileged and she did not know it. The assumptions were careless and because they were careless they were also cruel. She pictured a harsh exchange between them, bitter revelations, a dramatic exit.

But she knew she was not really angry with her friend. There was no point in trying to ground her frustration. No one was to blame. Retaliation would be unfair. She turned off the road again, this time onto a small country lane. She parked in a gravel lay-by and looked up at the hills. On the slopes the previous year's bracken was rust-coloured and collapsing, the fresh underlay was taking hold. With all the talk of carcinogens they did not burn it back as often as they used to. She had not smelled that fragrance in a long time. It would be dark soon. She knew she should visit her father, who did not live far away. But his endless hope would be too wearing. The cottage would be thick with dust and newspapers, unrinsed bottles. It would smell of mould and be full of loss. In her purse were the white boxes. After she had left the train station she had bought three packets of painkillers, from different pharmacies. It had been easy. Her mother had been the same age.

She had on heeled shoes from being in the city, from being with her lover, from moving among the public as if she was someone else. And the striped dress. What would they say about her attire, if they found her in the bracken? Perhaps they would say she had prepared. She sat in the car. She could still smell his wet hair, remember the feeling of its damp warmth between her fingers. Remembering their exchanges was like engaging in them again. The memories and the acts were almost the same. Whenever he came inside her it stung. Towards the end of their time together he would gauge how sore she was. He knew the difference between pleasure and discomfort, though the two were so closely aligned. She had brought him so close. And yet so much was unspeakable.

The hills were around her. She took up her purse, opened the car door and stepped into them. It was like opening a book.

ANDREW DAVIES

from:
GETTING HURT

SOMEONE HAD TAKEN down all the photographs of Viola. There were new photographs on the walls. They were of empty cardboard boxes and pieces of string, mostly separately, some in combination. I stood in the doorway feeling huge and clumsy and spare in my big suit, dangling a bottle of champagne and a bottle of Scotch like a couple of Indian clubs. She stood there looking at me, and I thought how irresolute we both were. She was wearing the same black dress, but no earrings this time. She looked very clean and her hair was damp. I was very clean too. I had showered and shaved myself mercilessly and washed my hair and doused myself in Chanel for Blokes and cut my fingernails and toenails. We were both so clean under our clothes.

She stepped towards me, her hands down by her side, until we were touching, and started to kiss my face with soft, little-girl kisses. Her body felt damp and cool but her lips were very warm and soft; she smelt of soap and shampoo, but also increasingly and unmistakeably of herself, and I felt my dick quicken to her and started to feel warm and safe. I wanted to put my Indian clubs down and hold her to me, and she sensed this, and pulled away, and took my hand and dragged me into the living room, smiling.

'I have to tell you I am very nervous,' she said. 'I had a little puke about an hour ago.'

'I'm nervous too,' I said.

'Good,' she said. 'Let's have a drink.'

269

* * *

I am not a man who sits on floors. I sat on the black sofa and she kicked her flat black shoes off and sat on the floor at my feet, and we drank some of the champagne. She talked a little about the Man with the Shelves: how she had tried to love him but he wouldn't let himself be loved; about how he couldn't bear her but couldn't let her go; how he couldn't get to sleep unless he had his arm tight around her like a vice so she lay all night like a rabbit in a trap; how they used each other. After not very much of this I could feel my genitalia quaking and shrivelling as if they wanted to squeeze back inside me and hide and I said that if she didn't mind, I'd rather we didn't talk about the Man with the Shelves any more.

'I'm sorry,' she said. 'Just one more thing. The other night, when I went back in the house, as soon as I came into the room, he says: that guy, you're having an affair with him, aren't you? I said, no, of course I'm not, I've just talked to him a couple of times in Guido's. He was giving me terrible hardeye you know, it was like third degree. And then he said: well, whether you're having an affair with him or not, he's having an affair with you. I go: oh, yes, and how do you make that out? He says: body language, you bitch. He thinks he can read body language, you know.' She grinned and scrambled up on the sofa, leaned back against the arm, facing me, and put her bare feet in my lap like a present. 'I think maybe what he can read is the future, yes?' she said.

I took her long pale feet in my hands; they felt cool, and still slightly damp, and I warmed them for her, remembering a time when Sal, aged two, had wrapped one of her fat little feet in Christmas paper and given it to me as a present. Viola curled her toes round my fingers. She had long and clever toes and I tried not to think about whose fingers she had curled them round before. She was with me now. After a

270

while, she wiggled them in my lap, in a gentle, exploratory way. Neither of us looked down. We looked into each other's eyes. She was smiling slightly and I was smiling increasingly broadly, probably grinning like an idiot, as her blind, clever toes fumbled and found their way.

'Listen,' she said, 'this is going to be all right, in a strange way, even if it isn't; you know what I mean?'

'Yes,' I said. I felt very grateful to her for saying that, because it is so rarely all right the first time, though very occasionally, even when it isn't, it is. In a strange way.

'OK,' she said, taking my hand. 'Let's go.'

She led me upstairs to a bedroom I didn't see, except that it had a bed in it and it had her in it. She lit two candles, turned to face me, smiling shyly, and pulled her dress over her head. She had nothing on underneath except a pair of skimpy black pants, and she slipped them off too – she was as quick as a fish – and stood resting her thin body lightly against me, her face against my chest. I could feel her warm breath through my shirt, and I felt huge and clumsy and encumbered, and wondered how she could possibly want this. It's so hard for us to understand what women want in men, when they want us, so easy to believe them when they don't.

She got into bed but she didn't pull the sheet over her. She lay propped up on her elbows smiling at me. 'So you're going to take your things off, or not?'

She looked at me all the time I was undressing, which seemed to take for ever, but it was my face she was looking at, not my body, which made things a little better. The candles threw big shadows. Her face was in shadow but her eyes were bright. I got in beside her and heard the springs creak: I weigh over thirteen stone. She looked so fragile. I had this irrational fear that I might break her in some way. She touched my shoulder lightly, and kissed me lightly on the lips, then took my cock on her hand and bent over it, as if in a biology lesson.

'You're not circumcised! You didn't tell me this!' She seemed astonished, though not displeased.

'Er . . . should I have?' I said.

'But of course. It's so surprising. I haven't seen one like this since I was thirteen, in Poland. It's very pretty, you know.' Together we watched the embarrassed sceptre of my manhood wilting under our scrutiny. 'I'm sorry,' she said. 'I think this is not very considerate of me. Come on. Lie down. Lie down quietly by me.'

I did what she told me, and felt the thin length of her against me, her breath against my face, and ran my fingers down the sweet knobbly road of her spine, and held one cheek of her tight muscular bum in my hand. Very lightly, so that she would feel free to move, remembering what she had said about the Man with the Shelves. We kissed so softly that our mouths seemed to have no shape, so long that we seemed to have one face between the two of us. I felt myself thickening and stiffening again, and felt her feel that too, and I was so sure that she would slither on top of me that I was surprised when she pulled my weight on top of her. My face was far enough away from hers to be able to see her properly now. She was smiling. She was smiling as if she trusted me not to hurt her, or as if she understood that I would hurt her but she trusted me just the same . . . no, that's not quite it, that's not all of it; it was a brave smile, but it was friendly, too, as if this was something that might hurt us both, but something we could get through together. Her thighs were wide apart, defenceless, and she moved delicately under me,

272

finding a conjunction that was pleasing for both of us, and after a while I could see her eyes go vague and misty and she started to sigh. I reached down, but she stopped me. 'No. Let him find his own way.'

It was a good trick she had there, and again I found myself trying not to think about where she had learnt it and how long it had taken her to perfect it, as her blind, clever sex reached for mine, circled round it and showed it where to go, while her wide intelligent eyes looked into my eyes. The eagle sees everything, except where the mole sees. She was wonderfully warm and wet and slippery, but narrow, and her eyes went very wide as I went into her. She was still smiling, though. I was up on my elbows, keeping my weight off her; I didn't want to crush her or stop her moving, and I thought it was so nice that she was smiling, as if she was telling me that this terrible thing that we were doing was all right and something that had to be done, and nothing that either of us should blame each other for. Her arms were up above her head, but very relaxed, and her small breasts had almost disappeared as breasts. Delicate pinky-fawn nipples that I bent and licked lightly: and she laughed and moved under me to take the whole length of me, and growled deep in her throat, and then laughed again at the sound of her growling; and suddenly it seemed like not a terrible thing at all, but something very relaxed and pleasant that we were sharing, like a witty conversation with no pressure to sparkle, but in which we were somehow quite effortlessly finding things to say to each other that were subtle and relevant and friendly and pleasing, and I thought: this actually is actually all right, not just all right even though it isn't, and I felt long and strong in her and lordly and safe, and as if I could go slowly on like this for ever; and I held still for what seemed like whole long minutes, while she moved around me and under me, pleasing herself and pleasing me, and smiling, smiling all the time; and I found myself smiling too; and then she laughed, and I thought she must be laughing at the daft grin I probably had all over my face; and I said, 'What?'

'Nothing,' she said. 'It's just so nice, this, you know? I didn't think you would be so gentle, I thought you would be a wham bang man.'

'I am, sometimes,' I said.

'Good,' she said.

She stretched out one of her long legs and dangled it gaily and nonchalantly over my shoulder, stroking the nape of my neck with her toes.

'Goodness me,' I said.

'What?'

'You're tremendously supple, aren't you?'

She put her hands behind her head and grinned up at me. 'Aren't we all?' She lifted her other leg and folded it companionably round my back, moving it gently up and down, while I wondered in a blurred sort of way what she had meant, and where I had heard that phrase before, in some recent but quite foreign context; something was moving, dark and blurred, in the shadows at the back of my mind . . .

'Come on,' she said. 'Concentrate.' And she pulled me down on top of her, sighing as my weight pressed her down into the bed, and stretched her arms straight up over her head, and opened her mouth wide under mine, and tilted her hips up to take even more of me, and I realized almost immediately that I had been quite wrong about being able to go on like that for ever, and that I didn't in the least want to.

'Yes,' she said. 'Come on. Come on. Come. Come in me.'

And I felt that she wanted me to drive hard into her, thud against her, jolt her into orgasm; but I couldn't, didn't want

274

to; what was happening to me felt so strange, as if I wanted to lose myself in her, dissolve in her, and I came almost motionless inside her, except that I was trembling all over, down to my toes, and weeping too, without sobs, the way women weep, women for whom weeping is easy; and I wanted to tell her how strange it felt, but my mouth was too soft and shapeless to form the message I couldn't find the words for, and she pulled my head down into her neck and held me until I had stopped trembling and weeping.

'Good,' she said, softly.

And I felt and thought absolutely nothing except good.

I wonder if everyone wants to die like that.

MARRIED
PASSION

JUNICHIRŌ TANIZAKI

from:
THE KEY

Translated by Howard Hibbett

January 29

MY WIFE HASN'T been up since last night's incident. It was about midnight when Kimura and I carried her to the bedroom, half-past twelve when I called Dr Kodama, and two o'clock when he left. I went to the door with him, and saw that it was a clear, starlight night, but extremely cold. Our bedroom stove usually keeps us comfortable till morning on a single scoopful of coal, which I throw in before I go to bed; last night, however, at Kimura's own suggestion, I had him fire it up enough to make the room quite warm.

'I'll be leaving, then, if there's nothing else I can do,' he said.

I couldn't send him home at that hour. 'Why not stay overnight?' I asked. 'I can find somewhere for you to sleep.'

'Please don't bother, sir,' he said. 'I haven't far to go.' After helping me carry Ikuko in, he had stood waiting uneasily between our beds (I was sitting in the only chair). It occurs to me that Toshiko disappeared just as he came into the bedroom.

He insisted on going home, and left, as I had hoped he would. A certain plan had been taking shape in my mind for a long time, and I needed privacy to carry it out. Once I was sure he had gone, and that Toshiko wouldn't come in again, I went over and took Ikuko's pulse. It was normal: the Vita-camphor seemed to have worked. As far as I could tell, she was in a deep slumber. Of course she may have been only shamming. But that needn't hinder me, I thought.

I began by firing the stove up even hotter, till it was roaring. Then I slowly drew off the black cloth that I had draped over the shade of the floor lamp. Stealthily I moved the lamp to my wife's bedside, placing it so that she was lying within its circle of light. I felt my heart pound. I was excited to think that what I had so long dreamed of was about to be realized.

Next, I quietly went upstairs to get the fluorescent lamp from my study, brought it back, and put it on the night table. This was by no means a sudden whim. Last fall I replaced my old desk lamp with a fluorescent one, because I foresaw that I might sooner or later have a chance like this. Toshiko and my wife were opposed to it at the time, saying it would affect the radio; but I told them that my eyesight was weakening and the old lamp was hard to read by – which was quite true. However, my real reason was a desire to see Ikuko's naked body in that white radiance. That had been my fantasy ever since I had first heard of fluorescent lighting.

Everything went as I had hoped. I took away her covers, carefully slipped her thin nightgown off, and turned her on her back. She lay there completely naked, exposed to the daylight brilliance of the two lamps. Then I began to study her in detail, as if I were studying a map. For a while, as I gazed on that beautiful, milk-white body, I felt bewildered. It was the first time I had ever had an unimpeded view of her in the nude.

I suppose the average husband is familiar with all the details of his wife's body, down to the very wrinkles on the soles of her feet. But Ikuko has never let me examine her that way. Of course in love-making I have had certain opportunities – but never below the waist, never more than she had to let me see. Only by touch have I been able to picture to myself the beauty of her body, which is why I wanted so desperately to look at her under that brilliant light. And what I saw far exceeded my expectations.

For the first time I was able to enjoy a full view of her, able to explore all her long-hidden secrets. Ikuko, who was born in 1911, doesn't have the tall, Western kind of figure so common among the young girls of today. Having been an expert swimmer and tennis player, she is well proportioned for a Japanese woman of her age; still, she is not particularly full-bosomed, nor sizeable in the buttocks, either. Moreover, her legs, as long and graceful as they are, can hardly be called straight. They bulge out at the calves, and her ankles are not quite trim. But, rather than slim, foreign-looking legs, I have always liked the slightly bowed ones of the old-fashioned Japanese woman, such as my mother and my aunt. Those slender, pipe-stem legs are uninteresting. And instead of overdeveloped breasts and buttocks, I prefer the gently swelling lines of the Bodhisattva in the Chuguji Temple. I had supposed that my wife's body must be shaped like that, and it turned out that I was right.

What surpassed anything I had imagined was the utter purity of her skin. Most people have at least a minor flaw, some kind of dark spot, a birthmark, mole, or the like; but although I searched her body with the most scrupulous care, I could find no blemish. I turned her face down, and even peered into the hollow where the white flesh of her buttocks swelled up on either side. . . . How extraordinary for a woman to have reached the age of forty-four, and to have experienced childbirth, without suffering the slightest injury to her skin! Never before had I been allowed to gaze at this superb body, but perhaps that is just as well. To be startled, after more than twenty years together, by a first awareness of the physical beauty of one's own wife – that, surely, is to begin a new marriage. We have long since passed the stage of disillusionment, and now I can love her with twice the passion I used to have.

I turned her on her back once again. For a while I stood there, devouring her with my eyes. Suddenly it appeared to me that she was only pretending to be asleep. She had been asleep at first, but had awakened; then, shocked and horrified at what was going on, she had tried to conceal her embarrassment by shamming. . . . Perhaps it was merely my own fantasy, but I wanted to believe it. I was captivated by the idea that this exquisite, fair-skinned body, which I could manipulate as boldly as if it were lifeless, was very much alive, was conscious of everything I did. But suppose that she really was asleep – isn't it dangerous for me to write about how I indulged myself with her? I can scarcely doubt that she reads this diary, in which case my revelations may make her decide to stop drinking. . . . No, I don't think so; stopping would confirm that she does read it. Otherwise she wouldn't have known what went on while she was unconscious.

For over an hour, beginning at three o'clock, I steeped myself in the pleasure of looking at her. Of course that wasn't all I did. I wanted to find out how far she would let me go, if she were only pretending to be asleep. And I wanted to embarrass her to the point that she would have to continue her pretence to the very end. One by one I tried all the sexual vagaries that she so much loathes – all the tricks that she calls annoying, disgusting, shameful. At last I fulfilled my desire to lavish caresses with my tongue, as freely as I liked, on those beautiful feet. I tried everything I could imagine – things, to use her words, 'too shameful to mention'.

Once, curious to see how she would respond, I bent over to kiss an especially sensitive place – and happened to drop my glasses on her stomach. Her eyelids fluttered open for a moment, as if she had been startled awake. I was startled too, and hastily switched off the fluorescent lamp. Then I poured some drinking water into a cup, added hot water from the kettle on the stove till it was lukewarm, chewed up a tablet of Luminal and half a tablet of Quadronox in a mouthful of it, and transferred the mixture directly from my mouth to hers. She swallowed it as if in a dream. Sometimes a dose of that size doesn't work; but I knew it would give her an excuse for pretending to be asleep.

As soon as I could see that she was sleeping (or at least shamming), I set out to accomplish my final purpose. Since I had already aroused myself to a state of intense excitement by the most thorough, unhampered preliminaries, I succeeded in performing the act with a vigour that quite astonished me. I was no longer my usual spineless, timid self, but a man powerful enough to subdue her lustfulness. From now on, I thought, I would have to get her drunk as often as possible.

And yet, in spite of the fact that she had had several orgasms, she still seemed to be only half awake. Occasionally she opened her eyes a little, but she would be looking off in another direction. Her hands were moving slowly, languidly, with the dreamlike movements of a somnambulist. Soon, what had never happened before, she began groping as if to explore my chest, arms, cheeks, neck, legs. . . . Up till now she had never touched or looked at any part of me that she could avoid.

It was then that Kimura's name escaped her lips. She said it in a kind of delirious murmur – faintly, very faintly indeed – but she certainly said it. I'm not sure whether she was really delirious or whether that was only a subterfuge. Was she dreaming of making love with Kimura, or was she telling me how much she longed to? Perhaps she was warning me never to humiliate her like this again.

Kimura telephoned around eight this evening to ask about Ikuko. 'I should have stopped in to see how she was,' he said.

'There's nothing to worry about,' I told him. 'I've given her a sedative, and she's still asleep.'

EXTRA-
MARITAL
EXCURSIONS

ANTON CHEKHOV

THE LADY
WITH THE DOG

Translated by Constance Garnett

I

IT WAS SAID that a new person had appeared on the sea-front: a lady with a little dog. Dmitri Dmitritch Gurov, who had by then been a fortnight at Yalta, and so was fairly at home there, had begun to take an interest in new arrivals. Sitting in Verney's pavilion, he saw, walking on the sea-front, a fair-haired young lady of medium height, wearing a *béret*; a white Pomeranian dog was running behind her.

And afterwards he met her in the public gardens and in the square several times a day. She was walking alone, always wearing the same *béret*, and always with the same white dog; no one knew who she was, and everyone called her simply 'the lady with the dog'.

'If she is here alone without a husband or friends, it wouldn't be amiss to make her acquaintance,' Gurov reflected.

He was under forty, but he had a daughter already twelve years old, and two sons at school. He had been married young, when he was a student in his second year, and by now his wife seemed half as old again as he. She was a tall, erect woman with dark eyebrows, staid and dignified, and, as she said of herself, intellectual. She read a great deal, used phonetic spelling, called her husband, not Dmitri, but Dimitri, and he secretly considered her unintelligent, narrow, in-elegant, was afraid of her, and did not like to be at home. He had begun being unfaithful to her long ago – had been unfaithful to her often, and, probably on that account, almost always spoke ill of women, and when they were talked about in his presence, used to call them 'the lower race'.

It seemed to him that he had been so schooled by bitter experience that he might call them what he liked, and yet he could not get on for two days together without 'the lower race'. In the society of men he was bored and not himself, with them he was cold and uncommunicative; but when he was in the company of women he felt free, and knew what to say to them and how to behave; and he was at ease with them even when he was silent. In his appearance, in his character, in his whole nature, there was something attractive and elusive which allured women and disposed them in his favour; he knew that, and some force seemed to draw him, too, to them.

Experience often repeated, truly bitter experience, had taught him long ago that with decent people, especially Moscow people – always slow to move and irresolute – every intimacy, which at first so agreeably diversifies life and appears a light and charming adventure, inevitably grows into a regular problem of extreme intricacy, and in the long run the situation becomes unbearable. But at every fresh meeting with an interesting woman this experience seemed to slip out of his memory, and he was eager for life, and everything seemed simple and amusing.

One evening he was dining in the gardens, and the lady in the *béret* came up slowly to take the next table. Her expression, her gait, her dress, and the way she did her hair told him that she was a lady, that she was married, that she was in Yalta for the first time and alone, and that she was dull there. . . . The stories told of the immorality in such places as Yalta are to a great extent untrue; he despised them, and knew that such stories were for the most part made up by persons who would themselves have been glad to sin if they had been able; but when the lady sat down at the next table three paces from him, he remembered these tales of easy conquests, of trips to the mountains, and the tempting thought of a swift, fleeting love affair, a romance with an unknown woman, whose name he did not know, suddenly took possession of him.

He beckoned coaxingly to the Pomeranian, and when the dog came up to him he shook his finger at it. The Pomeranian growled: Gurov shook his finger at it again.

The lady looked at him and at once dropped her eyes.

'He doesn't bite,' she said, and blushed.

'May I give him a bone?' he asked; and when she nodded he asked courteously, 'Have you been long in Yalta?'

'Five days.'

'And I have already dragged out a fortnight here.'

There was a brief silence.

'Time goes fast, and yet it is so dull here!' she said, not looking at him.

'That's only the fashion to say it is dull here. A provincial will live in Belyov or Zhidra and not be dull, and when he comes here it's "Oh, the dulness! Oh, the dust!" One would think he came from Grenada.'

She laughed. Then both continued eating in silence, like strangers, but after dinner they walked side by side; and there sprang up between them the light jesting conversation of people who are free and satisfied, to whom it does not matter where they go or what they talk about. They walked and talked of the strange light on the sea: the water was of a soft warm lilac hue, and there was a golden streak from the moon upon it. They talked of how sultry it was after a hot day. Gurov told her that he came from Moscow, that he had taken his degree in Arts, but had a post in a bank; that he had trained as an opera-singer, but had given it up, that he owned two houses in Moscow. . . . And from her he learnt that she had grown up in Petersburg, but had lived in S— since her marriage two years before, that she was staying another month in Yalta, and that her husband, who needed a holiday too, might perhaps come and fetch her. She was not sure whether her husband had a post in a Crown Department or under the Provincial Council – and was amused by her own ignorance. And Gurov learnt, too, that she was called Anna Sergeyevna.

Afterwards he thought about her in his room at the hotel – thought she would certainly meet him next day; it would he sure to happen. As he got into bed he thought how lately she had been a girl at school, doing lessons like his own daughter; he recalled the diffidence, the angularity, that was still manifest in her laugh and her manner of talking with a stranger. This must have been the first time in her life she had been alone in surroundings in which she was followed, looked at, and spoken to merely from a secret motive which she could hardly fail to guess. He recalled her slender, delicate neck, her lovely, grey eyes.

'There's something pathetic about her, anyway,' he thought, and fell asleep.

II

A week had passed since they had made acquaintance. It was a holiday. It was sultry indoors, while in the street the wind whirled the dust round and round, and blew people's hats off. It was a thirsty day, and Gurov often went into the pavilion, and pressed Anna Sergeyevna to have syrup and water or an ice. One did not know what to do with oneself.

In the evening when the wind had dropped a little, they went out on to the groyne to see the steamer come in. There were a great many people walking about the harbour; they had gathered to welcome someone, bringing bouquets. And two peculiarities of a well-dressed Yalta crowd were very conspicuous: the elderly ladies were dressed like young ones, and there were great numbers of generals.

Owing to the roughness of the sea, the steamer arrived late, after the sun had set, and it was a long time turning about before it reached the groyne. Anna Sergeyevna looked through her lorgnette at the steamer and the passengers as though looking for acquaintances, and when she turned to Gurov her eyes were shining. She talked a great deal and asked disconnected questions, forgetting next moment what she had asked; then she dropped her lorgnette in the crush.

The festive crowd began to disperse; it was too dark to see people's faces. The wind had completely dropped, but Gurov and Anna Sergeyevna still stood as though waiting to see someone else come from the steamer. Anna Sergeyevna was silent now, and sniffed the flowers without looking at Gurov.

'The weather is better this evening,' he said. 'Where shall we go now? Shall we drive somewhere?'

She made no answer.

Then he looked at her intently, and all at once put his arm round her and kissed her on the lips, and breathed in the moisture and the fragrance of the flowers; and he immediately looked round him, anxiously wondering whether anyone had seen them.

'Let us go to your hotel,' he said softly. And both walked quickly.

The room was close and smelt of the scent she had bought at the Japanese shop. Gurov looked at her and thought: 'What different people one meets in the world!' From the past he preserved memories of careless, good-natured women, who loved cheerfully and were grateful to him for the happiness he gave them, however brief it might be; and of women like his wife who loved without any genuine feeling, with superfluous phrases, affectedly, hysterically, with an expression that suggested that it was not love nor passion, but something more significant; and of two or three others, very beautiful, cold women, on whose faces he had caught a glimpse of a rapacious expression – an obstinate desire to snatch from life more than it could give, and these were capricious, unreflecting, domineering, unintelligent women not in their first youth, and when Gurov grew cold to them their beauty excited his hatred, and the lace on their linen seemed to him like scales.

But in this case there was still the diffidence, the angularity of inexperienced youth, an awkward feeling; and there was a sense of consternation as though someone had suddenly knocked at the door. The attitude of Anna Sergeyevna – 'the lady with the dog' – to what had happened was somehow peculiar, very grave, as though it were her fall – so it seemed, and it was strange and inappropriate. Her face dropped and faded, and on both sides of it her long hair hung down mournfully; she mused in a dejected attitude like 'the woman who was a sinner' in an old-fashioned picture.

'It's wrong,' she said. 'You will be the first to despise me now.'

There was a water-melon on the table. Gurov cut himself a slice and began eating it without haste. There followed at least half an hour of silence.

Anna Sergeyevna was touching; there was about her the purity of a good, simple woman who had seen little of life. The solitary candle burning on the table threw a faint light on her face, yet it was clear that she was very unhappy.

'How could I despise you?' asked Gurov. 'You don't know what you are saying.'

'God forgive me,' she said, and her eyes filled with tears. 'It's awful.'

'You seem to feel you need to be forgiven.'

'Forgiven? No. I am a bad, low woman; I despise myself and don't attempt to justify myself. It's not my husband but myself I have deceived. And not only just now; I have been deceiving myself for a long time. My husband may be a good, honest man, but he is a flunkey! I don't know what he does there, what his work is, but I know he is a flunkey! I was twenty when I was married to him. I have been tormented by curiosity; I wanted something better. "There must be a different sort of life," I said to myself. I wanted to live! To live, to live! . . . I was fired by curiosity . . . you don't understand it, but, I swear to God, I could not control myself; something happened to me: I could not be restrained. I told my husband I was ill, and came here. . . . And here I have been walking about as though I were dazed, like a mad creature; . . . and now I have become a vulgar, contemptible woman whom anyone may despise.'

Gurov felt bored already, listening to her. He was irritated by the naïve tone, by this remorse, so unexpected and inopportune; but for the tears in her eyes, he might have thought she was jesting or playing a part.

'I don't understand,' he said softly. 'What is it you want?'

She hid her face on his breast and pressed close to him.

'Believe me, believe me, I beseech you . . .' she said. 'I love a pure, honest life, and sin is loathsome to me. I don't know what I am doing. Simple people say: "The Evil One has beguiled me." And I may say of myself now that the Evil One has beguiled me.'

'Hush, hush! . . .' he muttered.

He looked at her fixed, scared eyes, kissed her, talked softly

297

and affectionately, and by degrees she was comforted, and her gaiety returned; they both began laughing.

Afterwards when they went out there was not a soul on the sea-front. The town with its cypresses had quite a death-like air, but the sea still broke noisily on the shore; a single barge was rocking on the waves, and a lantern was blinking sleepily on it.

They found a cab and drove to Oreanda.

'I found out your surname in the hall just now: it was written on the board – Von Diderits,' said Gurov. 'Is your husband a German?'

'No; I believe his grandfather was a German but he is an Orthodox Russian himself.'

At Oreanda they sat on a seat not far from the church, looked down at the sea, and were silent. Yalta was hardly visible through the morning mist; white clouds stood motionless on the mountain-tops. The leaves did not stir on the trees, grasshoppers chirruped, and the monotonous hollow sound of the sea, rising up from below, spoke of the peace, of the eternal sleep awaiting us. So it must have sounded when there was no Yalta, no Oreanda here; so it sounds now, and it will sound as indifferently and monotonously when we are all no more. And in this constancy, in this complete indifference to the life and death of each of us, there lies hid, perhaps, a pledge of our eternal salvation, of the unceasing movement of life upon earth, of unceasing progress towards perfection. Sitting beside a young woman who in the dawn seemed so lovely, soothed and spellbound in these magical surroundings – the sea, mountains, clouds, the open sky – Gurov thought how in reality everything is beautiful in this world when one reflects: everything except what we think or do ourselves when we forget our human dignity and the higher aims of our existence.

A man walked up to them – probably a keeper – looked at them and walked away. And this detail seemed mysterious and beautiful, too. They saw a steamer come from Theodosia, with its lights out in the glow of dawn.

'There is dew on the grass,' said Anna Sergeyevna, after a silence.

'Yes. It's time to go home.'

They went back to the town.

Then they met every day at twelve o'clock on the seafront, lunched and dined together, went for walks, admired the sea. She complained that she slept badly, that her heart throbbed violently; asked the same questions, troubled now by jealousy and now by the fear that he did not respect her sufficiently. And often in the square or gardens, when there was no one near them, he suddenly drew her to him and kissed her passionately. Complete idleness, these kisses in broad daylight while he looked round in dread of someone's seeing them, the heat, the smell of the sea, and the continual passing to and fro before him of idle, well-dressed, well-fed people, made a new man of him; he told Anna Sergeyevna how beautiful she was, how fascinating. He was impatiently passionate, he would not move a step away from her, while she was often pensive and continually urged him to confess that he did not respect her, did not love her in the least, and thought of her as nothing but a common woman. Rather late almost every evening they drove somewhere out of town, to Oreanda or to the waterfall; and the expedition was always a success, the scenery invariably impressed them as grand and beautiful.

They were expecting her husband to come, but a letter came from him, saying that there was something wrong with his eyes, and he entreated his wife to come home as quickly as possible. Anna Sergeyevna made haste to go.

'It's a good thing I am going away,' she said to Gurov. 'It's the finger of destiny!'

She went by coach and he went with her. They were driving the whole day. When she had got into a compartment of the express, and when the second bell had rung, she said:

'Let me look at you once more . . . look at you once again. That's right.'

She did not shed tears, but was so sad that she seemed ill, and her face was quivering.

'I shall remember you . . . think of you,' she said. 'God be with you; be happy. Don't remember evil against me. We are parting for ever – it must be so, for we ought never to have met. Well, God be with you.'

The train moved off rapidly, its lights soon vanished from sight, and a minute later there was no sound of it, as though everything had conspired together to end as quickly as possible that sweet delirium, that madness. Left alone on the platform, and gazing into the dark distance, Gurov listened to the chirrup of the grasshoppers and the hum of the telegraph wires, feeling as though he had only just waked up. And he thought, musing, that there had been another episode or adventure in his life, and it, too, was at an end, and nothing was left of it but a memory. . . . He was moved, sad, and conscious of a slight remorse. This young woman whom he would never meet again had not been happy with him; he was genuinely warm and affectionate with her, but yet in his manner, his tone, and his caresses there had been a shade of light irony, the coarse condescension of a happy man who was, besides, almost twice her age. All the time she had called him kind, exceptional, lofty; obviously he had seemed to her different from what he really was, so he had unintentionally deceived her. . . .

Here at the station was already a scent of autumn; it was a cold evening.

'It's time for me to go north,' thought Gurov as he left the platform. 'High time!'

III

At home in Moscow everything was in its winter routine; the stoves were heated, and in the morning it was still dark when the children were having breakfast and getting ready for school, and the nurse would light the lamp for a short time. The frosts had begun already. When the first snow has fallen, on the first day of sledge-driving it is pleasant to see the white earth, the white roofs, to draw soft, delicious breath, and the season brings back the days of one's youth. The old limes and birches, white with hoar-frost, have a good-natured expression; they are nearer to one's heart than cypresses and palms, and near them one doesn't want to be thinking of the sea and the mountains.

Gurov was Moscow born; he arrived in Moscow on a fine frosty day, and when he put on his fur coat and warm gloves, and walked along Petrovka, and when on Saturday evening he heard the ringing of the bells, his recent trip and the places he had seen lost all charm for him. Little by little he became absorbed in Moscow life, greedily read three newspapers a day, and declared he did not read the Moscow papers on principle! He already felt a longing to go to restaurants, clubs, dinner-parties, anniversary celebrations, and he felt flattered at entertaining distinguished lawyers and artists, and at playing cards with a professor at the doctors' club. He could already eat a whole plateful of salt fish and cabbage....

In another month, he fancied, the image of Anna Sergeyevna would be shrouded in a mist in his memory, and
only from time to time would visit him in his dreams with a
touching smile as others did. But more than a month passed,
real winter had come, and everything was still clear in his
memory as though he had parted with Anna Sergeyevna only
the day before. And his memories glowed more and more
vividly. When in the evening stillness he heard from his study
the voices of his children, preparing their lessons, or when
he listened to a song or the organ at the restaurant, or the
storm howled in the chimney, suddenly everything would
rise up in his memory: what had happened on the groyne,
and the early morning with the mist on the mountains, and
the steamer coming from Theodosia, and the kisses. He
would pace a long time about his room, remembering it all
and smiling; then his memories passed into dreams, and in
his fancy the past was mingled with what was to come. Anna
Sergeyevna did not visit him in dreams, but followed him
about everywhere like a shadow and haunted him. When he
shut his eyes he saw her as though she were living before him,
and she seemed to him lovelier, younger, tenderer than she
was; and he imagined himself finer than he had been in Yalta.
In the evenings she peeped out at him from the bookcase,
from the fireplace, from the corner – he heard her breathing,
the caressing rustle of her dress. In the street he watched the
women, looking for someone like her.

He was tormented by an intense desire to confide his
memories to someone. But in his home it was impossible to
talk of his love, and he had no one outside; he could not talk
to his tenants nor to anyone at the bank. And what had he to
talk of? Had he been in love, then? Had there been anything
beautiful, poetical, or edifying or simply interesting in his
relations with Anna Sergeyevna? And there was nothing for

him but to talk vaguely of love, of woman, and no one guessed what it meant; only his wife twitched her black eyebrows, and said: 'The part of a lady-killer does not suit you at all, Dimitri.'

One evening, coming out of the doctors' club with an official with whom he had been playing cards, he could not resist saying:

'If only you knew what a fascinating woman I made the acquaintance of in Yalta!'

The official got into his sledge and was driving away, but turned suddenly and shouted:

'Dmitri Dmitritch!'

'What?'

'You were right this evening: the sturgeon was a bit too strong!'

These words, so ordinary, for some reason moved Gurov to indignation, and struck him as degrading and unclean. What savage manners, what people! What senseless nights, what uninteresting, uneventful days! The rage for card-playing, the gluttony, the drunkenness, the continual talk always about the same thing. Useless pursuits and conversations always about the same things absorb the better part of one's time, the better part of one's strength, and in the end there is left a life grovelling and curtailed, worthless and trivial, and there is no escaping or getting away from it – just as though one were in a madhouse or a prison.

Gurov did not sleep all night, and was filled with indignation. And he had a headache all next day. And the next night he slept badly; he sat up in bed, thinking, or paced up and down his room. He was sick of his children, sick of the bank; he had no desire to go anywhere or to talk of anything.

In the holidays in December he prepared for a journey, and told his wife he was going to Petersburg to do something

303

in the interests of a young friend – and he set off for S——.
What for? He did not very well know himself. He wanted
to see Anna Sergeyevna and to talk with her – to arrange a
meeting, if possible.

He reached S—— in the morning, and took the best room
at the hotel, in which the floor was covered with grey army
cloth, and on the table was an ink-stand, grey with dust and
adorned with a figure on horseback, with its hat in its hand
and its head broken off. The hotel porter gave him the necessary information; Von Diderits lived in a house of his own
in Old Gontcharny Street – it was not far from the hotel: he
was rich and lived in good style, and had his own horses;
everyone in the town knew him. The porter pronounced the
name 'Dridirits'.

Gurov went without haste to Old Gontcharny Street and
found the house. Just opposite the house stretched a long
grey fence adorned with nails.

'One would run away from a fence like that,' thought
Gurov, looking from the fence to the windows of the house
and back again.

He considered: today was a holiday, and the husband
would probably be at home. And in any case it would be
tactless to go into the house and upset her. If he were to send
her a note it might fall into her husband's hands, and then
it might ruin everything. The best thing was to trust to
chance. And he kept walking up and down the street by the
fence, waiting for the chance. He saw a beggar go in at the
gate and dogs fly at him; then an hour later he heard a piano,
and the sounds were faint and indistinct. Probably it was
Anna Sergeyevna playing. The front door suddenly opened,
and an old woman came out, followed by the familiar white
Pomeranian. Gurov was on the point of calling to the dog,

but his heart began beating violently, and in his excitement he could not remember the dog's name.

He walked up and down, and loathed the grey fence more and more, and by now he thought irritably that Anna Sergeyevna had forgotten him, and was perhaps already amusing herself with someone else, and that that was very natural in a young woman who had nothing to look at from morning till night but that confounded fence. He went back to his hotel room and sat for a long while on the sofa, not knowing what to do, then he had dinner and a long nap.

'How stupid and worrying it is!' he thought when he woke and looked at the dark windows: it was already evening. 'Here I've had a good sleep for some reason. What shall I do in the night?'

He sat on the bed, which was covered by a cheap grey blanket, such as one sees in hospitals, and he taunted himself in his vexation:

'So much for the lady with the dog ... so much for the adventure. . . . You're in a nice fix. . . .'

That morning at the station a poster in large letters had caught his eye. 'The Geisha' was to be performed for the first time. He thought of this and went to the theatre.

'It's quite possible she may go to the first performance,' he thought.

The theatre was full. As in all provincial theatres, there was a fog above the chandelier, the gallery was noisy and restless; in the front row the local dandies were standing up before the beginning of the performance, with their hands behind them; in the Governor's box the Governor's daughter, wearing a boa, was sitting in the front seat, while the Governor himself lurked modestly behind the curtain with only his hands visible; the orchestra was a long time tuning up; the stage curtain swayed. All the time the audience were coming in and taking their seats Gurov looked at them eagerly.

Anna Sergeyevna, too, came in. She sat down in the third row, and when Gurov looked at her his heart contracted, and he understood clearly that for him there was in the whole world no creature so near, so precious, and so important to him; she, this little woman, in no way remarkable, lost in a provincial crowd, with a vulgar lorgnette in her hand, filled his whole life now, was his sorrow and his joy, the one happiness that he now desired for himself, and to the sounds of the inferior orchestra, of the wretched provincial violins, he thought how lovely she was. He thought and dreamed.

A young man with small side-whiskers, tall and stooping, came in with Anna Sergeyevna and sat down beside her; he bent his head at every step and seemed to be continually bowing. Most likely this was the husband whom at Yalta, in a rush of bitter feeling, she had called a flunkey. And there really was in his long figure, his side-whiskers, and the small bald patch on his head, something of the flunkey's obsequiousness; his smile was sugary, and in his buttonhole there was some badge of distinction like the number on a waiter.

During the first interval the husband went away to smoke; she remained alone in her stall. Gurov, who was sitting in the stalls, too, went up to her and said in a trembling voice, with a forced smile:

'Good-evening.'

She glanced at him and turned pale, then glanced again with horror, unable to believe her eyes, and tightly gripped the fan and the lorgnette in her hands, evidently struggling with herself not to faint. Both were silent. She was sitting, he was standing, frightened by her confusion and not venturing to sit down beside her. The violins and the flute began tuning up. He felt suddenly frightened; it seemed as though all the people in the boxes were looking at them. She got up and went quickly to the door; he followed her, and both walked senselessly along passages, and up and down stairs, and figures in legal, scholastic, and civil service uniforms, all wearing badges, flitted before their eyes. They caught glimpses of ladies, of fur coats hanging on pegs; the draughts blew on them, bringing a smell of stale tobacco. And Gurov, whose heart was beating violently, thought:

'Oh, heavens! Why are these people here and this orchestra!...'

And at that instant he recalled how when he had seen Anna Sergeyevna off at the station he had thought that everything was over and they would never meet again. But how far they were still from the end!

On the narrow, gloomy staircase over which was written 'To the Amphitheatre', she stopped.

'How you have frightened me!' she said, breathing hard, still pale and overwhelmed. 'Oh, how you have frightened me! I am half dead. Why have you come? Why?'

'But do understand, Anna, do understand...' he said hastily in a low voice. 'I entreat you to understand....'

She looked at him with dread, with entreaty, with love; she looked at him intently, to keep his features more distinctly in her memory.

'I am so unhappy,' she went on, not heeding him. 'I have thought of nothing but you all the time; I live only in the thought of you. And I wanted to forget, to forget you; but why, oh why, have you come?'

On the landing above them two schoolboys were smoking and looking down, but that was nothing to Gurov; he drew Anna Sergeyevna to him, and began kissing her face, her cheeks, and her hands.

'What are you doing, what are you doing!' she cried in

horror, pushing him away. 'We are mad. Go away today; go away at once. . . . I beseech you by all that is sacred, I implore you. . . . There are people coming this way!'

Someone was coming up the stairs.

'You must go away,' Anna Sergeyevna went on in a whisper. 'Do you hear, Dmitri Dmitritch? I will come and see you in Moscow. I have never been happy; I am miserable now, and I never, never shall be happy, never! Don't make me suffer still more! I swear I'll come to Moscow. But now let us part. My precious, good, dear one, we must part!'

She pressed his hand and began rapidly going downstairs, looking round at him, and from her eyes he could see that she really was unhappy. Gurov stood for a little while, listened, then, when all sound had died away, he found his coat and left the theatre.

IV

And Anna Sergeyevna began coming to see him in Moscow. Once in two or three months she left S——, telling her husband that she was going to consult a doctor about an internal complaint – and her husband believed her, and did not believe her. In Moscow she stayed at the Slaviansky Bazaar hotel, and at once sent a man in a red cap to Gurov. Gurov went to see her, and no one in Moscow knew of it.

Once he was going to see her in this way on a winter morning (the messenger had come the evening before when he was out). With him walked his daughter, whom he wanted to take to school: it was on the way. Snow was falling in big wet flakes.

'It's three degrees above freezing-point, and yet it is snowing,' said Gurov to his daughter. 'The thaw is only on the surface of the earth; there is quite a different temperature at a greater height in the atmosphere.'

'And why are there no thunderstorms in the winter, father?'

He explained that, too. He talked, thinking all the while that he was going to see *her*, and no living soul knew of it, and probably never would know. He had two lives: one open, seen and known by all who cared to know, full of relative truth and of relative falsehood, exactly like the lives of his friends and acquaintances; and another life running its course in secret. And through some strange, perhaps accidental, conjunction of circumstances, everything that was essential, of interest and of value to him, everything in which he was sincere and did not deceive himself, everything that made the kernel of his life, was hidden from other people; and all that was false in him, the sheath in which he hid himself to conceal the truth – such, for instance, as his work in the bank, his discussions at the club, his 'lower race', his presence with his wife at anniversary festivities – all that was open. And he judged of others by himself, not believing in what he saw, and always believing that every man had his real, most interesting life under the cover of secrecy and under the cover of night. All personal life rested on secrecy, and possibly it was partly on that account that civilized man was so nervously anxious that personal privacy should be respected.

After leaving his daughter at school, Gurov went on to the Slaviansky Bazaar. He took off his fur coat below, went upstairs, and softly knocked at the door. Anna Sergeyevna, wearing his favourite grey dress, exhausted by the journey and the suspense, had been expecting him since the evening before. She was pale; she looked at him, and did not smile, and he had hardly come in when she fell on his breast. Their kiss was slow and prolonged, as though they had not met for two years.

'Well, how are you getting on there?' he asked. 'What news?'

'Wait; I'll tell you directly. . . . I can't talk.'

She could not speak; she was crying. She turned away from him, and pressed her handkerchief to her eyes.

'Let her have her cry out. I'll sit down and wait,' he thought, and he sat down in an armchair.

Then he rang and asked for tea to be brought him, and while he drank his tea she remained standing at the window with her back to him. She was crying from emotion, from the miserable consciousness that their life was so hard for them; they could only meet in secret, hiding themselves from people, like thieves! Was not their life shattered?

'Come, do stop!' he said.

It was evident to him that this love of theirs would not soon be over, that he could not see the end of it. Anna Sergeyevna grew more and more attached to him. She adored him, and it was unthinkable to say to her that it was bound to have an end some day; besides, she would not have believed it!

He went up to her and took her by the shoulders to say something affectionate and cheering, and at that moment he saw himself in the looking-glass.

His hair was already beginning to turn grey. And it seemed strange to him that he had grown so much older, so much plainer during the last few years. The shoulders on which his hands rested were warm and quivering. He felt compassion for this life, still so warm and lovely, but probably already not far from beginning to fade and wither like his own. Why did she love him so much? He always seemed to women different from what he was, and they loved in him not himself, but the man created by their imagination, whom they had been eagerly seeking all their lives; and afterwards, when they noticed their mistake, they loved him all the same. And not one of them had been happy with him. Time passed, he had made their acquaintance, got on with them, parted, but he had never once loved; it was anything you like, but not love.

And only now when his head was grey he had fallen properly, really in love – for the first time in his life.

Anna Sergeyevna and he loved each other like people very close and akin, like husband and wife, like tender friends; it seemed to them that fate itself had meant them for one another, and they could not understand why he had a wife and she a husband; and it was as though they were a pair of birds of passage, caught and forced to live in different cages. They forgave each other for what they were ashamed of in their past, they forgave everything in the present, and felt that this love of theirs had changed them both.

In moments of depression in the past he had comforted himself with any arguments that came into his mind, but now he no longer cared for arguments; he felt profound compassion, he wanted to be sincere and tender. . . .

'Don't cry, my darling,' he said. 'You've had your cry; that's enough. . . . Let us talk now, let us think of some plan.'

Then they spent a long while taking counsel together, talked of how to avoid the necessity for secrecy, for deception, for living in different towns and not seeing each other for long at a time. How could they be free from this intolerable bondage?

'How? How?' he asked, clutching his head. 'How?'

And it seemed as though in a little while the solution would be found, and then a new and splendid life would begin; and it was clear to both of them that they had still a long, long way to go, and that the most complicated and difficult part of it was only just beginning.

D. H. LAWRENCE

from:
LADY
CHATTERLEY'S
LOVER

CONNIE WENT TO the wood directly after lunch. It was really a lovely day, the first dandelions making suns, the first daisies so white. The hazel thicket was a lace-work, of half-open leaves, and the last dusty perpendicular of the catkins. Yellow celandines now were in crowds, flat open, pressed back in urgency, and the yellow glitter of themselves. It was the yellow, the powerful yellow of early summer. And primroses were broad, and full of pale abandon, thick-clustered primroses no longer shy. The lush, dark green of hyacinths was a sea, with buds rising like pale corn, while in the riding the forget-me-nots were fluffing up, and columbines were unfolding their ink-purple ruches, and there were bits of blue bird's eggshell under a bush. Everywhere the bud-knots and the leap of life!

The keeper was not at the hut. Everything was serene, brown chickens running lustily. Connie walked on towards the cottage, because she wanted to find him.

The cottage stood in the sun, off the wood's edge. In the little garden the double daffodils rose in tufts, near the wide-open door, and red double daisies made a border to the path. There was the bark of a dog, and Flossie came running.

The wide-open door! so he was at home. And the sunlight falling on the red-brick floor! As she went up the path, she saw him through the window, sitting at the table in his shirt-sleeves, eating. The dog wuffed softly, slowly wagging her tail.

He rose, and came to the door, wiping his mouth with a red handkerchief, still chewing.

'May I come in?' she said.

'Come in!'

The sun shone into the bare room, which still smelled of a mutton chop, done in a dutch oven before the fire, because the dutch oven still stood on the fender, with the black potato-saucepan on a piece of paper, beside it on the white hearth. The fire was red, rather low, the bar dropped, the kettle singing.

On the table was his plate, with potatoes and the remains of the chop; also bread in a basket, salt, and a blue mug with beer. The table-cloth was white oil-cloth, he stood in the shade.

'You are very late,' she said. 'Do go on eating!'

She sat down on a wooden chair, in the sunlight by the door.

'I had to go to Uthwaite,' he said, sitting down at the table but not eating.

'Do eat,' she said.

But he did not touch the food.

'Shall y'ave something?' he asked her. 'Shall y'ave a cup of tea? t' kettle's on t' boil' – he half rose again from his chair.

'If you'll let me make it myself,' she said, rising. He seemed sad, and she felt she was bothering him.

'Well, tea-pot's in there' – he pointed to a little, drab corner cupboard; 'an' cups. An' tea's on t' mantel ower yer 'ead.'

She got the black tea-pot, and the tin of tea from the mantel-shelf. She rinsed the tea-pot with hot water, and stood a moment wondering where to empty it.

'Throw it out,' he said, aware of her. 'It's clean.'

She went to the door and threw the drop of water down the path. How lovely it was here, so still, so really woodland. The oaks were putting out ochre yellow leaves: in the garden the red daisies were like red plush buttons. She glanced at the big, hollow sandstone slab of the threshold, now crossed by so few feet.

'But it's lovely here,' she said. 'Such a beautiful stillness, everything alive and still.'

He was eating again, rather slowly and unwillingly, and she could feel he was discouraged. She made the tea in silence, and set the tea-pot on the hob, as she knew the people did. He pushed his plate aside and went to the back place; she heard a latch click, then he came back with cheese on a plate, and butter.

She set the two cups on the table; there were only two.

'Will you have a cup of tea?' she said.

'If you like. Sugar's in th' cupboard, an' there's a little cream-jug. Milk's in a jug in th' pantry.'

'Shall I take your plate away?' she asked him. He looked up at her with a faint ironical smile.

'Why ... if you like,' he said, slowly eating bread and cheese. She went to the back, into the pent-house scullery, where the pump was. On the left was a door, no doubt the pantry door. She unlatched it, and almost smiled at the place he called a pantry; a long narrow white-washed slip of a cupboard. But it managed to contain a little barrel of beer, as well as a few dishes and bits of food. She took a little milk from the yellow jug.

'How do you get your milk?' she asked him, when she came back to the table.

'Flints! They leave me a bottle at the warren end. You know, where I met you!'

But he was discouraged.

She poured out the tea, poising the cream-jug.

'No milk,' he said; then he seemed to hear a noise, and looked keenly through the doorway.

''Appen we'd better shut,' he said.

'It seems a pity,' she replied. 'Nobody will come, will they?'

'Not unless it's one time in a thousand, but you never know.'

'And even then it's no matter,' she said. 'It's only a cup of tea. Where are the spoons?'

He reached over, and pulled open the table drawer. Connie sat at the table in the sunshine of the doorway.

'Flossie!' he said to the dog, who was lying on a little mat at the stair foot. 'Go an' hark, hark!'

He lifted his finger, and his 'hark!' was very vivid. The dog trotted out to reconnoitre.

'Are you sad today?' she asked him.

He turned his blue eyes quickly, and gazed direct on her.

'Sad! no, bored! I had to go getting summonses for two poachers I caught, and, oh well, I don't like people.'

He spoke cold, good English, and there was anger in his voice.

'Do you hate being a game-keeper?' she asked.

'Being a game-keeper, no! So long as I'm left alone. But when I have to go messing around at the police-station, and various other places, and waiting for a lot of fools to attend to me . . . oh well, I get mad . . .' and he smiled, with a certain faint humour.

'Couldn't you be really independent?' she asked.

'Me? I suppose I could, if you mean manage to exist on my pension. I could! But I've got to work, or I should die. That is, I've got to have something that keeps me occupied. And I'm not in a good enough temper to work for myself. It's got to be a sort of job for somebody else, or I should throw it up in a month, out of bad temper. So altogether I'm very well off here, especially lately . . .'

He laughed at her again, with mocking humour.

'But why are you in a bad temper?' she asked. 'Do you mean you are *always* in a bad temper?'

'Pretty well,' he said, laughing. 'I don't quite digest my bile.'

'But what bile?' she said.

'Bile!' he said. 'Don't you know what that is?' She was silent, and disappointed. He was taking no notice of her.

'I'm going away for a while next month,' she said.

'You are! Where to?'

'Venice.'

'Venice! With Sir Clifford? For how long?'

'For a month or so,' she replied. 'Clifford won't go.'

'He'll stay here?' he asked.

'Yes! He hates to travel as he is.'

'Ay, poor devil!' he said, with sympathy.

There was a pause.

'You won't forget me when I'm gone, will you?' she asked. Again he lifted his eyes and looked full at her.

'Forget?' he said. 'You know nobody forgets. It's not a question of memory.'

She wanted to say: 'When then?' but she didn't. Instead, she said in a mute kind of voice: 'I told Clifford I might have a child.'

Now he really looked at her, intense and searching.

'You did?' he said at last. 'And what did he say?'

'Oh, he wouldn't mind. He'd be glad, really, so long as it seemed to be his.' She dared not look up at him.

He was silent a long time, then he gazed again on her face.

'No mention of *me*, of course?' he said.

'No. No mention of you,' she said.

'No, he'd hardly swallow me as a substitute breeder. – Then where are you supposed to be getting the child?'

'I might have a love-affair in Venice,' she said.

319

'You might,' he replied slowly. 'So that's why you're going?'

'Not to have the love-affair,' she said, looking up at him, pleading.

'Just the appearance of one,' he said.

There was silence. He sat staring out the window, with a faint grin, half mockery, half bitterness, on his face. She hated his grin.

'You've not taken any precautions against having a child then?' he asked her suddenly. 'Because I haven't.'

'No,' she said faintly. 'I should hate that.'

He looked at her, then again with the peculiar subtle grin out of the window. There was a tense silence.

At last he turned his head and said satirically:

'That was why you wanted me, then, to get a child?'

She hung her head.

'No. Not really,' she said.

'What then, *really*?' he asked rather bitingly.

She looked up at him reproachfully, saying: 'I don't know.'

He broke into a laugh.

'Then I'm damned if I do,' he said.

There was a long pause of silence, a cold silence.

'Well,' he said at last. 'It's as your Ladyship likes. If you get the baby, Sir Clifford's welcome to it. I shan't have lost anything. On the contrary, I've had a very nice experience, very nice indeed!' – and he stretched in a half-suppressed sort of yawn. 'If you've made use of me,' he said, 'it's not the first time I've been made use of; and I don't suppose it's ever been as pleasant as this time; though of course one can't feel tremendously dignified about it.' – He stretched again, curiously, his muscles quivering, and his jaw oddly set.

'But I didn't make use of you,' she said, pleading.

'At your Ladyship's service,' he replied.

'No,' she said. 'I liked your body.'

'Did you?' he replied, and he laughed. 'Well, then, we're quits, because I liked yours.'

He looked at her with queer darkened eyes.

'Would you like to go upstairs now?' he asked her, in a strangled sort of voice.

'No, not here. Not now!' she said heavily, though if he had used any power over her, she would have gone, for she had no strength against him.

He turned his face away again, and seemed to forget her.

'I want to touch you like you touch me,' she said. 'I've never really touched your body.'

He looked at her, and smiled again. 'Now?' he said.

'No! No! Not here! At the hut. Would you mind?'

'How do I touch you?' he asked.

'When you feel me.'

He looked at her, and met her heavy, anxious eyes.

'And do you like it when I feel you?' he asked, laughing at her still.

'Yes, do you?' she said.

'Oh, me!' Then he changed his tone. 'Yes,' he said. 'You know without asking.' Which was true.

She rose and picked up her hat. 'I must go,' she said.

'Will you go?' he replied politely.

She wanted him to touch her, to say something to her, but he said nothing, only waited politely.

'Thank you for the tea,' she said.

'I haven't thanked your Ladyship for doing me the honours of my tea-pot,' he said.

She went down the path, and he stood in the doorway, faintly grinning. Flossie came running with her tail lifted. And Connie had to plod dumbly across into the wood, knowing he was standing there watching her, with that incomprehensible grin on his face.

She walked home very much downcast and annoyed. She didn't at all like his saying he had been made use of; because, in a sense, it was true. But he oughtn't to have said it. Therefore, again, she was divided between two feelings: resentment against him, and a desire to make it up with him.

She passed a very uneasy and irritated tea-time, and at once went up to her room. But when she was there it was no good: she could neither sit nor stand. She would have to do something about it. She would have to go back to the hut; if he was not there, well and good.

She slipped out of the side door, and took her way direct and a little sullen. When she came to the clearing she was terribly uneasy. But there he was again, in his shirt-sleeves, stooping, letting the hens out of the coops, among the chicks that were now growing a little gawky, but were much more trim than hen-chickens.

She went straight across to him.

'You see I've come!' she said.

'Ay, I see it!' he said, straightening his back, and looking at her with a faint amusement.

'Do you let the hens out now?' she asked.

'Yes, they've sat themselves to skin and bone,' he said. 'An' now they're not all that anxious to come out an' feed. There's no self in a sitting hen; she's all in the eggs or the chicks.'

The poor mother-hens; such blind devotion! even to eggs not their own! Connie looked at them in compassion. A helpless silence fell between the man and the woman.

'Shall us go i' th' 'ut?' he asked.

'Do you want me?' she asked, in a sort of mistrust.

'Ay, if you want to come.'

She was silent.

'Come then!' he said.

And she went with him to the hut. It was quite dark when

he had shut the door, so he made a small light in the lantern, as before.

'Have you left your underthings off?' he asked her.

'Yes!'

'Ay, well, then I'll take my things off too.'

He spread the blankets, putting one at the side for a coverlet. She took off her hat, and shook her hair. He sat down, taking off his shoes and gaiters, and undoing his cord breeches.

'Lie down then!' he said, when he stood in his shirt. She obeyed in silence, and he lay beside her, and pulled the blanket over them both.

'There!' he said.

And he lifted her dress right back, till he came even to her breasts. He kissed them softly, taking the nipples in his lips in tiny caresses.

'Eh, but tha'rt nice, tha'rt nice!' he said, suddenly rubbing his face with a snuggling movement against her warm belly.

And she put her arms round him under his shirt, but she was afraid, afraid of his thin, smooth, naked body, that seemed so powerful, afraid of the violent muscles. She shrank, afraid.

And when he said, with a sort of little sigh: 'Eh, tha'rt nice!' something in her quivered, and something in her spirit stiffened in resistance: stiffened from the terribly physical intimacy, and from the peculiar haste of his possession. And this time the sharp ecstasy of her own passion did not overcome her; she lay with her hands inert on his striving body, and do what she might, her spirit seemed to look on from the top of her head, and the butting of his haunches seemed ridiculous to her, and the sort of anxiety of his penis to come to its little evacuating crisis seemed farcical. Yes, this was love, this ridiculous bouncing of the buttocks, and the wilting of the poor, insignificant, moist little penis. This was the divine love! After all, the moderns were right when they felt contempt for the performance; for it was a performance. It was quite true, as some poets said, that the God who created man must have had a sinister sense of humour, creating him a reasonable being, yet forcing him to take this ridiculous posture, and driving him with blind craving for this ridiculous performance. Even a Maupassant found it a humiliating anti-climax. Men despised the intercourse act, and yet did it.

Cold and derisive her queer female mind stood apart, and though she lay perfectly still, her impulse was to heave her loins, and throw the man out, escape his ugly grip, and the butting over-riding of his absurd haunches. His body was a foolish, impudent, imperfect thing, a little disgusting in its unfinished clumsiness. For surely a complete evolution would eliminate this performance, this 'function'.

And yet when he had finished, soon over, and lay very very still, receding into silence, and a strange motionless distance, far, farther than the horizon of her awareness, her heart began to weep. She could feel him ebbing away, ebbing away, leaving her there like a stone on a shore. He was withdrawing, his spirit was leaving her. He knew.

And in real grief, tormented by her own double consciousness and reaction, she began to weep. He took no notice, or did not even know. The storm of weeping swelled and shook her, and shook him.

'Ay!' he said. 'It was no good that time. You wasn't there.'
– So he knew! Her sobs became violent.

'But what's amiss?' he said. 'It's once in a while that way.'

'I . . . I can't love you,' she sobbed, suddenly feeling her heart breaking.

'Canna ter? Well, dunna fret! There's no law says as tha's got to. Ta'e it for what it is.'

324

He still lay with his hand on her breast. But she had drawn both her hands from him.

His words were small comfort. She sobbed aloud.

'Nay, nay!' he said. 'Ta'e the thick wi' th' thin. This wor a bit o' thin for once.'

She wept bitterly, sobbing. 'But I want to love you, and I can't. It only seems horrid.'

He laughed a little, half bitter, half amused.

'It isna horrid,' he said, 'even if tha thinks it is. An' tha canna ma'e it horrid. Dunna fret thysen about lovin' me. Tha'lt niver force thysen to 't. There's sure to be a bad nut in a basketful. Tha mun ta'e th' rough wi' th' smooth.'

He took his hand away from her breast, not touching her. And now she was untouched she took an almost perverse satisfaction in it. She hated the dialect: the *thee* and the *tha* and the *thysen*. He could get up if he liked, and stand there, above her, buttoning down those absurd corduroy breeches, straight in front of her. After all, Michaelis had had the decency to turn away. This man was so assured in himself, he didn't know what a clown other people found him, a half-bred fellow.

Yet, as he was drawing away, to rise silently and leave her, she clung to him in terror.

'Don't! Don't go! Don't leave me! Don't be cross with me! Hold me! Hold me fast!' she whispered in blind frenzy, not even knowing what she said, and clinging to him with un-canny force. It was from herself she wanted to be saved, from her own inward anger and resistance. Yet how powerful was that inward resistance that possessed her!

He took her in his arms again and drew her to him, and suddenly she became small in his arms, small and nestling. It was gone, the resistance was gone, and she began to melt in a marvellous peace. And as she melted small and wonderful in his arms, she became infinitely desirable to him, all his blood-vessels seemed to scald with intense yet tender desire, for her, for her softness, for the penetrating beauty of her in his arms, passing into his blood. And softly, with that marvellous swoon-like caress of his hand in pure soft desire, softly he stroked the silky slope of her loins, down, down between her soft warm buttocks, coming nearer and nearer to the very quick of her. And she felt him like a flame of desire, yet tender, and she felt herself melting in the flame. She let herself go. She felt his penis risen against her with silent amazing force and assertion and she let herself go to him. She yielded with a quiver that was like death, she went all open to him. And oh, if he were not tender to her now, how cruel, for she was all open to him and helpless!

She quivered again at the potent inexorable entry inside her, so strange and terrible. It might come with the thrust of a sword in her softly-opened body, and that would be death. She clung in a sudden anguish of terror. But it came with a strange slow thrust of peace, the dark thrust of peace and a ponderous, primordial tenderness, such as made the world in the beginning. And her terror subsided in her breast, her breast dared to be gone in peace, she held nothing. She dared to let go everything, all herself, and be gone in the flood.

And it seemed she was like the sea, nothing but dark waves rising and heaving, heaving with a great swell, so that slowly her whole darkness was in motion, and she was ocean rolling its dark, dumb mass. Oh, and far down inside her the deeps parted and rolled asunder, in long, far-travelling billows, and ever, at the quick of her, the depths parted and rolled asunder, from the centre of soft plunging, as the plunger went deeper and deeper, touching lower, and she was deeper and deeper and deeper disclosed, the heavier the billows of her rolled away to some shore, uncovering her, and closer and closer plunged the palpable unknown, and further and further rolled the waves of herself away from herself, leaving her, till suddenly, in a soft, shuddering convulsion, the quick of all her plasm was touched, she knew herself touched, the consummation was upon her, and she was gone. She was gone, she was not, and she was born: a woman.

Ah, too lovely, too lovely! In the ebbing she realized all the loveliness. Now all her body clung with tender love to the unknown man, and blindly to the wilting penis, as it so tenderly, frailly, unknowingly withdrew, after the fierce thrust of its potency. As it drew out and left her body, the secret, sensitive thing, she gave an unconscious cry of pure loss, and she tried to put it back. It had been so perfect! And she loved it so!

And only now she became aware of the small, bud-like reticence and tenderness of the penis, and a little cry of wonder and poignancy escaped her again, her woman's heart crying out over the tender frailty of that which had been the power.

'It was so lovely!' she moaned. 'It was so lovely!' But he said nothing, only softly kissed her, lying still above her. And she moaned with a sort of bliss, as a sacrifice, and a newborn thing.

And now in her heart the queer wonder of him was awakened.

He bent down and kissed her soft flank, rubbed his cheek against it, then covered it up.

'And will you never leave me?' she said.

'Dunna ask them things,' he said.

'But you do believe I love you?' she said.

'Tha loved me just now, wider than iver tha thout tha would. But who knows what'll 'appen, once tha starts thinkin' about it!'

327

'No, don't say those things! – And you don't really think that I wanted to make use of you, do you?'

'How?'

'To have a child –?'

'Now anybody can 'ave any childt i' th' world,' he said, as he sat down fastening on his leggings.

'Ah no!' she cried. 'You don't mean it?'

'Eh well!' he said, looking at her under his brows. 'This wor t' best.'

She lay still. He softly opened the door. The sky was dark blue, with crystalline, turquoise rim. He went out, to shut up the hens, speaking softly to his dog. And she lay and wondered at the wonder of life, and of being.

When he came back she was still lying there, glowing like a gipsy. He sat on the stool by her.

'Tha mun come one naight ter th' cottage, afore tha goos; sholl ter?' he asked, lifting his eyebrows as he looked at her, his hands dangling between his knees.

'Sholl ter?' she echoed, teasing.

He smiled.

'Ay, sholl ter?' he repeated.

'Ay!' she said, imitating the dialect sound.

'Yi!' he said.

'Yi!' she repeated.

'An' slaip wi' me,' he said. 'It needs that. When sholt come?'

'When sholl I?' she said.

'Nay,' he said, 'tha canna do't. When sholt come then?'

''Appen Sunday,' she said.

''Appen a' Sunday! Ay!'

He laughed at her quickly.

'Nay, tha canna,' he protested.

'Why canna I?' she said.

He laughed. Her attempts at the dialect were so ludicrous, somehow.

'Coom then, tha mun goo!' he said.

'Mun I?' she said.

'Maun Ah!' he corrected.

'Why should I say *maun* when you said *mun*?' she protested. 'You're not playing fair.'

'Arena Ah!' he said, leaning forward and softly stroking her face.

'Th'art good cunt, though, aren't ter? Best bit o' cunt left on earth. When ter likes! When tha'rt willin'!'

'What is cunt?' she said.

'An' doesn't ter know? Cunt! It's thee down theer; an' what I get when I'm i'side thee, and what tha gets when I'm i'side thee; it's a' as it is, all on't.'

'All on't,' she teased. 'Cunt! It's like fuck then.'

'Nay nay! Fuck's only what you do. Animals fuck. But cunt's a lot more than that. It's thee, dost see: an' tha'rt a lot besides an animal, aren't ter? – even ter fuck? Cunt! Eh, that's the beauty o' thee, lass!'

She got up and kissed him between the eyes, that looked at her so dark and soft and unspeakably warm, so unbearably beautiful.

'Is it?' she said. 'And do you care for me?'

He kissed her without answering.

'Tha mun goo, let me dust thee,' he said.

His hand passed over the curves of her body, firmly, without desire, but with soft, intimate knowledge.

As she ran home in the twilight the world seemed a dream; the trees in the park seemed bulging and surging at anchor on a tide, and the heave of the slope to the house was alive.

ALLAN GURGANUS

FORCED USE

A naughty story for David Del Tredici

THREE BROWN BEETLES – meeting windshield at 61 mph – smeared green paste three ways: I took this as a sign to finally stop and phone my wife.

I pulled into a rest area on 87 South – a grassy stretch without bathrooms, just six picnic tables, one dempsy dumpster, tall anchor fencing stretched all around and keeping back the woods. I reversed charges and noticed a young man sunning on one table. 'Darling,' I told Alice, 'I survived.' Big arms were interlocked across his forehead. He wore only shorts, no shoes, no shirt. Good legs dangled off the table's end, the kid's toes kept flexing, pointing, bobbling as he thought his thoughts; otherwise he looked asleep. To my wife, I described the convention. I reported who'd inquired about her; I repeated their compliments: Alice's charm, her brightness. She asked how my paper was received; I admitted Wilkinson claimed it was the first *new* thing he'd heard since discussing the subject with Berenson once in Rome.

'*Wilkinson* said that?' My loyal wife reads all the journals in my field and her own. Alice's voice was elated, lovely, 'So, a triumph, right? You must be feeling very smug.'

'I guess,' I said; his hair was brown, (some blue, some copper in it) tangled ringlets full of light. Behind me, the highway sounded sickening: I'd driven since dawn; it was nearly noon now, it was mid-July, pure humidity, pure heat. I told Alice when I would arrive this evening. I asked if she had mailed the tuition cheque to our young son's day school.

As I talked I wondered if the table underneath him – flecked with picnic drippings, gouged with lovers' carved initials – if it weren't sticking to the fellow's skin, didn't wood cut into his fine wide back? Driving, I'd been feeling wasted, old. Nothing I did ever called for total energy.

Of all my strengths, I utilized maybe thirty per cent at a time. The career, I thought, it's been too easy. After my success at the convention, after getting every possible rave from the people I respected most, I felt oddly let down. Thirty-one years old, too soon at the top of my profession, secure, in good health – and yet, nothing, nothing whatso-ever had ever really *happened* to me. I was in my prime, or rather it was in me, a vat full of goods but wasting, like surplus food – curdling due to some silly hold-up in paper-work – spoiling while the whole world starved.

Standing here, all nerves and worries, I longed to feel drained, to know I'd given something absolutely everything. Oh, to be used up so perfectly – it would feel like getting understood!

The only others in the park – a family – sat eating at a distant table in the shade. Nearer, he was belly-up in the light. I studied him, unable to say exactly why he interested me so. Did he look like a friend of friends? – I hadn't seen his face yet. Did he remind me of myself at twenty-two or -three, making those long cross-country drives (gas twenty-nine cents a gallon) napping in the sun along the way? Just now, as I listened to my wife (her argument with a boss' secretary, our son's latest funny saying), the well-made boy lowered his arms, displayed a squarish jaw, opened his eyes, then stretched. It was a simple and effective and profound animal stretch. Big toes curled under as both legs lifted, hovering – effortless – level with the tabletop. Seeming to wake, he looked to where I stood – me, all awkward and exposed in the glass booth, me, caught gawking at him.

The kid propped one cheek on one fist and stared over here in a bored unembarrassed way. When I didn't turn my head at once, he lazily reached down with his free hand and, index finger crooked, tugged at the groin of his cut-off khaki shorts; he kept his thumb and forefinger nuzzling around up under the fabric, testing, pinching loose skin there. He gave me this steady noncommittal smirk. His bearing was a smart aleck's. His dark face, oval like some boy saint's. The body was wide, valuable with use as a seasoned stevedore's – only, his looked newer.

I turned my back on him. He was a kid, some punk. I faced interstate but – counting cars parked in the lot here – tried guessing which was his. My wife announced that the food processor had arrived at last and was working like a whizz. 'Good,' I said. She'd made watercress soup just this morning and, served cool later, it would be fantastic in weather as brutal as this. 'Great,' I said. I chose an old red Jaguar convertible, its front end so bitten with rust, the grille hung half dislodged. I invented a story: he was from a poor working family, second generation, seven brothers and sisters, his father – a plasterer – drank, kept an expensive mistress. The boy had saved to buy this used car, he bagged groceries and cut people's yards; he repaired the car himself but, when he saw it wouldn't do what he hoped for his local reputation (on the street, everybody knew him) he lost interest in it. He just drove it now – to hell with maintenance. He drove it out to rest stops on the interstate where strangers were. Dressed in next-to-nothing, he stretched out on tables at the rest stops, hoping to get noticed by these strangers. He got noticed. The Jaguar, still sleek, was pocked with lacy excremental rust, gills and flecks and finger-length brown holes of it. The ruined car looked expensive and disreputable, both. Like him. Like him.

'What?' my wife asked. Alice knows me.

'Nothing. Just tired from driving and the heat.'

'Stop somewhere. Take a break, take one of your famous ten-minute naps.'

'I will. I think I will.'

I turned around and watched him stand, uneasy as a child on his bare feet, both arms out, balancing. In one fist, he held a pack of cigarettes; from the other, car keys dangled. He meandered towards the woods that started, one lush surface, just where the clearing ceased. Since there were no bathrooms here, some merciful planner had left a few high bushes before the fence and you could see well-worn foot paths slipping around behind them. The kid stepped into leafy shade then, leaning against fence, turned to face me. Alongside either hip, his fingers jammed through metal mesh. In shadow, he looked even browner. He just stood there, waiting.

Only I could see him. At a far table, the small family ate, glum, overheated. Skinny little twin girls, shirtless in seer-sucker shorts, tied motel handtowels around their necks as capes. They modelled these for one another. Parents – red-faced, silent – watched their own fast-moving, witty kids. The twins kept stooping, talking to an animal's carrying case – its roof was all polka-dotted, holes pierced for something's breathing. The boy simply looked towards me. I did not know what he wanted. Still, anyone could guess. I'd been around. I knew human nature, that all is possible. Myself, I couldn't do that sort of thing. But anybody could figure why he eyed me in that steady, breathing way.

Alice: 'Laura had the piece in the *Times* on Tuesday, see it? I told her to cut out all the sociology double-talk and she did drop some. I do think it's better than when she showed it to me first. Kevin's school is going to the Planetarium and he's impossible with quasars and black holes and all that mess. His teacher said ... '

Shouldn't the ordinary matter of your own life interest you? Today it did not. Today, in this humidity, in this young thug's gaze, I and my wife and our gabby little prodigy seemed monotonous and greedy, trivial. I thought, the best part of me will go wholly wasted. It'll die untapped, unknown. The sweetest secret energies will never once get used, never even hinted at or touched.

Alice said, 'You know it really is amazing about these gaps in outer space, ones our encyclopaedia claimed nothing could withstand, raw holes that use up everything as temporary heat, vacuums snorting in whatever meteoric junk drifts near. Scientists call such pockets anti-matter.'

'That's how I feel,' I said. 'That's what I need.'

Maternally, Alice ignored this grumpiness, sped right along with household news.

He was hidden from the others. Above him, 'Trespassers Will Be Prosecuted Beyond This Point. State Land Ends.' The sign was clamped to fence, along its top, a crown and garland of barbed wire. He tipped back and, fingers in its gaps, rocked fencing some; three birch branches, growing through it, moved. He simply stared. His feet spread wide apart. His head kept tilting slightly left. I could look him over. I thought he wanted me to. I did ...

He wasn't quite grinning, wasn't quite frowning either but offered me this wry half-secretive expression as if waiting to be recognized. His face – sulky, sour, pretty – was anything but neutral. A dimple cut the right side of his mouth. He squinted at me knowingly then turned and, knuckles locked within steel webbing, did some angled push ups – lumpy back expanding. He flipped around to watch me noticing.

He was somewhat stubbily constructed, built with a smooth round chest. The brown torso was halved then quartered; lower fourths, across a flat belly, were quilted into separate eighths. One dark strip of hair, growing in herringbone pattern, kept pulling sight down towards and into his green shorts. The brass buckle, like the ones they sell in tourist traps, advertised a local beer. To me, it looked cheap. Even as a joke, I'd never wear a thing like that. It made you feel sorry for the kind of jerky kid who'd go out and pay good money for that. But, on him, somehow, it did look sort of good. The longer I stared, the better it looked. By now, already, it appeared almost . . . excellent. Yes, I fussily decided, excellent, on him.

Heat had laid a sombre sheen along every notch and facet of his chest. He glanced down at himself, casually interested in whatever I, right now and from out here in light, could find to size up and admire. He seemed to like the spectacle he made; he looked at me, mugged an expression, gave one funny charming shrug as if to say, Not so bad, huh? – He was right, of course. That's just it.

Both thighs were black with hair; he now reached down to scratch a furry knee that plainly did not itch. Then, grinning, this punk, this small-time champ, crossed his arms and, eyes fluttering shut, let his whole head roll sideways, a smeared and languid kind of smile. It was part dare, part plea, part snarl. I thought, He surely knows what he's doing. He wants me to know he knows. Now I do. OK, but the answer is still negative. No way.

I listened to Alice's final comments, personal important ones. I wished she wouldn't hang up on me. I felt glad she was about to. I heard some yelps and, twisting right, saw one twin flip open the animal's case. A fat white Persian cat fluffed out, hurrying this way, scuddling along weeded fence, keeping

338

low to the ground, bolting and stopping. One child chased it. The creature made towards shrubbery, where the sullen boy stood watching me. Hearing squeals, he straightened.

I leaned towards him. The creature dodged under a low limb, the child scooped up her pet, its plump tail flipping forward. Then the girl stomped away. She jerked cat's face near her own, hollered at its eyes and muzzle, 'Bad, *bad* Snowflake. You always run off. Don't you even like us any more?' Nearing the listless family, she said, 'I think Flake just *hates* vacations. To her, if it's not our yard it's way too weird to handle!' I laughed. Kids are incredible, aren't they. The things they come out with. I missed my talkative son.

Then the boy in the bushes ('The Bushes', I marvelled at the words, last heard when I was sixteen, fifteen), he wagged his head towards the woods. He signalled I should follow. Watching him, my grin died. Kids are something, all right. Watching him, I knew I would not. Do what he wanted. Could not do . . . that, he'd planned – I was someone's husband, someone's actual dad. Even if nothing if life ever *had* occurred or overwhelmed me, even if I did feel under-utilized, I couldn't sacrifice whatever'd piled up by lucky accident, right? Couldn't jeopardize all of that for one motley little roadside risk, for this one interesting wrong, right? Right. Still, I rushed last-minute conversation with my wife, said, Yes the car was fine, the food had been good but not so good as hers, as ours.

I leaned back on stainless-steel shelf. Phonebooks had been linked here till someone ripped them out. Tufts of paper binding, one white, one yellow, spun from long and sturdy chains. I doubted I could stand much longer. I blamed July. My voice got cramped and wavery, my wife accepted all emotions as ones she had inspired, Alice said, 'You'll be home in under four hours. Your talk was a great success. There are two telegrams here. Kyle, between his asteroids and black holes, keeps asking about you. We'll make ice-cream with our new thing. It's in the booklet.' I said I loved her. I hung up. I *did* love her, and very much. So much I felt quite dizzy, so much I needed to walk over and sit down on a table just conveniently abandoned.

I settled upon upper slats. Deck shoes rested on the bench part. I settled faced away from highway, phones; I aimed towards trees, towards him. I wondered how I looked – my old chinos, blue buttondown – would I pass? Would I do, if so, why? Under the back of my workpants, planks felt splintery and slick. Wincing in this light, I noted a ragged crescent along woodgrain – dark oil, wetness showing where one smooth shoulder had just pressed. Sun dried a corner of this mark. I touched my index fingertip to the dampest spot then tested finger against thumb. Moisture felt like lanolin; I sniffed it. He was watching me. Let him. I was closer to the cars than he. I could, at any moment, run for it.

Twins dashed in circles, they pretended to fly, their arms poked out, they admired how capes looked luffing out behind. 'Am above *build*ings,' one squealed. 'All this air is our air. We're way way up now, look.' Parents appeared bored. Sunstroked, numb, unworthy of their girls' imaginations. Watching, I felt something like stagefright. I'd seen the boy ('my' boy, I almost said, 'my' boy) slide right; he was now lost behind the wilted shrubbery. Odd, I already missed him.

Years back, I confessed a college misdeed to Alice – how, with my sophomore room mate, all-state lacrosse, exams over, him with a sprained muscle in one leg, needing help with that, both of us drunk as our excuse and amnesia … Alice, ready with statistics from a famous national survey, blurted out the odds for this occurring, said it was incredibly

340

widespread, between boys, the occasional lapse. After all, Alice said, when you think of it: the world's half male, half female – occasionally, given those odds, one *had* to notice and long for a member of one's own fifty per cent. Statistically, it was bound to happen, right? 'That,' I told her gently, 'makes sense.'

Options. I sat on a picnic table, in sun, mid-summer, off highway, nowhere in particular between two minor towns upstate. I pinched the bridge of my nose; with elbows propped on knees, I pressed both hands across my face. I could feel eye sockets, goggles in the bone. I imagined him behind greenery not fifteen feet away. (I found I *could* picture him, 20/20.) He was backed against heavy-gauge steel wiring, shoulders printed with it, plaid and zigzagged, pink. He was a swarthy boy used to minimum wage, a mechanic's helper. Today, he was all itch, all smirk and certainty. He was back there, he had something back there with him, 'he had something in his pants'. Sick of my highminded life, I savoured the sleazy sound of this – 'something *good* in his pants'.

Decide. To hurry to your car, do right, speed away, lock every door and, for at least six months (till willpower bleached this memory) wonder what smut he'd had in mind for you, you two? Speeding, you could squirt detergent, purge the windshield of four states' insect life and – cleansed – appear a model citizen, pretend you'd only seen some mild rancid mirage brought on by loneliness, professional jitters, too long a drive.

Or: risk it just this once? To just risk getting nabbed by cops or hurt by him? Or catching something you might pass on to Alice? To just haul off and chance everything you've earned, to put that on the line and just stand up and follow him right now and see what might at last unlatch itself and happen finally? Which? You choose. One only.

I could not control my thoughts. I mashed butt-ends of hands against closed eyes, attempting to be rational. But, eye spheres, twitchy and slippery within skin so fine, reminded me of certain famous masculine underparts, matched sets and issued by the millions to make mischief among the world's populace, to make the world's populace. So one hand quickly shifted, pressed across my mouth, the other slammed to forehead in a fever test. Yes, heat. Yeah, leave. But it was a hundred and two degrees out here; logic was nowhere. I perspired; it probably showed. Had I been parked here for half an hour or just under seven minutes? What was the topic of a paper of someone my age and weight delivered yesterday? Applause, that I recalled. I also understood my destination, my marital condition, Mother's maiden name. But as for decency, this swarm of recollected wrongs kept interfering.

– How when I was ten, my older brother invited friends to sleep over, and how I barged into our shared attic bathroom and saw, lit by dim glow from the shower, two of brother's rangy pals (blond kids well-known at school) both studying a prized pornographic postcard (three women busy on one bony sailor in a bad hotel) and how the boys' tennis shorts were jammed around their upper legs, binding upper legs, and how – with the picture delicately suspended (a card trick) between them – they had serious hold on, of, around one another's crucials, long arms grasped to make a sinewy brown X and how – as I lunged in, then fell back against doorjamb – they gaped my way while staying bodily locked into this odd cross-referenced pose. It seems, in memory, a bond like Siamese twins' – some slab of mutual gristle, tubular and linking them – boys hooked like this for ever, sharing one rosy erection, but forked.

Their stricken faces seemed to speak: We can't help it.

342

It grew like this. Awful, yeah, but all we've got. It is growing, still. What are we to *do* with it but what feels best? It is a fact that we can't help or stop. We check on it a lot. Here it is. We can't believe it has to look like this but ... does. It's a monster. We're its hobby. They stared down at it – a humid brittle thing between them, pronged.

– How, in the Army, after my spinal injury on the obstacle course, a physical therapist kept rubbing my lower back with some heated implement for minute after minute; alone in the room with me, door closed, he ran this burning thing across the tops of my legs, across and all around my butt then up over my neck, burrowing it, hurtful, into scalp and how I didn't stop him, didn't ask if this were therapy and necessary. When he said I should turn over, I felt ashamed to. I refused. I pretended not to hear him, I faked sleep. I was just a kid and scared to death. He had to slap my ass, first jokingly, then not, then even less so. Again he told me to get on my back, 'You think you're the first that's happened to, man? Know how many GIs I have in here every workday? You touch guys where I've got to, just to help them – on most guys it'll happen. It's supposed to, see? You think you're special or something, think you interest me? Roll over, soldier. I'm getting pretty sick of this.'

And so I did, turn over, show him. Had to, it was all right there, right there to see. He was my age, about my build, perspiring too. He looked down at the whole raw front of me. He diagnosed, like a vet. It seemed I was this dog brought in to him, some dog just hit by a car or something; he stared down with such pity, like he thought maybe he could save me. '*Look* at you,' he said, admiring. He gazed at me, at it, then on up to my face, comparing.

'I'm an Army therapist,' he said. 'Been trained in this. I know everything about a guy's body.' Having explained himself, he reached for it, he, he had it, he proved – I felt at once – he was expert.

And, in a voice you had to believe, my fellow soldier said, 'The backbone is one thing, real real easy to throw off. And then, of course, there's all of this, isn't there, buddy? – There's all of this down here that needs attention, too. Am I right?'

I didn't answer. He consulted my face again – his eyes solemn.

Gently then, he got me by the hair, he shook my whole head back and forth, a coerced Yes to his question about need, my need. His doing this seemed odd to me, but funny. I laughed and so did he. It was a nice moment. I can't explain. I trusted him more. He let my hair loose but this head, my head, kept kept kept on nodding Yes.

'That an answer?' Again I bowed my head. Tears filled either eye. One spilled over. I shook some.

His was a decent worthy grin. I settled back. I watched him. And others, sure, some others. And now, in July, within hearing of a major highway at this minor patch of grass, a nameless place, some new kid was waiting for me, hidden, thinking I knew why he hid. He might be back there ready to rob me. If I disappeared here, if he took my wallet and keys, if he murdered me and buried the body deep in a hole in that birch wood past the fence, and if he stole my car and drove it to another state, nobody would know where to look for me. I would be lost for good. I would deserve to be. I followed him. I shoved off from the bench as if pushing off a pool's edge. Air had texture. I moved through it. I walked in a studied casual way. I worried that the family over there might see me step behind these bushes, I worried what the twins would think; I wanted to protect them from all know-ledge of me – Since there were no bathrooms here, they

344

would probably remember that. Yes, they'd think my motives were as innocent as that.

I stepped behind the bushes.

Somebody had clipped the fence open. Each sturdy wire was cut then peeled aside in a cylindrical coil the way you might twirl the lid off a can of smoked oysters. This made a neat narrow six-foot passage in the fence, no jagged edges, done with professional care. I was glad that some other outlaw had thought to perform this service, that he owned (or rented) the equipment, that he knew how to use it. The sign hanging over this gap still warned: 'Trespassers Will Be Prosecuted. State Land Ends.' In red spray-paint, somebody'd underlined 'Trespassers' and scrawled a ten-inch exclamation mark; the dot beneath had bled a long red droplet off the edge.

Amazed I could, this terrified, still move – I stepped through fencing. Only thought: My father would kill me. Here was a wide and downhill wood. It felt fifteen degrees cooler, it was muddy. I looked for the boy, couldn't see him. Underbrush was scuffed with paths. Other people, needing cover, also up to no good, knew this place and used it. Fastfood wrappers (red, yellow) were scattered underfoot but the birches' fine white trunks made the space look beautiful and almost planned. Then, to the left, forty feet downhill and in a grove of saplings, I saw motion. Skin was half hidden in blue shade but it was skin, his skin, his shoulder's skin, I knew that. I couldn't get a full breath. Should leave, should run out into sun and phone my wife again. Hearing her would get me past this.

Yesterday, I delivered my paper: 'The Influence of Prairie Architecture on Henry Adams' Appreciation of Mont St Michel', a work praised for its structure, vision, wit. Today I was an idiot blundering into woods, stalking nearer what

I wanted (while pretending I'd come back in here to see what a typical rustic upstate glade looks like). I felt very foolish. Not enough to stop, but foolish. What I wanted wanted doing so much, it seemed mostly done already. I would just be finishing up a messy required task. Inhaling got me one quarter of the oxygen adults need.

My shoe crunched broken bottle. I wondered how he'd run so far into forest without cutting his bare feet. I worried for his feet as I'd fretted for the twins. I told myself he needs help, he is far from the road, is in some kind of trouble – I knew exactly what I wanted and yet, offering myself this lie (sad boy in need of first aid) I believed my lie at once.

Hadn't been in woods, real woods, for years. Just off highway yet it looked untamed – dense ferns, this strange lushness. I moved, was getting there, but memories – the worst ones yet – kept going off in spasm warnings. How (do you mind my telling this?) at Wiggins' Lake, when I was nine, how Father caught me with the older son of a Greek that ran the bait shop. We were in high reeds, way away from everything; I never knew how Dad found us – smell, fury? Just, suddenly, he was there, hands on hips – above us on the bank. He acted polite to the other kid. 'You may leave now,' he said, cordial. The big kid was zipping up, there was some whimpering, there was his limping off, his calling back through dense rushes, 'We didn't mean it.'

That left two of us, the right father, the wrong son. Days before, at a science fair, I'd seen the electromagnet demonstrated – a thumbtack was dropped six feet away, it skipped towards attraction and struck that magnet, humming there, immobilized and whining with such force. I felt like that. Getting trapped quadrupled gravity. I considered explaining, couldn't – found I didn't even understand. 'I wish,' Dad said, 'that I could blame him. Spiro's boy is older but I know it

346

was you again, wasn't it, son?' I stood there. 'Why?' he asked. I looked at my tennis shoes – stained grass colour: I studied reeds bent under my soles, I pitied those reeds our weight had flattened – the wrestling, our laughing, unbuttoning; it had seemed almost natural till getting nabbed.

Dad came over, within reach. Someone like him started hitting me. 'This,' he said, 'And this.' Rocked side to side and yet detached, I thought I knew why – in cartoons – they show stars when some funny animal gets clubbed or belted in the head a lot. It's *like* stars. Points of light, sudden, jagged, coloured, out of nowhere, decorating what is otherwise the total dark. I heard my father groaning, the exertion of beating me this thoroughly. I thought: I am nine, he is thirty-four. It seemed important, a score. I heard lapping water, distant jukebox music from the bait shop, his grunts like ones he made while sawing wood. My T-shirt was not the colour it'd been. Day was ending. Reeds were slick with all I'd lost. I found myself falling, then in arms being carried down to water.

He worried aloud (the lake cold around me) that my mother'd faint or kill me, me coming home this cut up, this big mess. He grumbled, blaming me for the amount I'd bled. 'I do all this for you, Willy. Trying to get *at* whatever's in you makes you act like this – not like your mother's family, not like me. It's just that one part I'm after, son. Not *you*. I'd like to find that one bad spot and ... lance it, like I would a sty, son. Cure you.'

Bathing me, he muttered as the day gave out. Sky was slatted with all colours bruises turn – the golden-greens, the plums, the sulphur-yellows. 'We'll say you fell in. Yeah, tell her you fell in. Say it like you really *did* fall. Say it, now.'

'I felw inw.' My mouth was full of misplaced liquids. Upset, slapping water to my open face, he unbuttoned

347

sleeves, unfastened the front and pulled his whole shirt off and all around me, shelter, I was shivering. In late light, his neck and shoulders looked part pink, part blue – a new colour. He saw me noticing his chest, admiring what the late light did. I was dazed. I couldn't judge or move my head. Whatever came into my sight I looked at. 'Haven't *learned*?' he yelled and, backhand, cuffed me. 'I hit at *it*, not you.' He called down through all the stars he'd sired. 'I hate it as much as I love you. That much, Will.' He pulled me close against him so I couldn't see his front side buckling. I felt sorry for him. I heard sounds come through his ribs; I thought, whatever's in me that he hopes to get at – it's too far gone already – you can't lance that far in and have the person live.

He lugged me to the car. The sky was over us, I knew that. My features aimed towards its features. My own face was numb with stars, inlaid, a jaw alive with green implanted ones. For nose I had a bright-red hole, five pointed. My eyes were swollen into shiny planets I could not see through.

'Practise. Say it.'

I hollered what we'd planned, what Dad and I had planned. I called that up towards stars – cousins of my own. I hollered straight up, blind. ' "Flew in"?' I hollered, blinded.

– Now, adult. Deep in the woods, I heard water running, a brook, a ditch. Birds sang – a male called, a female answered. – I'd only done this kind of thing maybe four or ten times since meeting Alice. I love my wife. I remember Dad's effective lessons. This has helped me avoid nightspots where men dance close with men, it has helped me ignore the dark places around my hometown – under the memorial bridge, out on certain dirt roads near the ice plant – where men go to meet boys and other men – I've been good, I haven't even missed it all that much.

But, sometimes, when you blunder on to something by mistake, (you know how it is?) when Alice is two full states away, Dad good and dead, and you find you're in an unknown place with an even quieter more private woods to wander into (like a bonus), and when you're coaxed back here by some kid who is no more important than how he looks to you and how the way he looks makes you feel while looking at him hard because he wants you to, (can you even half imagine how it is?) and when he's some sweet idiot kid you'll never have to see again or even speak to much ... sometimes, in July heat this bad, no amount of fear or will or planning can quite help prevent it. And you will probably go ahead because doing it's involuntary as a heartbeat's next lurch is, helpless as the eyesight that made you notice him first, that forced you back in here, that drew you into shadow where he's waiting, where – it appears – he's fooling with himself. This isn't some deed you choose to do or not to do, this is not some minor infection you can pierce and empty out and heal, it is – scalding, simple: your eyesight, air supply, blood type, your history and aims – you, it's You.

I was shivering, had to cross my arms to hide the worst of it, to keep from jogging towards full light, back past the nice pet-owning family, back into the locked car my wife's folks had given us, back to that and out of here to safety – lack of choice. Civilization.

The kid's whole back was a show, varnish-brown, slick. I stood maybe twenty feet behind him when he scowled over one shoulder at me. He fixed me with a mean welcoming glower. Up this close, the boy looked coarser than I'd believed, he looked a little older. He looked poorer. He looked better.

I studied the calves' boxy shapes, how his legs flexed far apart. Some mud smeared across the top of one pale foot, gummed along his bristled ankle. His back was a knot-tying manual; I studied every plane and segment, how his shoulder, working in steady yanking on the front of him, widened, that arm buckling with force, dents and notches in it flattening then deepening as he – squinting at my face, my legs – pulled at something hidden, something he wanted to show me and I wanted to see.

'What do you want,' I said, and loud, to the kid's back. It sounded stupid.

He just swung his head, bull neck spreading, showing I should walk around in front of him, to look at him. I began to circle. I kept my distance, skirting the grove so far I had to steal back into it. Passing some low pines, I could see the whole front of him now. That arm was straight. I saw its big blunt fist. Across the hands' back, a cusp of black hair grew; I watched fist working on the stubby solid fact he held. He kept clamping fingers across the whole top of it. He wouldn't let me see.

I felt half-dead with this much numbing guilt, with this much excitement, same thing, same thing. On the highway, semis skimmed and blustered. Through leaves behind the kid, rectangles of silver glided North.

Step nearer. I reached into the pocket of my trousers – unable not to – I took hold of myself; my whole skull rolled back along its axis, a sigh rushed out like steam escaping. At last, I thought. Why denied so long? – If you're like me – when it starts again, when you feel how powerful, how pure, how sharp it is, (of everything, the best) you wonder: How can I have lived a day of life without this in it? From one time to the next, how can I forget how good it is?

Only then did he move his hand aside, he let me see it poking out the khaki shorts' stretched opening. It looked buoyant, worked up with a colour like dark oak. The domed tip of it was sheeny wet, split in half, all slick. He laughed at how I gawked (I guess my mouth was open). Then, amused, superior, he reached down and with an almost comic doctorly gesture – using thumb and forefinger, pulled brown skin back. The ending gap was ragged; as covering eased back, it opened like an eye. He showed me the wet thing's true shade – an almost bloody coral orange. Blunt and wide and glossy, it was the colour of a brick.

In a harsh voice, low, with what sounded like an accent, 'Come here.' Now he'd spoken, he seemed more real, more dangerous. OK, I would leave. Definitely. Under my sole, backing away, two twigs popped. Then I heard four car doors slam – first three and then a last – the family. Their car snapped across gravel, raised blue dust. When it lowered, everything went still. We were alone here. We were two young men in the woods for reasons of mischief. We were wrong to be here. Not exactly depraved, not criminal really, just mistaken. This we wanted was illegal. We were strangers but eager for the same thing. All we knew about each other was how the other looked. It seemed enough.

Who would be hurt? Who, but maybe me? I still felt afraid of him. He was like a monster in a monster movie – the one you dread seeing again, the one you paid to see – the one that eats people, the one they name the film for.

What the brown boy held out for me, there was too much of it. It belonged grafted on to someone else, some guy larger, some pro athlete, giant. His parts were like some beautiful deformity, too colourful and lurid, too ethnic – somehow too lower class, too possibly unclean, too unlike me, too swollen up with sudden black blood, too available, too . . . too nasty.

'You heard me – Said, come here.' I felt ill. Under my feet, brittle stems and paper litter crackled as I eased back two steps then paused then moved three full steps nearer. I could see his whole chest bucking now with steady breaths, expecting something. Hands hung by his sides. He glanced down at it, amused and tolerant – as at some stunt or accomplishment. On ground near his feet, the pack of Camels, a throwaway lighter, a few silver keys on a heavy brass ring.

'Look,' I said, 'don't hate me, but I'm just not sure. I saw you come back in here. I thought you were . . . in trouble or something. I didn't really know.' I hated how I sounded. Why is it so easy for some people and, for me, such perfect torture? Every victory, a relapse.

What made me ask, 'Tell me something . . . about yourself.' He cocked his head, said, 'What's to tell.' He laughed, amused by my attempt at getting personal. 'Nothing *to* tell. I got a job. Got a wife. I hate the job. Plus, lost a lot of interest in the wife – Come here. You gone this far, means you got to. You're not about to leave now, no way.' Part statement, part threat. Mostly, I thought, threat.

A sapling stood to my right; somebody'd hung a prophylactic from one branchtip; it drooped full of heavy liquid, rain and more rain. I moved past that, I moved towards him. It seemed important to, the one polite choice left me. The rasp of my own breathing alarmed me but his silence spooked me more. I thought, if I don't do something now, he'll hurt me probably. He's been too long between times. He's a garage employee; it's his one afternoon off, this is his only pleasure. He never had my advantages. I inspected the belt buckle; this near, it looked superb. I felt sorrier for him. His eyes were flirting, earnest, poisonous.

He nodded towards what waited, angled out of parted shorts. 'You didn't come way back in here just to look at it, jerk – What, have I got to spell stuff out for you, or what?

First, get your own one out, let me see it.' Sleepwalking, taking orders, I did that, what he'd said.

He said he wanted I should come over there, get down on to my knees, said he had something to show me, close up, said he had plans for it and me, asked if I had a mouth, right? And if it led to a throat, right?

He smiled in a bitter tender insinuating way. The grin disgusted me. I thought, this is really a mistake. He's a crazy one. This is dangerous. I'm definitely leaving now; he read my face.

He cut between me and the road, my car. Advancing, barefoot over mud, he made no sound at all.

I felt trapped.

He stopped six feet before me.

'Look,' I tried again. 'I never do this. I'm married. Let's just say it was a lapse OK? Let's say I'm just mixed up. OK? – All right.'

He shook his head Yes, laughed, sounded decent, from a big family, forgiving. I'd risked a smile when he was on me, right hand flipped way back up near his jaw then it sped, that hand was speeding down, came flipping out and blurring past a face, my face. It weighed exactly eight pounds, the hand. It left a sound, a knock, in air, a noise upright, it was just the size of a piece of toast. It connected hard before the thought gathered, This punk is slapping you, has just cuffed you a good one, has knocked you over, down. Fool, run. My right knee hit dirt first.

A strong yellow sound whined into my right ear, that side of my face said, 'But . . .' (He couldn't even get into a junior college. Why's he allowed to do this to me? Doesn't he know who I *am*? I will have to pull rank on him now. He will cower before such credentials. He'll be sorry, he'll . . .)

My hair was being grabbed. Curly hairs that grow on your

skull's backside. It burned how he was yanking those. I heard a tearing sound as his stern clutch tore some loose. This was maybe happening to someone else. He rattled my whole head so hard, top teeth hit bottoms, cut tongue, hurt. I felt a bloody nose begin, that odd ringing like a smell. 'Wait,' I called, expecting a time out. Then the metal taste as it inched and curled into my open mouth.

'OK,' I spoke towards his feet, my right eye smarting, swelling some. I knelt here – truck and birds, those sounds. At least I'm conscious. I looked up through a quarter less of everything as the blackened eye widened fast. I could see a grownman's shorts and, jammed out into air, underside fore-most, the lower half of it, his. It was even stiffer now, with four fat dorsal ridges and, from down here beneath, looked very light and weighty (a trout) made of artery and knot. It bobbed, expectant. Turned straight up, its girth was wor-ried with forked veins wide as fingers, blue-green, some blackish. Coarse brown hair spilled, coiling, out the shorts' split and some of it – kind of mossy quills – grew in a stripe half up the front of it. I felt my nose's blood spill off the jaw, each droplet warming my pants' front then chilling there. Stooped, I thought, It's deep woods, who would hear my screaming; if they found us, what to *say*?

No, I must accept this, have to, he will kill me, my whole life'll be used up in this one bad mistake, my fault. Just have to find a way to live by giving him enough of what he wants so he won't hurt me even more.

He lifted me by hair. 'Please, no.' I grabbed nearest sup-ports, legs, blunt backs of legs. I clutched the mass of either vertical, their bristles stiff but skin beneath as smooth as soapstone. Being down here, tucked underneath, his legs formed the steepled shelter that I knelt in – doghouse/temple – home.

'OK,' I said. 'I know now what I want.' I could only see one thing, his, a mess, a beauty.

My face got smeared against shorts, rough texture. Belt buckle caught between one eye, a hip, and cut into my cheek; it didn't really ache but made a sort of tremor, tickle. He still had me by scalp. He yanked me away, seeing I'd bloodied his pants. Then he pushed my upper body back so I could view all of it, thumping in place, over-ready as he yanked me, lowered, on to it, pulled my whole head overtop.

I could not see. Blind, the opening my mouth made got shoved into then past and on until my throat was open wider than a human throat can be. In my nostrils, blood rattled (a sound like frying) as I tried to breathe around the total size. All I wanted was to breathe, to live through this and it.

Legs duckwalked farther apart, all his toes went curling into soft mud out beyond my own soiled knees. Straddling me, he kept shoving, stuffing, glutting my whole gullet, his full weight pitched and funnelled through hip bones as he muttered names of women, as he tore hard at my hair, as he clamped hands over my ringing ears, as he lightly slapped me till he started to hit harder. He was forcing me, kept cuffing me whenever I gagged too much in some way he didn't like. He was making me a core and hollow. I became the gap where he was throwing everything he had. I held on, was getting used – but also getting used to being used like this, I (*summa cum laude*, Bones at Yale, PhD, the thirty published articles, three books) became whatever he would choose to make of me. Released from IQ, duties, for once I knew my earthly function, perfectly: relieving him. One use. – Then I felt the boy give a low jolt, felt his pelvis lock, felt what fingers I'd worked up by accident into his back opening, the quick and jelly tucked inside, get clamped down on, bitten in spasms as he bucked, as he said, loud,

'Can't, can't, man, got . . . ah,' as he was going off whole pints, all triggered out of it and him and piped into and down me, some even rushing out edges of my mouth's gorged corners, slopping down (in shapes and pieces) flat on to my legs. It had weight, the stuff, like fibre in it, weight, a value. Then, done, he threw my head away. I went keeling back with it, half strangled, my clothes striped with his white, my red. I now shot across his legs' black hair. Everything I had spouted out of me and I felt so good it hurt. My whole history evacuating, liquid, leaving me a fresh start where it's been packed, accumulating, surplus soured by its own long wait for light.

I was hollow, blind, his opening.

He dodged away from me, scraping wet stuff off his belly and flinging it – disgusted – on to clattering leaves, was running, deftly bending to snag up cigarettes and keys, and was gone.

I heard an engine start. It gunned. I managed to half-stand just long enough to see a rusted hulk wheel past and veer out, screeching, on to interstate. Then the stillness of just me here. I fell back, fell down again, was out at once, asleep. I slept right here. Needed blackness lasted an uncertain time. Reprieve from everything.

I woke; had Alice phoned the state police? Earth pressed – cooling – against half my face, blood there solid. I'd slept curled in on myself as children do. Spillage across clothes (stuff I'd bled, what he'd shot, all that aimed up out of me towards him) this holy slop had merged and stiffened. So now, as I tried sitting, melded liquid separated, made this awful tearing sound as if my viscera were ripping open like a pod. Despite the noise, I found it hadn't hurt a bit. I found I could have lived through the whole thing again, again. There was more of me than I'd guessed – no precious limited commodity but ore as rich as uses it was put to. I propped

356

myself half up on arms. Where and what time, who expected me, in what house?

Evening now, and blue all over, deep in a wood. I heard something from a clearing twenty feet away. In half light, I saw one boy standing, his back to me, smeared painters' pants bunched around white ankles, his shoulders flecked with a day's work, dark-green dripped enamel. He heaved into another kid's backparts – a kid who looked too young for this, who kept whimpering, who bent face-first into a forked birch, was propped there and enduring. A striped tie curled back over his left shoulder, shirt-tail was peeled neatly from the bottom as he leaned into the sapling whose leaves shivered around him with each solid thrust, as he kept crying in a small voice, 'Shouldn't, shouldn't have, shouldn't do such, shouldn't be, we shouldn't, shouldn't, shouldn't.'

Listening to worse moans, sharper sobs, to muttered pleas, much offered thanks, then breaths breathed deeply, I heard one boy laugh at a joke, heard the other urinate, then both got wading back through ferns and, finally, the sound of some car or truck crunching into the smooth realm of head-lights, traffic, legality again.

Flat on my back, staring up through tree limbs at evening sky, I thought, Stars. Only reason we can see them is: they are so busy using everything they own. Fires that end them are the only things that make them visible – a show and message – to us down here.

I wanted that. For me, my back pressed in mud (a luxury!) swollen eyes aimed up, both arms flung out as if pinned to earth for good, the face a nest of numbness and itch, I longed to stay in woods, sated, ripped, used so thoroughly I'd feel no interest in seeing sunlight ever again. I would sleep and live here, he would visit me. He would come back every evening with others. He would do more to me, they would do everything to me, in turn, in groups. I would be kept right here for ever, suspended in this creature equilibrium, ready for pleasure, anyone's, my own. I'd never need an address again. I'd be past reputation, free from any single use but this. Nobody would miss me long. Nobody would know where to look for who I'd been. They would soon give up. I'd have disappeared through perfect use.

I flattened out, a secret. Ferns helped hide me. I listened, hoping others would scuff back into this grove towards me.

Cars still moved along four lanes north, four south. I waited. I would wait. A mild breeze moved each leaf in hearing and – showing through a gap in foliage overhead, high, way high above my stunned muddy face – three white stars were out already, burning, burning – burning up.

NIGHTLIGHT

'There must always be two to a kiss.'
R. L. STEVENSON, 'An Apology for Idlers'

SHE COMES TO him late on Wednesdays, only for sex, the cab waiting outside. Four months ago someone recommended her to him for a job but he has no work she can do. He doesn't even pay himself now. They talk of nothing much, and there are silences in which they can only look at one another. But neither wants to withdraw and something must be moving between them, for they stand up together and lie down beside the table, without speaking.

Same time next week she is at the door. They undress immediately. She leaves, not having slept, but he has felt her dozing before she determinedly shakes herself awake. She collects herself quickly without apology, and goes without looking back. He has no idea where she lives or where she is from.

Now she doesn't come into the house, but goes straight down into the basement he can't afford to furnish, where he has thrown blankets and duvets on the carpet. They neither drink nor play music and can barely see one another. It's a mime show in this room where everything but clarity, it seems, is permitted.

At work his debts increase. What he has left could be taken away, and no one but him knows it. He is losing his hold and does it matter? Why should it, except that it is probably terminal; if one day he feels differently, there'll be no way back.

For most of his life, particularly at school, he's been successful, or en route to somewhere called Success. Like most people he has been afraid of being found out, but unlike most he probably has been. He has a small flat, an old car and a shabby feeling. These are minor losses. He misses steady quotidian progress, the sense that his well-being, if not happiness, is increasing, and that each day leads to a recognizable future. He has never anticipated this extent of random desolation.

Three days a week he picks up his kids from school, feeds them, and returns them to the house into which he put most of his money, and which his wife now forbids him to enter. Fridays he has dinner with his only male friend. After, they go to a black bar where he likes the music. The men, mostly in their thirties, and whose lives are a mystery to him, seem to sit night after night without visible discontent, looking at women and at one another. He envies this, and wonders if their lives are without anxiety, whether they have attained a stoic resignation, or if it is a profound uselessness they are stewing in.

On this woman's day he bathes for an hour. He can't recall her name, and she never says his. She calls him, when necessary, 'man'. Soon she will arrive. He lies there thinking how lucky he is to have one arrangement which costs nothing.

Five years ago he left the wife he didn't know why he married for another woman, who then left him without explanation. There have been others since. But when they come close he can only move backwards, without comprehending why.

His wife won't speak. If she picks up the phone and hears his voice, she calls for the kids, those intermediaries growing up between immovable hatreds. A successful woman, last year she found she could not leave her bed at all. She will have no help and the children have to minister to her. They are inclined to believe that he has caused this. He begins to think he can make women insane, even as he understands that this flatters him.

Now he has this inexplicable liaison. At first they run tearing at one another with middle-aged recklessness and then lie silently in the dark, until desire, all they have, rekindles. He tells himself to make the most of the opportunity.

When she's gone he masturbates, contemplating what they did, imprinting it on his mind for ready reference: she on her stomach, him on the boat of her back, his face in her black hair for ever. He thinks of the fluffy black hairs, flattened with sweat, like a toff's parting, around her arsehole.

Walking about later he is both satisfied and unfulfilled, disliking himself for not knowing why he is doing this – balked by the puzzle of his own mind and the impossibility of grasping why one behaves so oddly, and why one ends up resenting people for not providing what one hasn't been able to ask for. Surely this new thing is a web of illusion, and he is a fool? But he wants more foolishness, and not only on Wednesdays.

The following weeks she seems to sense something. In the space where they lie beneath the level of the street, almost underground – a mouse's view of the world – she invites him to lie in different positions; she bids him touch different parts of her body. She shows him they can pore over one another.

Something intriguing is happening in this room, week after week. He can't know what it might be. He isn't certain she will turn up; he doesn't trust her, or any woman, not to let him down. Each week she surprises him, until he wonders what might make her stop.

One Wednesday the cab doesn't draw up. He stands at the window in his dressing gown and slippers for three hours, feeling in the first hour like Casanova, in the second like a child awaiting its mother, and during the third like an old man. Is she sick, or with her husband? He lies on the floor where she usually lies, in a fever of desire and longing, until, later, he feels a presence in the room, a hanging column of air, and sits up and cries out at this ghost.

He assumes he is toxic. For him, lacking disadvantages has been a crime in itself. He grasps the historical reasons for this, since his wife pointed them out. Not that this prevented her living off him. For a while he did try to be the sort of man she might countenance. He wept at every opportunity, and communicated with animals wherever he found them. He tried not to raise his voice, though for her it was 'liberating' to get wild. Soon he didn't know who he was supposed to be. They both got lost. He dreaded going home. He kept his mouth shut, for fear of what would come out; this made her search angrily for a way in.

Now he worries that something has happened to this new woman and he has no way of knowing. What wound or hopelessness has made her want only this?

Next week she does come, standing in the doorway, coat-wrapped, smiling, in her early thirties, about fifteen years younger than him. She might have a lover or husband; might be unemployed; might be disillusioned with love, or getting married next week. But she is tender. How he has missed what they do together.

The following morning he goes downstairs and smells her on the sheets. The day is suffused with her, whoever she is. He finds himself thinking constantly of her, pondering the peculiar mixture of ignorance and intimacy they have. If sex is how you meet and get to know people, what does he know of her? On her body he can paint only imaginary figures, as in the early days of love, when any dreams and desires can be flung onto the subject, until reality upsets and rearranges them. Not knowing, surely, is beautiful, as if everything one learns detracts from the pleasures of pure imagination. Fancy could provide them with more satisfaction than reality.

But she is beginning to make him wonder, and when one night he touches her and feels he has never loved anything so much – if love is loss of the self in the other then, yes, he loves her – he begins to want confirmation of the notions which pile up day after day without making any helpful shape. And, after so many years of living, the expensive education, the languages he imagined would be useful, the books and newspapers studied, can he be capable of love only with a silent stranger in a darkened room? But he dismisses the idea of speaking, because he can't take any more disappointment. Nothing must disturb their perfect evenings.

You want sex and a good time, and you get it; but it usually comes with a free gift – someone like you, a person. Their arrangement seems an advance, what many people want, the best without the worst, and no demands – particularly when he thinks, as he does constantly, of the spirit he and his wife wasted in dislike and sniping, and the years of taking legal and financial revenge. He thinks often of the night he left.

He comes in late, having just left the bed of the woman he is seeing, who has said she is his. The solid bulk of his wife, her back turned, is unmoving. His last night. In the morning he'll talk to the kids and go, as so many men he knows have done, people who'd thought that leaving home was something you did only once. Most of his friends, most of the people he knows, are on the move from wife to wife, husband to husband, lover to lover. A city of love vampires, turning from person to person, hunting the one who will make the difference.

He puts on the light in the hall, undresses and is about to lie down when he notices that she is now lying on her back and her eyes are open. Strangely she looks less pale. He realizes she is wearing eyeshadow and lipstick. Now she reaches out to him, smiling. He moves away; something is wrong. She throws back the covers and she is wearing black and red underwear. She has never, he is certain, dressed like this before.

'It's too late,' he wants to cry.

He picks up his clothes, rushes to the door and closes it behind him. He doesn't know what he is doing, only that he has to get out. The hardest part is going into the children's room, finding their faces in the mess of blankets and toys, and kissing them goodbye.

This must have turned his mind, for, convinced that people have to take something with them, he hurries into his study and attempts to pick up his computer. There are wires; he cannot disconnect it. He gathers up the television from the shelf. He's carrying this downstairs when he turns and sees his wife, still in her tart garb, with a dressing gown on top, screaming, 'Where are you going? Where? Where?'

He shouts, 'You've had ten years of me, ten years and no more, no more!'

He slips on the step and falls forward, doubling up over the TV and tripping down the remaining stairs. Without stopping to consider his injuries, he flees the house without affection or dislike and doesn't look back, thinking only, strange, one never knows every corner of the houses one lives in as an adult, not as one knew one's childhood house. He leaves the TV in the front garden.

*   *   *

The woman he sees now helps kill the terrible fear he constantly bears that his romantic self has been crushed. He feels dangerous but wants to wake up in love. Soft, soft; he dreams of opening a door and the person he will love is standing behind it.

This longing can seize him at parties, in restaurants, at friends' and in the street. He sits opposite a woman in the train. With her the past will be redeemed. He follows her. She crosses the street. So does he. She is going to panic. He grabs her arm and shouts, 'No, no, I'm not like that!' and runs away.

He doesn't know how to reach others, but disliking them is exhausting. Now he doesn't want to go out, since who is there to hold onto? But in the house his mind devours itself; he is a cannibal of his own consciousness. He is starving for want of love. The shame of loneliness, a dingy affliction! There are few creatures more despised than middle-aged men with strong desires, and desire renews itself each day, returning like a recurring illness, crying out, more life, more!

At night he sits in the attic looking through a box of old letters from women. There is an abundance of pastoral description. The women sit in cafés drinking good coffee; they eat peaches on the patio; they look at snow. Everyday sensations are raised to the sublime. He wants to be scornful. It is easy to imagine 'buzzes' and 'charges' as the sole satisfactions. But what gratifies him? It is as if the gears of his life have become disengaged from the mechanism that drove him forward. When he looks at what other people yearn for, he can't grasp why they don't know it isn't worth wanting. He asks to be returned to the ordinary with new eyes. He wants to play a child's game: make a list of what you noticed today, adding desires, regrets and contentments, if any, to the list, so that your life doesn't pass without your having noticed it. And he requires the extraordinary, on Wednesdays.

He lies on his side in her, their mouths are open, her legs holding him. When necessary they move to maintain the level of warm luxury. He can only gauge her mood by the manner of her love-making. Sometimes she merely grabs him; or she lies down, offering her neck and throat to be kissed.

He opens his eyes to see her watching him. It has been a long time since anyone has looked at him with such attention. His hope is boosted by a new feeling: curiosity. He thinks of taking their sexuality into the world. He wants to watch others looking at her, to have others see them together, as confirmation. There is so much love he almost attempts conversation.

For several weeks he determines to speak during their love-making, each time telling himself that on this occasion the words will come out. 'We should talk,' is the sentence he prepares, which becomes abbreviated to 'Want to talk?' and even 'Talk?'

However his not speaking has clearly gladdened this woman. Who else could he cheer up in this way? Won't clarity wreck their understanding, and don't they have an alternative vocabulary of caresses? Words come out bent, but who can bend a kiss? If only he didn't have to imagine continually that he has to take some action, think that something should happen, as if friendships, like trains, have to go somewhere.

He has begun to think that what goes on in this room is his only hope. Having forgotten what he likes about the world, and thinking of existence as drudgery, she reminds him, finger by finger, of the worthwhile. All his life, it seems, he's been seeking sex. He isn't certain why, but he must have gathered that it was an important thing to want. And now he has it, it doesn't seem sufficient. But what does that matter? As long as there is desire there is a pulse; you are alive; to want is to reach beyond yourself, into the world, finger by finger.

ACKNOWLEDGMENTS

APULEIUS: Excerpt from 'Under the Trainer' from *The Golden Ass* by Apuleius, translated by Robert Graves. Copyright © 1951, renewed 1979 by Robert Graves. Reprinted by permission of Farrar, Straus and Giroux, LLC. Reprinted by permission of United Agents on behalf of The Trustees of Robert Graves Copyright Trust.

NICHOLSON BAKER: Chapter 1 from *The Fermata* by Nicholson Baker. Published by Chatto & Windus. Reprinted by permission of The Random House Group Limited. Chapter 1 from *The Fermata* by Nicholson Baker, copyright © 1994 by Nicholson Baker. Used by permission of Random House, an imprint of The Random House Publishing Group, a division of Random House LLC. All rights reserved.

GIOVANNI BOCCACCIO: Excerpt from J. G. Nichols' translation of Boccaccio's *Decameron* © Alma Classics.

ANTON CHEKHOV: 'The Lady with the Dog' (approx. 6,400 words) taken from *My Life and Other Stories* by Anton Chekhov, translated by Constance Garnett. Reprinted by permission of A. P. Watt at United Agents on behalf of The Executors of the Estate of Constance Garnett.

ANDREW DAVIES: From *Getting Hurt* by Andrew Davies. Published by Vintage. Reprinted by permission of The Random House Group Limited.

E. M. FORSTER: *Dr Woolacott* by E.M. Forster, reprinted with permission from The Provost and Scholars of King's College, Cambridge and The Society of Authors as the representatives